Presbytarian Board of Publication

Social Hymn Book

Being the Hymns of the Social Hymn and Tune Book, for the Lecture ....

Presbytarian Board of Publication

Social Hymn Book
Being the Hymns of the Social Hymn and Tune Book, for the Lecture ....

ISBN/EAN: 9783337089641

Printed in Europe, USA, Canada, Australia, Japan

Cover: Foto ©Andreas Hilbeck / pixelio.de

More available books at **www.hansebooks.com**

SOCIAL HYMN BOOK,

BEING THE HYMNS OF THE

SOCIAL HYMN AND TUNE BOOK.

FOR

THE LECTURE ROOM,

PRAYER MEETING, FAMILY,

AND CONGREGATION.

SECOND EDITION.

PHILADELPHIA:
PRESBYTERIAN BOARD OF PUBLICATION,
1334 CHESTNUT STREET.

PREFACE.

"*The Social Hymn and Tune Book*" has commanded the highest praise, and met with a most marked success. But, in many churches where it has been introduced, there are those to whom it would be a convenience to have the hymns alone. To meet the wishes of such persons the committee now issue "THE SOCIAL HYMN BOOK," which comprises the psalms and hymns contained in The Social Hymn and Tune Book, and is, in arrangement and numbering, identical with it.

We trust that the publication of the psalms and hymns without the tunes will not be permitted to interfere with the use of The Social Hymn and Tune Book, where the possession of the tunes will add to the interest and value of the songs of worship in the lecture-room or the church.

SOCIAL HYMN BOOK.

---

1   *General Invocation.*   **L. M.**

1 COME, dearest Lord! descend and dwell,
   By faith and love, in every breast;
Then shall we know, and taste, and feel,
   The joys that cannot be express'd.

2 Come, fill our hearts with inward strength;
   Make our enlarged souls possess,
And learn the height, and breadth, and length
   Of thine eternal love and grace.

---

2   *Father, Son, and Spirit Invoked.*   **6s & 4s.**

1 COME, thou almighty King!
  Help us thy name to sing,
    Help us to praise:
  Father, all glorious,
  O'er all victorious,
  Come and reign over us,
    Ancient of days.

2 Come, thou incarnate Word!
  Gird on thy mighty sword;
    Our prayer attend:

Come, and thy people bless,
And give thy word success;
Spirit of holiness!
On us descend.

3 Come, holy Comforter!
Thy sacred witness bear,
In this glad hour:
Thou, who almighty art,
Now rule in every heart,
And ne'er from us depart,
Spirit of power!

————◆————

3   *Praise to the Redeemer.*   *6s & 4s.*

1 COME, all ye saints of God!
Wide through the earth abroad,
Spread Jesus' name;
Tell what his love has done,
Trust in his grace alone;
Shout to his lofty throne,
"Worthy the Lamb!"

2 Hence, gloomy doubts and fears,
Dry up your mournful tears;
Swell the glad theme;
Praise ye our gracious King,
Strike each melodious string,
Join heart and voice to sing,
"Worthy the Lamb!"

4   *Praise for the Mercy-seat.*   *S. M.*

1 How charming is the place,
    Where my Redeemer God
Unveils the glories of his face,
    And sheds his love abroad!

2 Not the fair palaces,
    To which the great resort,
Are once to be compared with this,
    Where Jesus holds his court.

3 Here on the mercy-seat,
    With radiant glory crowned,
Our joyful eyes behold thee sit,
    And smile on all around.

4 To thee, our prayers and cries
    Each humble soul presents;
Oh! listen to our broken sighs,
    And grant us all our wants.

5 Give us, O Lord! a place,
    Within thy blest abode,
Among the children of thy grace,
    The servants of our God.

5   *Praise for Preserving Grace.*   *S. M.*

1 To God, the only-wise,
    Our Saviour and our King,
Let all the saints, below the skies,
    Their humble praises bring.

2 'Tis his almighty love,
  His counsel and his care,
Preserves us safe from sin and death,
  And every hurtful snare.

3 He will present our souls,
  Unblemished and complete,
Before the glory of his face,
  With joys divinely great.

4 Then all the chosen seed
  Shall meet around the throne;
Shall bless the conduct of his grace,
  And make his wonders known.

———— •◇• ————

6   *Praise from God's Servants. 5s & 6s.*

1 YE servants of God!
    Your Master proclaim,
  And publish abroad,
    His wonderful name;
  The name, all victorious,
    Of Jesus extol;
  His kingdom is glorious,
    And rules over all.

2 God ruleth on high,
    Almighty to save,
  And still he is nigh,
    His presence we have:
  The great congregation
    His triumph shall sing,

Ascribing salvation
    To Jesus, our King.

3 "Salvation to God,
    Who sits on the throne!"
Let all cry aloud,
    And honor the Son·
Immanuel's praises
    The angels proclaim;
Fall down on their faces,
    And worship the Lamb.

4 Then let us adore,
    And give him his right;
All glory and power,
    And wisdom and might;
All honor and blessing,
    With angels above,
And thanks never ceasing.
    And infinite love.

----•◦•----

7   *Praise to Jehovah.*   *S. M.*

1 COME, sound his praise abroad,
    And hymns of glory sing;
Jehovah is the Sovereign God,
    The universal King.

2 He formed the deeps unknown;
    He gave the seas their bound;
The watery worlds are all his own,
    And all the solid ground.

3 Come, worship at his throne;
  Come, bow before the Lord:
We are his works, and not our own;
  He formed us by his word.

————◦◦◦————

8   *Praise to the Lord of Heaven.*   II. M.

1 LORD of the worlds above!
    How pleasant, and how fair,
  The dwellings of thy love,
    Thine earthly temples are!
  To thine abode my heart aspires,
    With warm desires to see my God.

2 Oh! happy souls who pray,
    Where God appoints to hear;
  Oh! happy men who pay
    Their constant service there;
  They praise thee still, and happy they,
    Who love the way to Zion's hill.

3 They go from strength to strength,
    Through this dark vale of tears,
  Till each arrives at length,
    Till each in heaven appears;
  Oh! glorious seat, when God, our King,
    Shall thither bring our willing feet.

————◦◦◦————

9   *Praise to the King of Glory.*   II. M.

1 THE Lord Jehovah reigns;
    His throne is built on high;

The garments he assumes
  Are light and majesty:
His glories shine with beams so bright,
No mortal eye can bear the sight.

2 The thunders of his hand
  Keep the wide world in awe;
His wrath and justice stand
  To guard his holy law:
And, where his love resolves to bless,
His truth confirms and seals the grace.

3 And can this mighty King
  Of glory condescend,
And will he write his name,
  My Father and my Friend?
I love his name,—I love his word;
Join, all my powers! and praise the Lord.

10   *Praise to the God of Israel. L. P. M.*

1 I'LL praise My Maker with my breath,
And, when my voice is lost in death,
  Praise shall employ my nobler powers:
My days of praise shall ne'er be past,
While life, and thought, and being last,
  Or immortality endures.

2 Happy the man, whose hopes rely
On Israel's God; he made the sky,
  And earth, and seas, with all their train:

His truth forever stands secure;
He saves the oppressed, he feeds the poor;
    And none shall find his promise vain.

3 He loves his saints, he knows them well,
But turns the wicked down to hell:
    Thy God, O Zion! ever reigns;
Let ev'ry tongue, and ev'ry age,
In this exalted work engage;
    Praise him in everlasting strains. ·

4 I'll praise him while he lends me breath,
And, when my voice is lost in death,
    Praise shall employ my nobler powers:
My days of praise shall ne'er be past,
While life, and thought, and being last,
    Or immortality endures.

————◆◆————

11　　　*Praise from all the Earth.　L. P. M.*

1 LET all the earth their voices raise,
To sing the choicest psalms of praise;
    To sing and bless Jehovah's name:
His glory let the heathen know;
His wonders to the nations show;
    And all his saving works proclaim.

2 He framed the globe, he built the sky,
He made the shining worlds on high,
    And reigns complete in glory there;
His beams are majesty and light;
His beauties,—how divinely bright!
    His temple,—how divinely fair!

12 *Praise for the redeemed Soul.* S. M.

1 Oh! bless the Lord, my soul!
  Let all within me join,
And aid my tongue to bless his name,
  Whose favors are divine.

2 Oh! bless the Lord, my soul!
  Nor let his mercies lie
Forgotten in unthankfulness,
  And without praises die.

3 'Tis he forgives thy sins,
  'Tis he relieves thy pain,
'Tis he who heals thy sicknesses,
  And makes thee young again.

4 He crowns thy life with love,
  When ransomed from the grave;
He, who redeemed my soul from hell,
  Hath sovereign power to save.

———◆———

13 *Praise for God's Mercies.* S. M.

1 My soul! repeat his praise,
  Whose mercies are so great;
Whose anger is so slow to rise,
  So ready to abate.

2 High as the heavens are raised
  Above the ground we tread,
So far the riches of his grace
  Our highest thoughts exceed.

3 His power subdues our sins,
   And his forgiving love,
 Far as the east is from the west,
   Doth all our guilt remove.

4 The pity of the Lord,
   To those who fear his name,
 Is such as tender parents feel;
   He knows our feeble frame.

5 Our days are as the grass,
   Or like the morning-flower:
 If one sharp blast sweep o'er the field,
   It withers in an hour.

6 But thy compassions, Lord!
   To endless years endure;
 And children's children ever find
   Thy words of promise sure.

———•◇•———

14   *Praise for Divine Grace.*   C. M.

1 EARLY, my God! without delay,
   I haste to seek thy face;
 My thirsty spirit faints away,
   Without thy cheering grace.

2 So pilgrims on the scorching sand,
   Beneath a burning sky,
 Long for a cooling stream at hand,
   And they must drink or die.

3 I've seen thy glory and thy power
  Through all thy temple shine;
My God! repeat that heavenly hour,
  That vision so divine.

4 Not life itself, with all its joys,
  Can my best passions move;
Or raise so high my cheerful voice,
  As thy forgiving love.

----

15   *Praise for Redemption.*   C. M.

1 FATHER! how wide thy glory shines!
  How high thy wonders rise!
Known through the earth by thousand signs,
  By thousand through the skies.

2 Those mighty orbs proclaim thy power,
  Their motions speak thy skill;
And, on the wings of every hour,
  We read thy patience still.

3 But, when we view thy strange design
  To save rebellious worms,
Where vengeance and compassion join
  In their divinest forms,

4 Here the whole Deity is known;
  Nor dare a creature guess,
Which of the glories brightest shone,
  The justice, or the grace.

16   *Praise from God's People.*   *L. M.*

1 BEFORE Jehovah's awful throne,
    Ye nations! bow with sacred joy:
Know that the Lord is God alone:
    He can create, and he destroy.

2 His sovereign power, without our aid,
    Made us of clay, and formed us men;
And when like wand'ring sheep we stray'd,
    He brought us to his fold again.

3 We are his people, we his care,
    Our souls, and all our mortal frame:
What lasting honors shall we rear,
    Almighty Maker! to thy name?

4 We'll crowd thy gates with thankful songs;
    High as the heavens our voices raise;
And earth, with her ten thousand tongues,
    Shall fill thy courts with sounding praise.

5 Wide as the world is thy command,
    Vast as eternity thy love;
Firm as a rock thy truth must stand,
    When rolling years shall cease to move.

---

17   *Public Worship.*   *L. M.*

1 GREAT God! attend, while Zion sings
    The joy that from thy presence springs;
To spend one day with thee on earth,
    Exceeds a thousand days of mirth.

2 Might I enjoy the meanest place
  Within thy house, O God of grace!
  Not tents of ease, nor thrones of power,
  Should tempt my feet to leave thy door.

3 God is our sun, he makes our day;
  God is our shield, he guards our way
  From all th' assaults of hell and sin,
  From foes without, and foes within.

4 All needful grace will God bestow,
  And crown that grace with glory too;
  He gives us all things, and withholds
  No real good from upright souls.

18   *Praise to the Redeemer.*   *C. M.*

1 COME, thou desire of all thy saints!
    Our humble strains attend,
  While, with our praises and complaints,
    Low at thy feet we bend.

2 How should our songs, like those above,
    With warm devotion rise!
  How should our souls, on wings of love
    Mount upward to the skies!

3 Come, Lord! thy love alone can raise
    In us the heavenly flame;
  Then shall our lips resound thy praise,
    Our hearts adore thy name.

2 *

4 Dear Saviour! let thy glory shine,
   And fill thy dwellings here,
Till life, and love, and joy divine
   A heaven on earth appear.

5 Then shall our hearts enraptured say,
   Come, great Redeemer! come,
And bring the bright, the glorious day,
   That calls thy children home.

---

19   *Praise to the Saviour.*   *C. M.*

1 OH! for a thousand tongues to sing
   My dear Redeemer's praise!
The glories of my God and King,
   The triumphs of his grace!

2 My gracious Master and my God!
   Assist me to proclaim,
To spread, through all the earth abroad,
   The honors of thy name.

3 Jesus—the name that calms my fears,
   That bids my sorrows cease;
'Tis music to my ravished ears;
   'Tis life, and health, and peace.

4 He breaks the power of reigning sin,
   He sets the pris'ner free;
His blood can make the foulest clean;
   His blood availed for me.

20   *God of Love Invoked.*   *S. M.*

1 My God, my life, my love!
    To thee, to thee I call;
I cannot live, if thou remove,
    For thou art all in all.

2 To thee, and thee alone,
    The angels owe their bliss;
They sit around thy gracious throne,
    And dwell where Jesus is.

3 Not all the harps above
    Can make a heavenly place,
If God his residence remove,
    Or but conceal his face.

4 Nor earth, nor all the sky,
    Can one delight afford:
No, not a drop of real joy,
    Without thy presence, Lord!

5 Thou art the sea of love,
    Where all my pleasures roll,
The circle where my passions move
    And center of my soul.

---

21   *Holy Spirit Invoked.*   *S. M.*

1 Come, Holy Spirit! come,
    Let thy bright beams arise;
Dispel the sorrow from our minds,
    The darkness from our eyes.

2 Convince us of our sin,
 Then lead to Jesus' blood;
And, to our wondering view, reveal
 The secret love of God.

3 'Tis thine to cleanse the heart,
 To sanctify the soul,
To pour fresh life in every part,
 And new-create the whole.

4 Revive our drooping faith;
 Our doubts and fears remove;
And kindle in our breast the flame
 Of never-dying love.

---

22 *Praising Jehovah.* 7s.

1 GREAT the joy when Christians meet;
Christian fellowship, how sweet,
When, their theme of praise the same,
They exalt Jehovah's name!

2 Sing we then eternal love,
Such as did the Father move;
He beheld the world undone,
Loved the world, and gave his Son.

3 Sing the Son's unbounded love;
How he left the realms above,
Took our nature and our place,
Lived and died to save our race.

4 Sing we too the Spirit's love;
   With our stubborn hearts he strove,
   Chased the mists of sin away,
   Turned our night to glorious day.

5 Great the joy, the union sweet,
   When the saints in glory meet!
   Where the theme is still the same;
   Where they praise Jehovah's name.

---

23   *Rejoicing in Hope.*   **7s.**

1 CHILDREN of the heavenly King!
   As ye journey, sweetly sing;
   Sing your Saviour's worthy praise,
   Glorious in his works and ways.

2 Ye are traveling home to God,
   In the way the fathers trod;
   They are happy now, and ye
   Soon their happiness shall see.

3 Shout, ye little flock and blest!
   You on Jesus' throne shall rest;
   There, your seat is now prepared;
   There, your kingdom and reward.

4 Fear not, brethren! joyful stand
   On the borders of your land;
   Jesus Christ, your Father's Son,
   Bids you undismayed go on.

5 Lord! submissive make us go,
   Gladly leaving all below;
   Only thou our leader be,
   And we still will follow thee.

---

24   *Vowing Service.*   *C. M.*

1 WHAT shall I render to my God,
   For all his kindness shown?
   My feet shall visit thine abode,
   My songs address thy throne.

2 How much is mercy thy delight,
   Thou ever blessed God!
   How dear thy servants in thy sight,
   How precious is their blood!

3 How happy all thy servants are!
   How great thy grace to me!
   My life, which thou hast made thy care,
   Lord! I devote to thee.

4 Now I am thine—for ever thine;
   Nor shall my purpose move;
   Thy hand hath loosed my bonds of pain,
   And bound me with thy love.

5 Here, in thy courts, I leave my vow,
   And thy rich grace record;
   Witness, ye saints! who hear me now,
   If I forsake the Lord.

25   *Singing Salvation.*   C. M.

1 My Saviour! my almighty Friend!
    When I begin thy praise,
  Where will the growing numbers end,
    The numbers of thy grace?

2 Thou art my everlasting trust:
    Thy goodness I adore;
  And, since I knew thy graces first,
    I speak thy glories more.

3 My feet shall travel all the length
    Of the celestial road;
  And march, with courage, in thy strength,
    To see my Father God.

4 How will my lips rejoice to tell
    The vict'ries of my King!
  My soul, redeemed from sin and hell,
    Shall thy salvation sing.

5 Awake, awake, my tuneful powers!
    With this delightful song,
  I'll entertain the darkest hours,
    Nor think the season long.

THE SCRIPTURES.

26   *The Word.*   C. M.

1 FATHER of mercies! in thy word
    What endless glory shines!
  For ever be thy name adored,
    For these celestial lines.

2 Here the Redeemer's welcome voice,
　　Spreads heav'nly peace around;
　And life, and everlasting joys,
　　Attend the blissful sound.

3 Oh! may those heavenly pages be
　　My ever-dear delight;
　And still new beauties may I see,
　　And still increasing light.

4 Divine instructor, gracious Lord!
　　Be thou for ever near;
　Teach me to love thy sacred word,
　　And view my Saviour there.

27　　*The Spirit and the Word.*　　*C. M.*

1 THE Spirit breathes upon the word,
　　And brings the truth to sight;
　Precepts and promises afford
　　A sanctifying light.

2 A glory gilds the sacred page,
　　Majestic like the sun:
　It gives a light to every age;
　　It gives, but borrows none.

3 The hand, that gave it, still supplies,
　　The gracious light and heat;
　His truths upon the nations rise,
　　They rise, but never set,

4 Let everlasting thanks be thine,
   For such a bright display,
As makes a world of darkness shine
   With beams of heavenly day.

5 My soul rejoices to pursue
   The steps of him I love,
Till glory breaks upon my view,
   In brighter worlds above.

---

28   *Revelation.*   *L. M.*

1 God, in the gospel of his Son.
Makes his eternal counsels known,
Where love in all its glory shines,
And truth is drawn in fairest lines.

2 Here, sinners of a humble frame
May taste his grace, and learn his name;
May read, in characters of blood,
The wisdom, pow'r, and grace of God.

3 Here, faith reveals, to mortal eyes,
A brighter world beyond the skies;
Here, shines the light which guides our way
From earth to realms of endless day.

4 Oh! grant us grace, almighty Lord!
To read and mark thy holy word,
Its truths with meekness to receive,
And by its holy precepts live.

3

5 May this blest volume ever lie
   Close to my heart, and near mine eye,
Till life's last hour, my soul engage,
   And be my chosen heritage.

---

29   *Nature and Revelation.*   *L. M.*

1 THE heavens declare thy glory, Lord!
   In every star thy wisdom shines;
But, when our eyes behold thy word,
   We read thy name in fairer lines.

2 Sun, moon, and stars convey thy praise,
   Round the whole earth, and never stand:
So, when thy truth began its race,
   It touched and glanced on every land.

3 Nor shall thy spreading gospel rest,
   Till through the world thy truth has run,
Till Christ has all the nations blest,
   That see the light, or feel the sun.

4 Great Sun of Righteousness! arise;
   Bless the dark world with heavenly light;
Thy gospel makes the simple wise,
   Thy laws are pure, thy judgments right.

GOD.

30   *God's Eternity.*   *C. M.*

1 GREAT God! how infinite art thou!
   What worthless worms are we!

Let the whole race cf creatures bow,
And pay their praise to thee.

2 Thy throne eternal ages stood,
Ere seas or stars were made:
Thou art the ever-living God,
Were all the natiɔns dead.

3 Eternity, with all its years,
Stands present in thy view:
To thee there's nothing old appears;
Great God! there's nothing new.

4 Our lives through various scenes are drawn,
And vexed with trifling cares;
While thine eternal thought moves on
Thine undisturbed affairs.

5 Great God! how infinite art thou!
What worthless worms are we!
Let the whole race of creatures bow,
And pay their praise to thee.

---

31   *God's Omnipresence.*   *C. M.*

1 IN all my vast concerns with thee,
In vain my soul would try,
To shun thy presence, Lord! or flee
The notice of thine eye.

2 Thine all-surrounding sight surveys
My rising and my rest,
My public walks, my private ways,
And secrets of my breast.

3 My thoughts lie open to the Lord,
    Before they're formed within;
  And, ere my lips pronounce the word,
    He knows the sense I mean.

4 Oh! wondrous knowledge, deep and high,
    Where can a creature hide?
  Within thy circling arms I lie,
    Enclosed on every side.

5 So let thy grace surround me still,
    And like a bulwark prove,
  To guard my soul from every ill,
    Secured by sovereign love.

------◆------

32　　　　　*God's Perfection.*　　　　　*L. M.*

1 HIGH in the heav'ns, eternal God!
    Thy goodness in full glory shines;
  Thy truth shall break through every cloud,
    That veils or darkens thy designs.

2 Forever firm thy justice stands,
    As mountains their foundations keep;
  Wise are the wonders of thy hands,
    Thy judgments are a mighty deep.

3 My God! how excellent thy grace,
    Whence all our hope, our comfort springs!
  The sons of Adam, in distress,
    Fly to the shadow of thy wings.

4 Life, like a fountain, rich and free,
  Springs from the presence of my Lord;
And, in thy light, our souls shall see,
  The glories promised in thy word.

---

33   *God's Omniscience.*   *L. M.*

1 LORD! thou hast searched and seen me
      through:
Thine eye commands with piercing view,
My rising and my resting hours,
My heart and flesh, with all their powers.

2 My thoughts, before they are my own,
Are to my God distinctly known;
He knows the words I mean to speak,
Ere from my opening lips they break.

3 Within thy circling power I stand,
On every side I find thy hand:
Awake, asleep, at home abroad,
I am surrounded still with God.

4 Oh! may these thoughts possess my breast,
Where'er I rove, where'er I rest;
Nor let my weaker passions dare
Consent to sin, for God is there.

---

34   *God's Goodness.*   *S. M.*

1 My Maker and my King!
    To thee my all I owe;

3 *

Thy sov'reign bounty is the spring,
 Whence all my blessings flow.

2 The creature of thy hand,
 On thee alone I live;
My God! thy benefits demand
 More praise than life can give.

3 Shall I withhold thy due?
 And shall my passions rove?
Lord! form this wretched heart anew,
 And fill it with thy love.

4 Oh! let thy grace inspire
 My soul with strength divine;
Let all my powers to thee aspire,
 And all my days be thine.

---

35   *The Good Shepherd.*   S. M.

1 THE Lord my Shepherd is,
 I shall be well supplied;
Since he is mine, and I am his,
 What can I want beside?

2 He leads me to the place,
 Where heavenly pasture grows,
Where living waters gently pass,
 And full salvation flows.

3 If e'er I go astray,
 He doth my soul reclaim,
And guides me in his own right way,
 For his most holy name.

4 While he affords his aid,
 I cannot yield to fear;
Tho' I should walk thro' death's dark shade,
 My Shepherd's with me there.

———◄◆►———

36   *God's Mercy.*   C. M.

1 WHEN all thy mercies, O my God!
 My rising soul surveys,
Transported with the view, I'm lost
 In wonder, love, and praise.

2 Ten thousand thousand precious gifts
 My daily thanks employ;
Nor is the least a cheerful heart,
 That tastes those gifts with joy.

3 Through every period of my life,
 Thy goodness I'll pursue;
And after death, in distant worlds,
 The glorious theme renew.

4 Through all eternity to thee
 A joyful song I'll raise;
But oh! eternity's too short
 To utter all thy praise.

———◄◆►———

37   *Providence.*   C. M.

1 GOD moves in a mysterious way,
 His wonders to perform;
He plants his footsteps in the sea,
 And rides upon the storm.

2 Deep, in unfathomable mines
   Of never-failing skill,
He treasures up his bright designs,
   And works his sovereign will.

3 Ye fearful saints! fresh courage take;
   The clouds ye so much dread
Are big with mercy, and shall break
   In blessings on your head.

4 Judge not the Lord by feeble sense,
   But trust him for his grace;
Behind a frowning providence,
   He hides a smiling face.

5 His purposes will ripen fast,
   Unfolding every hour;
The bud may have a bitter taste,
   But sweet will be the flower.

6 Blind unbelief is sure to err,
   And scan his work in vain;
God is his own interpreter,
   And he will make it plain.

---

38   *God a Rock.*   *C. M.*

1 God! my supporter and my hope,
   My help for ever near,
Thine arm of mercy held me up,
   When sinking in despair.

2 Thy counsels, Lord! shall guide my feet,
   Through this dark wilderness;
Thy hand conduct me near thy seat,
   To dwell before thy face.

3 Were I in heav'n without my God,
   'T would be no joy to me;
And, while this earth is my abode,
   I long for none but thee.

4 What if the springs of life were broke,
   And flesh and heart should faint?
God is my soul's eternal rock;
   The strength of every saint.

5 But to draw near to thee, my God!
   Shall be my sweet employ;
My tongue shall sound thy works abroad,
   And tell the world my joy.

---

39   *God a Shepherd.*   *C. M.*

1 My Shepherd will supply my need,
   Jehovah is his name;
In pastures fresh he makes me feed,
   Beside the living stream.

2 He brings my wandering spirit back,
   When I forsake his ways;
And leads me, for his mercy's sake,
   In paths of truth and grace.

3 When I walk through the shades of death,
 Thy presence is my stay;
A word of thy supporting breath
 Drives all my fears away.

4 The sure provisions of my God
 Attend me all my days;
Oh! may thy house be mine abode,
 And all my work be praise.

5 There would I find a settled rest,
 While others go and come,
No more a stranger or a guest,
 But like a child at home.

40 *God a Comforter.* *11s.*

1 The Lord is my Shepherd, no want shall I
 know;
 I feed in green pastures, safe folded I rest;
He leadeth my soul where the still waters
 flow,
 Restores me when wand'ring, redeems
 when oppress'd.

2 Through the valley and shadow of death,
 though I stray,
 Since thou art my guardian no evil I fear;
Thy rod shall defend me, thy staff be my stay;
 No harm can befall, with my Comforter
 near.

3 In the midst of affliction my table is spread;
  With blessings unmeasured my cup run-
      neth o'er;
  With perfume and oil thou anointest my
      head;
  Oh! what shall I ask of thy providence
      more?

41   *God a Guide.*   C. M.

1 My soul! triumphant in the Lord,
    Proclaim thy joys abroad,
  And march with holy vigor on,
    Supported by thy God.

2 Through every winding maze of life,
    His hand has been my guide;
  And, in his long-experienced care,
    My heart shall still confide.

3 His grace through all the desert flows,
    An unexhausted stream;
  That grace, on Zion's sacred mount,
    Shall be my endless theme.

42   *God a Protector.*   C. M.

1 Dear Father! to thy mercy-seat
    My soul for shelter flies:
  'Tis here I find a safe retreat,
    When storms and tempests rise.

2 My cheerful hope can never die,
     If thou, my God! art near;
  Thy grace can raise my comforts high,
     And banish ev'ry fear.

3 My great Protector, and my Lord!
     Thy constant aid impart;
  Oh! let thy kind, thy gracious word,
     Sustain my trembling heart.

4 Oh! never let my soul remove
     From this divine retreat:
  Still let me trust thy power and love,
     And dwell beneath thy feet.

———◆———

43   *God a Refuge.*   *C. M.*

1 DEAR refuge of my weary soul!
     On thee, when sorrows rise,
  On thee, when waves of trouble roll,
     My fainting hope relies.

2 To thee I tell each rising grief,
     For thou alone canst heal:
  Thy word can bring a sweet relief,
     For every pain I feel.

3 But oh! when gloomy doubts prevail,
     I fear to call thee mine;
  The springs of comfort seem to fail,
     And all my hopes decline.

4 Hast thou not bid me seek thy face?
    And shall I seek in vain?
  And can the ear of sovereign grace
    Be deaf when I complain?

5 No,—still the ear of sovereign grace
    Attends the mourner's prayer:
  Oh! may I ever find access
    To breathe my sorrows there!

6 Thy mercy-seat is open still;
    Here let my soul retreat;
  With humble hope attend thy will,
    And wait beneath thy feet.

CHRIST.

44   *Angels' Song.*   8s & 7s.

1 HARK! what mean those holy voices,
    Sweetly sounding through the skies?
  Lo! th' angelic host rejoices,
    Heav'nly hallelujahs rise.

2 Listen to the wondrous story,
    Which they chant in hymns of joy:
  "Glory in the highest, glory,
    Glory be to God most high!

3 "Peace on earth, good-will from heaven,
    Reaching far as man is found;
  Souls redeemed, and sins forgiven;
    Loud our golden harps shall sound.
    4

4 "Christ is born, the great Anointed;
  Heaven and earth! his praises sing:
Oh! receive whom God appointed,
  For your prophet, priest, and king.

5 "Hasten, mortals! to adore him;
  Learn his name, and taste his joy;
Till in heaven ye sing before him,
  Glory be to God most high!"

----

45   *Christ born.*   8s & 7s.

1 HAIL, thou long-expected Jesus!
    Born to set thy people free;
  From our sins and fears release us,
    Let us find our rest in thee.

2 Israel's strength and consolation,
    Hope of all the saints, thou art;
  Long-desired of every nation,
    Joy of every waiting heart.

3 Born, thy people to deliver,
    Born a child, yet God our King,
  Born to reign in us for ever,
    Now thy gracious kingdom bring.

4 By thine own eternal Spirit,
    Rule in all our hearts alone;
  By thine all-sufficient merit,
    Raise us to thy glorious throne.

46 *Glad Tidings.* *C. M.*

1 WHILE shepherds watched their flocks by
  night,
  All seated on the ground,
The angel of the Lord came down,
  And glory shone around.

2 "Fear not," said he, for mighty dread,
  Had seized their troubled mind,
"Glad tidings of great joy I bring,
  To you and all mankind.

3 "To you, in David's town, this day,
  Is born of David's line,
The Saviour, who is Christ, the Lord,
  And this shall be the sign.

4 "The heavenly babe you there shall find,
  To human view displayed,
All meanly wrapped in swathing bands,
  And in a manger laid."

5 Thus spake the seraph—and forthwith
  Appeared a shining throng
Of angels, praising God, who thus
  Addressed their joyful song:—

6 "All glory be to God on high,
  And to the earth be peace;
Good-will henceforth from heaven to men
  Begin, and never cease!"

47 *The Saviour Comes.* **C. M.**

1 HARK, the glad sound! the Saviour comes,
  The Saviour, promised long;
Let every heart prepare a throne,
  And every voice a song.

2 On him the Spirit, largely poured,
  Exerts his sacred fire;
Wisdom, and might, and zeal, and love,
  His holy breast inspire.

3 He comes,—the pris'ners to release,
  In Satan's bondage held;
The gates of brass before him burst,
  The iron fetters yield.

4 He comes,—the broken heart to bind,
  The bleeding soul to cure;
And, with the treasures of his grace,
  T' enrich the humble poor.

---

48 *Christ, the Star of Bethlehem.* **L. M.**

1 WHEN, marshaled on the nightly plain,
  The glitt'ring host bestud the sky,
One star alone, of all the train,
  Can fix the sinner's wand'ring eye.
Hark! hark! to God the chorus breaks,
  From ev'ry host, from ev'ry gem:
But one alone the Saviour speaks—
  It is the Star of Bethlehem.

2 Once on the raging seas I rode,
   The storm was loud, the night was dark,
The ocean yawn'd, and rudely blow'd
   The wind that toss'd my found'ring bark;
Deep horror then my vitals froze,
   Death-struck, I ceased the tide to stem;
When suddenly a Star arose—
   It was the Star of Bethlehem.

3 It was my guide, my light, my all;
   It bade my dark forebodings cease:
And, through the storm, and danger's thrall,
   It led me to the port of peace.
Now safely moored—my perils o'er,
   I'll sing, first in night's diadem,
For ever and for evermore,
   The Star—the Star of Bethlehem!

---

49   *Christ, the Way, Truth, and Life.*   C. M.

1 THOU art the Way;—to thee alone
   From sin and death we flee;
And he, who would the Father seek,
   Must seek him, Lord! in thee.

2 Thou art the Truth;—thy word alone
   True wisdom can impart;
Thou only canst instruct the mind,
   And purify the heart.

4 *

3 Thou art the Life;—the rending tomb,
　Proclaims thy conquering arm;
And those who put their trust in thee
Not death nor hell shall harm.

50　　*Christ, the Star of the East. 11s & 10s.*

1 BRIGHTEST and best of the sons of the morn-
　　　ing!
　Dawn on our darkness and lend us thine
　　　aid;
Star of the East!—the horizon adorning—
　Guide where the infant Redeemer is laid.

2 Cold on his cradle, the dew-drops are shining;
　Low lies his head, with the beasts of the
　　　stall:
Angels adore him, in slumber reclining,
　Maker, and Monarch, and Saviour of all.

3 Say, shall we yield him, in costly devotion,
　Odors of Edom, and offerings divine?
Gems of the mountain, and pearls of the
　　　ocean,
　Myrrh from the forest, or gold from the
　　　mine?

4 Vainly we offer each ample oblation,
　Vainly with gold, would his favor secure;
Richer, by far, is the heart's adoration,
　Dearer to God are the prayers of the poor.

5 Brightest and best of the sons of the morning!
   Dawn on our darkness and lend us thine
      aid;
Star of the East!—the horizon adorning—
   Guide where our infant Redeemer is laid.

* * *

51   *Christ, the Day-Star.*   *11s.*

1 DAUGHTER of Zion! awake from thy sadness;
   Awake, for thy foes shall oppress thee no
      more;
Bright o'er thy hills dawns the day-star of
      gladness;
   Arise,—for the night of thy sorrow is o'er.

2 Strong were thy foes; but the arm that sub-
      dued them,
   And scattered their legions, was mightier
      far:
They fled, like the chaff, from the scourge
      that pursued them;
   Vain were their steeds and their chariots
      of war.

3 Daughter of Zion! the power that hath saved
      thee,
   Extolled with the harp and the timbrel
      should be;
Shout,—for the foe is destroyed that enslaved
      thee,
   Th' oppressor is vanquished. and Zion is
      free.

52   *Christ adored by Seraphs.*   H. M

1 HARK! hark! the notes of joy
    Roll o'er the heavenly plains,
And seraphs find employ
    For their sublimest strains;
Some new delight in heaven is known;
Loud sound the harps around the throne.

2 Hark! hark! the sounds draw nigh,
    The joyful hosts descend;
Jesus forsakes the sky,
    To earth his footsteps bend;
He comes to bless our fallen race;
He comes with messages of grace.

3 Bear, bear the tidings round;
    Let every mortal know
What love in God is found,
    What pity he can show;
Ye winds that blow! ye waves that roll!
Bear the glad news from pole to pole.

4 Strike—strike the harps again,
    To great Immanuel's name;
Arise, ye sons of men!
    And all his grace proclaim;
Angels and men! wake every string,
'Tis God the Saviour's praise we sing!

53 *Christ heralded by Angels.* 7s.

1 HARK! the herald angels sing,
  "Glory to the new-born King;
Peace on earth, and mercy mild,
  God and sinners reconciled."

2 Joyful, all ye nations! rise,
  Join the triumph of the skies;
With th' angelic host proclaim,
  "Christ is born in Bethlehem."

3 Mild he lays his glory by,
  Born that man no more may die;
Born to raise the sons of earth;
  Born to give them second birth.

---

54 *Christ's Cross.* L. M.

1 WHEN I survey the wondrous cross,
  On which the Prince of glory died,
My richest gain I count but loss,
  And pour contempt on all my pride.

2 Forbid it, Lord! that I should boast,
  Save in the death of Christ, my God!
All the vain things that charm me most,
  I sacrifice them to his blood.

3 See,—from his head, his hands, his feet,
  Sorrow and love flow mingled down!
Did e'er such love and sorrow meet,
  Or thorns compose so rich a crown?

4 Were the whole realm of nature mine,
  That were a present far too small;
Love, so amazing, so divine,
  Demands my soul, my life, my all.

---

55   *The Crucified Saviour.*   *L. M.*

1 STRETCHED on the cross, the Saviour dies!
Hark! his expiring groans arise:
See—from his hands, his feet, his side,
Fast flows the sacred crimson tide!

2 But life attends the deathful sound,
And flows from every bleeding wound;
The vital stream,—how free it flows,
To save and cleanse his rebel foes!

3 Can I survey this scene of woe,
Where mingling grief and wonder flow,
And yet my heart unmoved remain,
Insensible to love or pain?

4 Come, dearest Lord! thy grace impart
To warm this cold, this stupid heart;
Till all its powers and passions move,
In melting grief and ardent love.

---

56   *Christ's Cry on the Cross.*   *8s, 7s & 4s.*

1 HARK! the voice of love and mercy
  Sounds aloud from Calvary;

See! it rends the rocks asunder,
    Shakes the earth and veils the sky:
  "It is finished!"
Hear the dying Saviour cry.

2 "It is finished!"—Oh! what pleasure
    Do these charming words afford!
Heavenly blessings, without measure,
    Flow to us through Christ, the Lord:
  "It is finished!"
Saints! the dying words record.

3 Tune your harps anew, ye seraphs!
    Join to sing the pleasing theme:
All in earth and heaven, uniting,
    Join to praise Immanuel's name:
    Hallelujah!
Glory to the bleeding Lamb!

----

57   *Christ on the Cross.*   *C. M.*

1 BEHOLD the Saviour of mankind,
    Nailed to the shameful tree;
How vast the love that him inclined
    To bleed and die for me!

2 Hark! how he groans, while nature shakes,
    And earth's strong pillars bend!
The temple's veil asunder breaks,
    The solid marbles rend.

3 'Tis done! the precious ransom 's paid;
    "Receive my soul!" he cries:
See—how he bows his sacred head!
    He bows his head and dies.

4 But soon he'll break death's iron chain,
    And in full glory shine:
O Lamb of God! was ever pain,
    Was ever love like thine?

58   *Power of the Cross.*   *L. M.*

1 WE sing the praise of him who died,
    Of him who died upon the cross:
The sinner's hope let men deride,
    For this we count the world but loss.

2 Inscribed upon the cross we see,
    In shining letters, "God is love:"
He bears our sins upon the tree,
    He brings us mercy from above.

3 The cross! it takes our guilt away,
    It holds the fainting spirit up;
It cheers with hope the gloomy day,
    And sweetens every bitter cup.

4 It makes the coward spirit brave,
    And nerves the feeble arm for fight:
It takes its terrors from the grave,
    And gilds the bed of death with light.

5 The balm of life, the cure of woe,
    The measure and the pledge of love;
'Tis all that sinners want below,
    'Tis all that angels know above.

---

59   *Wonders of the Cross.*   **L. M.**

1 NATURE with open volume stands,
    To spread her Maker's praise abroad;
And every labor of his hands
    Shows something worthy of a God.

2 But, in the grace that rescued man,
    His brightest form of glory shines;
Here, on the cross, 'tis fairest drawn,
    In precious blood and crimson lines.

3 Oh! the sweet wonders of that cross,
    Where Christ, the Saviour, loved and died:
Her noblest life my spirit draws,
    From his dear wounds and bleeding side.

4 I would forever speak his name,
    In sounds to mortal ears unknown;
With angels join to praise the Lamb,
    And worship at his Father's throne.

---

60   *Christ Rising.*   **7s.**

1 MORNING breaks upon the tomb,
    Jesus scatters all its gloom;
    Day of triumph through the skies,
    See the glorious Saviour rise!

2 Ye, who are of death afraid,
Triumph in the scattered shade;
Drive your anxious cares away;
See the place where Jesus lay!

3 Christian! dry your flowing tears,
Chase your unbelieving fears;
Look on his deserted grave;
Doubt no more his power to save.

------

61 *Christ Risen.* **S. M.**

1 "THE Lord is risen indeed!
Then is his work performed;
The mighty captive now is freed,
And death, our foe, disarmed.

2 "The Lord is risen indeed!"
He lives to die no more;
He lives, the sinner's cause to plead,
Whose curse and shame he bore.

3 "The Lord is risen indeed!"
Then hell has lost his prey;
With him is risen the ransomed seed,
To reign in endless day.

4 "The Lord is risen indeed!"
Attending angels! hear;
Up to the courts of heaven, with speed,
The joyful tidings bear.

5 Then wake your golden lyres,
    And strike each tuneful chord;
Join, all ye bright, celestial choirs!
    To sing our risen Lord.

----◆----

62   *Christ Conquering.*   *H. M.*

1 YES, the Redeemer rose;
    The Saviour left the dead;
And o'er our hellish foes
    High raised his conquering head:
In wild dismay,
    The guards around,
Fall to the ground,
    And sink away.

2 Lo! the angelic bands
    In full assembly meet,
To wait his high commands,
    And worship at his feet:
Joyful they come,
    And wing their way,
From realms of day,
    To Jesus' tomb.

3 Then back to heaven they fly,
    The joyful news to bear:
Hark, as they soar on high,
    What music fills the air!

Their anthems say,
　"Jesus, who bled,
Has left the dead;
　He rose to-day."

63　　　*Christ, King.*　　　H. M.

1 REJOICE! the Lord is King!
　　Your God and King adore;
Mortals, give thanks, and sing,
　　And triumph evermore:
Lift up the heart, lift up the voice,
Rejoice aloud, ye saints! rejoice.

2 His kingdom cannot fail;
　　He rules o'er earth and heaven;
The keys of death and hell
　　Are to our Jesus given:
Lift up the heart, lift up the voice,
Rejoice aloud, ye saints! rejoice.

3 Rejoice in glorious hope;
　　Jesus, the Judge shall come,
And take his servants up
　　To their eternal home:
We soon shall hear the archangel's voice,
The trump of God shall sound,—Rejoice.

64　　　*Christ, Intercessor.*　　　L. M.

1 HE lives, the great Redeemer lives!
　What joy the blest assurance gives!

And now, before his Father-God,
Pleads the full merits of his blood.

2 Repeated crimes awake our fears,
And justice, armed with frowns, appears;
But, in the Saviour's lovely face,
Sweet mercy smiles, and all is peace.

3 In every dark, distressful hour,
When sin and Satan join their power,
Let this dear hope repel the dart,
That Jesus bears us on his heart.

4 Great Advocate, almighty Friend!
On thee our humble hopes depend:
Our cause can never, never fail,
For Jesus pleads, and must prevail,

———

65   *Christ, High-Priest and King.*   **L. M.**

1 Now to the Lord, who makes us know
The wonders of his dying love,
Be humble honors paid below,
And strains of nobler praise above.

2 'Twas he that cleansed our foulest sins,
And washed us in his richest blood;
'Tis he that makes us priests and kings,
And brings us rebels near to God.

3 To Jesus, our atoning priest,
To Jesus, our superior king,
Be everlasting power confessed,
And every tongue his glory sing.

5 *

4 Behold! on flying clouds he comes,
   And every eye shall see him move:
Though with our sins we pierced him once,
   Then he displays his pardoning love.

5 The unbelieving world shall wail,
   While we rejoice to see the day:
Come, Lord! nor let thy promise fail,
   Nor let thy chariot long delay.

---

66   *Christ Ruling the World.*   **C. M.**

1 Joy to the world,—the Lord is come;
   Let earth receive her King;
Let ev'ry heart prepare him room,
   And heav'n and nature sing.

2 Joy to the earth,—the Saviour reigns;
   Let men their songs employ!
While fields, and floods, rocks, hills, and
     plains,
   Repeat the sounding joy.

3 No more let sins and sorrows grow,
   Nor thorns infest the ground;
He comes to make his blessings flow,
   Far as the curse is found.

4 He rules the world with truth and grace,
   And makes the nations prove
The glories of his righteousness,
   And wonders of his love.

67   *Christ worthy to Reign.*   **L. M.**

1 WORTHY the Lamb of boundless sway,
     In earth and heaven, the Lord of all!
Let all the powers of earth obey,
     And low before his footstool fall.

2 Higher—still higher swell the strain:
     Creation's voice the note prolong!
Jesus the Lamb shall ever reign:
     Let hallelujahs crown the song.

68   *Christ Reigning in Heaven.*   **8s & 7s.**

1 HARK! ten thousand harps and voices
     Sound the notes of praise above,
Jesus reigns, and heaven rejoices;
     Jesus reigns, the God of love;
See! he sits on yonder throne;
Jesus rules the world alone.
     Hallelujah! hallelujah! hallelujah! amen.

2 Jesus! hail! whose glory brightens
     All above, and gives it worth;
Lord of life! thy smile enlightens,
     Cheers, and charms thy saints on earth!
When we think of love like thine,
Lord! we own it love divine.

3 King of glory! reign forever,
     Thine an everlasting crown;
Nothing from thy love shall sever
     Those whom thou hast made thine own;

Happy objects of thy grace,
Destined to behold thy face.

4 Saviour! hasten thine appearing;
　　Bring—oh! bring the glorious day,
When, the awful summons hearing,
　　Heaven and earth shall pass away:
Then, with golden harps, we'll sing,
"Glory, glory to our King."

69　　*Christ's Lordship.*　　*H. M.*

1 JOIN all the glorious names
　　Of wisdom, love, and power,
That ever mortals knew,
　　That angels ever bore:
All are too mean to speak his worth,
To mean to set my Saviour forth.

2 Great Prophet of our God!
　　Our tongues would bless thy name;
By thee the joyful news
　　Of our salvation came:
The joyful news of sins forgiven,
Of hell subdued, and peace with heaven.

3 Jesus, our great high-priest,
　　Hath shed his blood and died;
My guilty conscience needs
　　No sacrifice beside:
His precious blood did once atone,
And now it pleads before the throne.

4 O thou almighty Lord,
    Our Conqueror and our King!
Thy scepter and thy sword,
    Thy reigning grace, we sing;
Thine is the power; oh! make us sit,
In willing bonds, beneath thy feet.

———◦❖◦———

70   *Christ's Mission.*   *H. M.*

1 COME, every pious heart,
    That loves the Saviour's name!
Your noblest powers exert,
    To celebrate his fame;
Tell all above, and all below,
The debt of love to him you owe.

2 He left his starry crown,
    And laid his robes aside;
On wings of love came down,
    And wept, and bled, and died:
What he endured, no tongue can tell,
To save our souls from death and hell.

3 From the dark grave he rose,
    The mansion of the dead;
And thence his mighty foes
    In glorious triumph led:
Up through the sky the conqueror rode,
And reigns on high, the Saviour God.

4 From thence he'll quickly come,
    His chariot will not stay,

And bear our spirits home
To realms of endless day:
There shall we see his lovely face,
And ever be in his embrace.

— ◦◦◦ —

71   *Christ's Exaltation.*   *8s & 7s.*

1 JESUS! hail! enthroned in glory,
    There forever to abide;
All the heav'nly host adore thee,
    Seated at thy Father's side.

2 There for sinners thou art pleading,
    There thou dost our place prepare;
Ever for us interceding,
    Till in glory we appear.

3 Worship, honor, power, and blessing,
    Thou art worthy to receive;
Loudest praises, without ceasing,
    Meet it is for us to give.

4 Help, ye bright angelic spirits!
    Bring your sweetest, noblest lays;
Help to sing our Saviour's merits,
    Help to chant Immanuel's praise.

— ◦◦◦ —

72   *Christ's Love.*   *C. M.*

1 PLUNGED in a gulf of dark despair,
    We wretched sinners lay,
Without one cheerful beam of hope,
    Or spark of glimmering day.

2 With pitying eyes the Prince of grace
  Beheld our helpless grief;
He saw, and—oh! amazing love!—
  He ran to our relief.

3 Down from the shining seats above,
  With joyful haste he fled,
Entered the grave in mortal flesh,
  And dwelt among the dead.

4 Oh! for this love let rocks and hills
  Their lasting silence break;
And all harmonious human tongues
  The Saviour's praises speak.

5 Angels! assist our mighty joys;
  Strike all your harps of gold;
But, when you raise your highest notes,
  His love can ne'er be told.

---

73   *Christ's Majesty.*   *L. M.*

1 AROUND the Saviour's lofty throne,
  Ten thousand times ten thousand sing;
They worship him as God alone,
  And crown him, everlasting King.

2 Approach, ye saints! this God is yours,
  'Tis Jesus fills the throne above:
Ye cannot want while God endures;
  Ye cannot fail while God is love.

3 Jesus, thou everlasting King!
  To thee the praise of heaven belongs!
Yet smile on us who fain would bring
  The tribute of our humble songs.

4 Though sin defile our worship here,
  We hope ere long thy face to view;
And, when our souls in heaven appear,
  We'll praise thy name as angels do.

------◦◦◦------

74   *Christ's Glory and Grace.*   *L. M.*

1 Now to the Lord a noble song!
  Awake, my soul! awake, my tongue!
Hosanna to th' eternal name,
  And all his boundless love proclaim.

2 See where it shines in Jesus' face,
  The brightest image of his grace!
God, in the person of his Son,
  Has all his mightiest works outdone.

3 Grace!—'tis a sweet, a charming theme;
  My thoughts rejoice at Jesus' name:
Ye angels! dwell upon the sound;
  Ye heavens! reflect it to the ground.

4 Oh! may I reach that happy place,
  Where he unveils his lovely face,
Where all his beauties you behold,
  And sing his name to harps of gold.

75   *Christ's Godhead.*   *8s & 7s.*

1 MIGHTY GOD! while angels bless thee,
    May a mortal lisp thy name?
Lord of men, as well as angels!
    Thou art every creature's theme:
Lord of every land and nation!
    Ancient of eternal days!
Sounded through the wide creation,
    Be thy just and lawful praise.

2 For the grandeur of thy nature—
    Grand beyond a seraph's thought;
For the wonders of creation,
    Works with skill and kindness wrought;
For thy providence, that governs
    Through thine empire's wide domain,
Wings an angel, guides a sparrow;
    Blessed be thy gentle reign.

3 For thy rich, thy free redemption,
    Bright, though veiled in darkness long,
Thought is poor, and poor expression;
    Who can sing that wondrous song?
Brightness of the Father's glory!
    Shall thy praise unuttered lie?
Break, my tongue, such guilty silence,
    Sing the Lord who came to die:

4 From the highest throne of glory
    To the cross of deepest woe,

6

Came to ransom guilty captives!
　Flow, my praise! forever flow.
Reascend, immortal Saviour!
　Leave thy footstool, take thy throne;
Thence return and reign forever;
　Be the kingdom all thine own!

76　　*Christ's Righteousness.*　　**S. M.**

1 How heavy is the night
　That hangs upon our eyes
Till Christ, with his reviving light,
　Over our souls arise.

2 Our guilty spirits dread
　To meet the wrath of heav'n:
But in his righteousness array'd,
　We see our sins forgiv'n.

3 Unholy and impure
　Are all our thoughts and ways;
His hands infected nature cure,
　With sanctifying grace.

4 The powers of hell agree
　To hold our souls in vain;
He sets the sons of bondage free,
　And breaks the cursed chain.

5 Lord! we adore thy ways
　To bring us near to God;
Thy sovereign power, thy healing grace,
　And thine atoning blood.

77   *Christ's Mediation.*   *S. M.*

1 RAISE your triumphant songs
   To an immortal tune;
Let the wide earth resound the deeds
   Celestial grace has done.

2 'T was mercy filled the throne,
   And wrath stood silent by,
When Christ was sent with pardons, down
   To rebels doomed to die.

3 Now, sinners! dry your tears;
   Let hopeless sorrow cease;
Bow to the scepter of his love,
   And take the offered peace.

4 Lord! we obey thy call;
   We lay an humble claim
To the salvation thou hast brought,
   And love and praise thy name.

78   *Christ's Sympathy.*   C. M.

1 Now let our cheerful eyes survey
   Our great High-Priest above;
And celebrate his constant care,
   His sympathetic love.

2 Though raised to a superior throne,
   Where angels bow around,
And high o'er all the shining train,
   With matchless honors crowned;

3 The names of all his saints he bears
      Deep graven on his heart;
  Nor shall the meanest Christian say
      That he has lost his part.

4 Those characters shall fair abide,
      Our everlasting trust,
  When gems, and monuments, and crowns
      Are mouldered down to dust.

5 So, gracious Saviour! on my breast,
      May thy dear name be worn,
  A sacred ornament and guard,
      To endless ages borne.

————•◇•————

79   *Christ, the Reconciler.*   *C. M.*

  1 DEAREST of all the names above,
        My Jesus and my God!
    Who can resist thy heavenly love,
        Or trifle with thy blood?

  2 'Tis by the merits of thy death,
        The Father smiles again;
    'Tis by thine interceding breath,
        The Spirit dwells with men.

  3 Till God in human flesh I see,
        My thoughts no comfort find;
    The holy, just, and sacred Three
        Are terrors to my mind

4 But, if 'mmanuel's face appear,
   My hope, my joy begins;
His name forbids my slavish fear,
   His grace removes my sins.

5 While Jews on their own law rely,
   And Greeks of wisdom boast,
I love th' incarnate mystery,
   And there I fix my trust.

80   *Christ's Salvation.*   *C. M.*

1 THE Saviour! oh! what endless charms
   Dwell in the blissful sound!
Its influence ev'ry fear disarms,
   And spreads sweet peace around.

2 Here pardon, life, and joys divine,
   In rich effusion flow,
For guilty rebels, lost in sin,
   And doomed to endless woe.

3 Oh! the rich depths of love divine,
   Of bliss a boundless store!
Dear Saviour! let me call thee mine;
   I cannot wish for more.

4 On thee alone my hope relies,
   Beneath thy cross I fall;
My Lord, my life, my sacrifice,
   My Saviour, and my all.
6 *

81　　　　*Christ's Excellency.*　　　*C. M.*

1 INFINITE loveliness is thine,
　　Thou glorious Prince of grace!
Thine uncreated beauties shine,
　　With never-fading rays.

2 Sinners, from earth's remotest end,
　　Come bending at thy feet;
To thee their prayers and songs ascend,
　　In thee their wishes meet.

3 Millions of happy spirits live
　　On thine exhaustless store;
From thee they all their bliss receive,
　　And heaven can give no more.

4 Thou art their triumph and their joy,
　　They find their life in thee;
Thy glories will their tongues employ,
　　Through all eternity.

82　　　　*Christ's Blood.*　　　*C. M.*

1 THERE is a fountain fill'd with blood,
　　Drawn from Immanuel's veins;
And sinners, plung'd beneath that flood,
　　Lose all their guilty stains.

2 The dying thief rejoiced to see
　　That fountain in his day;
And there may I, though vile as he,
　　Wash all my sins away.

3 Dear dying Lamb! thy precious blood
　　Shall never lose its pow'r,
　Till all the ransom'd church of God
　　Be saved to sin no more.

4 E'er since, by faith, I saw the stream
　　Thy flowing wounds supply,
　Redeeming love has been my theme,
　　And shall be till I die.

5 Then, in a nobler, sweeter song.
　　I'll sing thy power to save,
　When this poor, lisping, stammering tongue
　　Lies silent in the grave.

83　　　　*Christ's Commission.*　　　*C. M.*

1 COME, happy souls! approach your God
　　With new melodious songs;
　Come, render to almighty grace
　　The tribute of your tongues.

2 So strange, so boundless was the love
　　That pitied dying men,
　The Father sent his equal Son
　　To give them life again.

3 Thy hands, dear Jesus! were not armed
　　With a revenging rod;
　No hard commission to perform
　　The vengeance of a God

4 But all was mercy, all was mild,
    And wrath forsook the throne
When Christ on the kind errand came,
    And brought salvation down.

5 Here, sinners! you may heal your wounds,
    And wipe your sorrows dry;
Trust in the mighty Saviour's name,
    And you shall never die.

84   *Christ's Sacrifice.*   *S. M.*

1 Not all the blood of beasts,
    On Jewish altars slain,
Could give the guilty conscience peace,
    Or wash away the stain.

2 But Christ, the heav'nly Lamb,
    Takes all our sins away;
A sacrifice of nobler name,
    And richer blood than they.

3 My faith would lay her hand
    On that dear head of thine,
While, like a penitent, I stand,
    And there confess my sin.

4 My soul looks back to see
    The burdens thou didst bear,
When hanging on th' accursed tree,
    And hopes her guilt was there.

5 Believing, we rejoice
  To see the curse remove;
We bless the Lamb with cheerful voice,
  And sing his bleeding love.

---

85   *Union to Christ.*   *S. M.*

1 DEAR Saviour! we are thine
  By everlasting bonds;
Our names, our hearts, we would resign;
  Our hearts are in thy hands.

2 To thee we still would cleave,
  With ever-growing zeal;
If millions tempt us Christ to leave,
  Oh! let them ne'er prevail.

3 Thy Spirit shall unite
  Our souls to thee, our head;
Shall form us to thine image bright,
  That we thy paths may tread.

4 Death may our souls divide
  From these abodes of clay;
But love shall keep us near thy side,
  Through all the gloomy way.

5 Since Christ and we are one,
  Why should we doubt and fear?
If he in heaven hath fixed his throne,
  He'll fix his members there.

86 *Life in Christ.* **L. M.**

1 When sins and fears prevailing rise,
    And fainting hope almost expires,
Jesus! to thee I lift mine eyes,
    To thee I breathe my soul's desires.

2 If my immortal Saviour lives,
    Then my immortal life is sure;
His word a firm foundation gives;
    Here let me build and rest secure.

3 Here let my faith unshaken dwell,
    Forever firm the promise stands;
Not all the powers of earth and hell
    Can e'er dissolve the sacred bands.

4 Here, O my soul! thy trust repose;
    If Jesus is forever mine,
Not death itself—that last of foes—
    Shall break a union so divine.

87 *Communion with Christ.* **L. M.**

1 Oh! that I could forever dwell,
    Delighted, at the Saviour's feet,
Behold the form I love so well,
    And all his tender words repeat:

2 The world shut out from all my soul,
    And heaven brought in with all its bliss:
Oh! is there aught, from pole to pole,
    One moment to compare with this?

3 This is the hidden life I prize,
    A life of penitential love;
When most my follies I despise,
    And raise my highest thoughts above:

4 When all I am, I clearly see,
    And freely own, with deepest shame;
When the Redeemer's love to me
    Kindles within a deathless flame.

5 Thus would I live till nature fail,
    And all my former sins forsake;
Then rise to God, within the veil,
    And of eternal joys partake.

---

88   *Forgiveness in Christ. 8s & 7s. Double.*

1 HAIL, my ever-blessed Jesus!
    Only thee I wish to sing;
To my soul thy name is precious,
    Thou, my Prophet, Priest, and King:
Oh, what mercy flows from heaven!
    Oh, what joy and happiness!
Love I much? I've much forgiven,
    I'm a miracle of grace.

2 Once with Adam's race in ruin,
    Unconcerned in sin I lay;
Swift destruction still pursuing,
    Till my Saviour passed that way:

Witness, all ye hosts of heaven,
  My Redeemer's tenderness:
Love I much?   I've much forgiven,
  I'm a miracle of grace!

3 Shout, ye bright angelic choir!
  Praise the Lamb enthroned above!
While, astonished, I admire
  God's free grace and boundless love:
That blest moment I received him
  Filled my soul with joy and peace;
Love I much?   I've much forgiven,
  I'm a miracle of grace!

89   *Cleansing in Christ.*   *C. M.*

1 FOREVER here my rest shall be,
  Close to thy bleeding side;
This all my hope and all my plea,
  For me the Saviour died.

2 My dying Saviour, and my God,
  Fountain for guilt and sin,
Sprinkle me ever with thy blood,
  And cleanse and keep me clean.

3 Th' atonement of thy blood apply,
  Till faith to sight improve;
Till hope in full fruition die,
  And all my soul be love.

90   *Refuge in Christ.*   *7s. Double.*

1 JESUS, lover of my soul!
      Let me to thy bosom fly,
    While the billows near me roll,
      While the tempest still is high;
    Hide me, O my Saviour! hide,
      Till the storm of life be past;
    Safe into the haven guide;
      Oh! receive my soul at last.

2 Other refuge have I none,
      Hangs my helpless soul on thee:
    Leave, ah! leave me not alone;
      Still support and comfort me:
    All my trust on thee is stayed;
      All my help from thee I bring;
    Cover my defenseless head,
      With the shadow of thy wing.

3 Plenteous grace with thee is found,
      Grace to pardon all my sin;
    Let the healing streams abound,
      Make and keep me pure within:
    Thou of life the fountain art,
      Freely let me take of thee;
    Spring thou up within my heart,
      Rise to all eternity.

7

91   *Hope in Christ.*   **7s.**

1 CHRIST, of all my hopes the ground,
     Christ, the spring of all my joy!
Still in thee let me be found,
     Still for thee my powers employ.
Let thy love my heart inflame;
     Keep thy fear before my sight;
Be thy praise my highest aim;
     Be thy smile my chief delight.

2 Fountain of o'erflowing grace!
     Freely from thy fullness give;
Till I close my earthly race,
     Be it "Christ for me to live!"
Firmly trusting in thy blood,
     Nothing shall my heart confound:
Safely I shall pass the flood,
     Safely reach Immanuel's ground.

---

92   *Comfort in Christ.*   **C. M.**

1 How sweet the name of Jesus sounds
     In a believer's ear!
It soothes his sorrows, heals his wounds,
     And drives away his fear.

2 It makes the wounded spirit whole,
     And calms the troubled breast:
'Tis manna to the hungry soul,
     And, to the weary, rest.

3 Jesus! my shepherd, husband, friend,
    My prophet, priest, and king,
My Lord, my life, my way, my end,
    Accept the praise I bring.

4 Weak is the effort of my heart,
    And cold my warmest thought;
But, when I see thee as thou art,
    I'll praise thee as I ought.

5 Till then I would thy love proclaim,
    With every fleeting breath;
And may the music of thy name
    Refresh my soul in death.

----♦----

93   *The Name, Jesus.*   *C. M.*

1 JESUS! I love thy charming name,
    'Tis music to my ear;
Fain would I sound it out so loud,
    That earth and heaven should hear.

2 Yes,—thou art precious to my soul,
    My joy, my hope, my trust;
Jewels to thee are gaudy toys,
    And gold is sordid dust.

3 All my capacious powers can wish,
    In thee most richly meet;
Not to mine eyes is light so dear,
    Nor friendship half so sweet.

4 Thy grace still dwells upon my heart,
    And sheds its fragrance there;
The healing balm of all its wounds,
    The cordial of its care.

5 I'll speak the honors of thy name,
    With my last lab'ring breath;
Then, speechless, clasp thee in mine arms,
    The antidote of death.

---

94   *Christ, the Robe of Righteousness.*   *L. M.*

1 JESUS! thy robe of righteousness
    My beauty is, my glorious dress:
    'Mid flaming worlds, in this arrayed,
    With joy shall I lift up my head,

2 When, from the dust of death, I rise
    To claim my mansion in the skies,
    E'en then shall this be all my plea,
  "Jesus hath lived and died for me."

3 This spotless robe the same appears,
    When ruined nature sinks in years;
    No age can change its glorious hue;
    The robe of Christ is ever new.

4 Oh! let the dead now hear thy voice,
    Now bid thy banished ones rejoice;
    Their beauty this—their glorious dress,
    Jesus, the Lord, our righteousness.

95 *Christ, the only Refuge.* L. M.

1 THOU only Sovereign of my heart,
My refuge, my almighty Friend!
And can my soul from thee depart,
On whom alone my hopes depend?

2 Whither, ah! whither shall I go,
A wretched wanderer from my Lord?
Can this dark world of sin and woe
One glimpse of happiness afford?

3 Eternal life thy words impart,
On these my fainting spirit lives;
Here sweeter comforts cheer my heart
Than all the round of nature gives.

4 Let earth's alluring joys combine;
While thou art near, in vain they call;
One smile, one blissful smile of thine,
My dearest Lord! outweighs them all.

5 Low at thy feet my soul would lie,
Here safety dwells and peace divine:
Still let me live beneath thine eye,
For life, eternal life is thine.

96 *Christ, our Example.* C. M.

1 BEHOLD! where, in a mortal form,
Appears each grace divine:
The virtues all in Jesus met,
With mildest radiance shine.

7 *

2 To spread the rays of heav'nly light,
   To give the mourner joy,
To preach glad tidings to the poor,
   Was his divine employ.

3 'Mid keen reproach and cruel scorn,
   He, meek and patient stood,
His foes ungrateful sought his life,
   Who labor'd for their good.

4 When, in the hour of deep distress,
   Before his Father's throne,
With soul resigned, he bowed, and said,
   "Thy will, not mine, be done!"

5 Be Christ our pattern and our guide,
   His image may we bear;
Oh! may we tread his holy steps,
   His joy and glory share.

———◆———

97   *Love to Christ desired.*   *C. M.*

1 THOU lovely source of true delight,
   Whom I unseen adore!
Unveil thy beauties to my sight,
   That I may love thee more.

2 Thy glory o'er creation shines;
   But in thy sacred word,
I read in fairer, brighter lines
   My bleeding, dying Lord.

3 'Tis here, whenc'er my comforts droop,
    And sin and sorrow rise,
Thy love, with cheering beams of hope,
    My fainting heart supplies.

4 But, ah! too soon the pleasing scene
    Is clouded o'er with pain;
My gloomy fears rise dark between,
    And I again complain.

5 Jesus, my Lord, my life, my light!
    Oh! come with blissful ray;
Break radiant through the shades of night,
    And chase my fears away.

———•◦•———

98   *Christ's Worth Celebrated.*   *C. P. M.*

1 Oh! could I speak the matchless worth,
  Oh! could I sound the glories forth,
    Which in my Saviour shine;
I'd soar and touch the heav'nly strings,
And vie with Gabriel, while he sings,
    In notes almost divine.

2 I'd sing the characters he bears,
  And all the forms of love he wears,
    Exalted on his throne;
In loftiest songs of sweetest praise,
I would, to everlasting days,
    Make all his glories known.

3 Soon the delightful day will come,
  When my dear Lord shall bring me home.
    And I shall see his face;
  Then, with my Saviour, brother, friend,
  A blest eternity I'll spend,
    Triumphant in his grace.

---

99   *Completeness in Christ.*   *C. P. M.*

1 COME join, ye saints, with heart and voice,
  Alone in Jesus to rejoice,
    And worship at his feet;
  Come, take his praises on your tongues,
  And raise to him your thankful songs,
    "In him ye are complete!"

2 In him, who all our praise excels,
  The fullness of the Godhead dwells,
    And all perfections meet;
  The head of all celestial powers,
  Divinely theirs, divinely ours;
    "In him ye are complete!"

3 Still onward urge your heavenly way,
  Dependent on him day by day,
    His presence still entreat;
  His precious name forever bless,
  Your glory, strength, and righteousness,
    "In him ye are complete!"

4 Nor fear to pass the vale of death;
  In his dear arms resign your breath,

He'll make the passage sweet;
The gloom and fears of death shall flee,
And your departing souls shall see
"In him ye are complete!"

100   *Christ's Loving-Kindness.*   *L. M.*

1 Awake, my soul! in joyful lays,
  And sing the great Redeemer's praise;
  He justly claims a song from me;
  His loving-kindness, Oh! how free!

2 He saw me ruined by the fall,
  Yet loved me notwithstanding all;
  He saved me from my lost estate;
  His loving-kindness, Oh! how great!

3 When trouble, like a gloomy cloud,
  Has gathered thick and thundered loud,
  He near my soul has always stood;
  His loving-kindness, Oh! how good!

4 Soon shall I pass the gloomy vale,
  Soon all my mortal powers shall fail;
  Oh! may my last expiring breath
  His loving-kindness sing in death.

5 Then let me mount, and soar away
  To the bright world of endless day,
  And sing, with rapture and surprise,
  His loving-kindness in the skies.

101 *Christ's Love.* *L. M.*

1 I WAS a traitor doomed to die,
    Bound to endure eternal pains;
When Jesus saw me from on high,
    Was moved by love, and broke my chains.

2 Did melting pity stoop so low,
    The Lord of heaven pour out his blood,
To save our rebel race from woe,
    And be our Advocate with God?

3 Infinite mercy! boundless love!
    Stand in amaze, ye rolling skies!
The Son of God, his grace to prove,
    Hangs on a tree, and groans, and dies!

102 *Christ, the Way to Heaven.* *L. M.*

1 JESUS, my all, to heaven is gone,
    He whom I fix my hopes upon;
His track I see, and I'll pursue
    The narrow way, till him I view.
This is the way I long have sought,
    And mourned because I found it not.
Till late I heard my Saviour say,
"Come hither, soul! I am the way."

2 Lo! glad I come, and thou blest Lamb!
    Shalt take me to thee as I am;
My sinful self to thee I give,
    Nothing but love shall I receive,

Then will I tell to sinners round,
What a dear Saviour I have found ;
I'll point to thy redeeming blood,
And say, "Behold the way to God."

---

103 *Christ's Example.* *L. M.*

1 My dear Redeemer, and my Lord !
I read my duty in thy word,
But in thy life the law appears,
Drawn out in living characters.

2 Such was thy truth, and such thy zeal,
Such deference to thy Father's will,
Such love and meekness so divine,
I would transcribe and make them mine.

3 Cold mountains, and the midnight air,
Witnessed the fervor of thy prayer ;
The desert thy temptations knew,
Thy conflict, and thy vict'ry too.

4 Be thou my pattern ; make me bear
More of thy gracious image here ;
Then God, the judge, shall own my name,
Among the followers of the Lamb.

---

104 *Christ, the Rock of Ages.* *7s.*

1 Rock of ages, cleft for me !
Let me hide myself in thee ;

Let the water and the blood,
From thy wounded side that flowed,
Be of sin the perfect cure;
Save me, Lord! and make me pure.

2 Should my tears for ever flow,
Should my zeal no languor know,
This for sin could not atone,
Thou must save, and thou alone:
In my hand no price I bring;
Simply to thy cross I cling.

3 While I draw this fleeting breath,
When mine eyelids close in death,
When I rise to worlds unknown,
And behold thee on thy throne,
Rock of ages, cleft for me!
Let me hide myself in thee.

105　　*Christ, the Lamb of Calvary.*　**6s & 4s.**

1 My faith looks up to thee,
Thou Lamb of Calvary!
　　Saviour divine!
Now hear me, while I pray,
Take all my guilt away,
Oh! let me, from this day,
　　Be wholly thine.

2 May thy rich grace impart
Strength to my fainting heart,

My zeal inspire;
As thou hast died for me,
Oh! may my love to thee,
Pure, warm, and changeless be,
  A living fire.

3 While life's dark maze I tread,
And griefs around me spread,
  Be thou my guide;
Bid darkness turn to day,
Wipe sorrow's tears away,
Nor let me ever stray
  From thee aside.

4 When ends life's transient dream,
When death's cold sullen stream
  Shall o'er me roll,
Blest Saviour! then in love,
Fear and distrust remove;
Oh! bear me safe above,
  A ransomed soul.

---

106   *Christ Trusted.*   **7s & 6s.**

1 I LAY my sins on Jesus,
  The spotless Lamb of God;
He bears them all, and frees us
  From the accursed load.
I bring my guilt to Jesus,
  To wash my crimson stains
White, in his blood most precious,
  Till not a spot remains.

2 I lay my wants on Jesus,
    All fullness dwells in him;
He healeth my diseases,
    He doth my soul redeem.
I lay my griefs on Jesus,
    My burdens and my cares;
He from them all releases,
    He all my sorrow shares.

3 I long to be like Jesus,
    Meek, loving, lowly, mild;
I long to be like Jesus,
    The Father's holy child.
I long to be with Jesus,
    Amid the heavenly throng,
To sing with saints his praises,
    To learn the angels' song.

---

107   *Christ Adored.*   *7s & 6s.*

1 To thee my God and Saviour!
    My heart exulting sings,
Rejoicing in thy favor,
    Almighty King of kings!
I'll celebrate thy glory,
    With all thy saints above,
And tell the joyful story
    Of thy redeeming love.

2 Soon as the morn, with roses
    Bedecks the dewy east,

And when the sun reposes
  Upon the ocean's breast
My voice, in supplication,
  Well pleased the Lord shall hear,
Oh! grant me thy salvation,
  And to my soul draw near.

3 By thee through life supported,
  I'll pass the dangerous road,
With heavenly hosts escorted,
  Up to thy bright abode;
Then cast my crown before thee,
  And, all my conflicts o'er,
Unceasingly adore thee:
  What could an angel more?

---

108   *Christ Chosen.*   *C. M.*

1 To whom, my Saviour, shall I go,
  If I depart from thee?
My guide through all this vale of woe,
  And more than all to me.

2 The world reject thy gentle reign,
  And pay thy death with scorn;
Oh! they could plait thy crown again,
  And sharpen every thorn.

3 But I have felt thy dying love
  Breathe gently through my heart,
To whisper hope of joys above;
  And can we ever part?

4 Ah! no, with thee I'll walk below,
　My journey to the grave:
To whom, my Saviour, shall I go,
　When only thou canst save.

109　　*Jesus in the Heart.*　　C. M.

1 O JESUS! King most wonderful!
　Thou Conqueror renowned!
Thou Sweetness most ineffable!
　In whom all joys are found.

2 When once thou visitest the heart,
　Then truth begins to shine;
Then earthly vanities depart;
　Then kindles love divine.

3 O Jesus! light of all below!
　Thou Fount of life and fire!
Surpassing all the joys we know,
　All that we can desire.

4 Thee may our tongues forever bless,
　Thee may we love alone,
And ever in our lives express
　The image of thine own.

110　　*Satisfaction in Jesus.*　　C. M.

1 I HEARD the voice of Jesus say,
　Come unto me and rest:
Lay down, thou weary one, lay down
　Thy head upon my breast.

I came to Jesus as I was,
   Weary, and worn, and sad,
I found in him a resting-place,
   And he has made me glad.

2 I heard the voice of Jesus say,
   Behold, I freely give
The living water; thirsty one
   Stoop down and drink and live.
I came to Jesus, and I drank
   Of that life-giving stream;
My thirst was quench'd, my soul revived,
   And now I live in him.

3 I heard the voice of Jesus say,
   I am this dark world's light:
Look unto me, thy morn shall rise
   And all thy day be bright.
I looked to Jesus, and I found
   In him my Star, my Sun;
And in that light of life I'll walk,
   Till all my journey 's done.

111   *Rest in Jesus.*   *7s.*

1 COME! said Jesus' sacred voice,
Come, and make my paths your choice:
I will guide you to your home:
Weary wanderer, hither come.

2 Thou, who homeless and forlorn,
Long hast borne the proud world's scorn,

Long hast roamed the barren waste
Weary wanderer, hither haste.

3 Ye, who tossed on beds of pain
Seek for ease, but seek in vain;
Ye, by fiercer anguish torn,
In remorse for guilt who mourn:—

4 Hither come, for here is found
Balm that flows for every wound!
Peace, that ever shall endure,
Rest eternal, sacred, sure.

---

112   *Christ, the Great Physician.*   **L. M.**

1 DEEP are the wounds which sin has made;
    Where shall the sinner find a cure?
In vain, alas! is nature's aid;
    The work exceeds her utmost pow'r.

2 But can no sov'reign balm be found?
    And is no kind physician nigh
To ease the pain and heal the wound,
    Ere life and hope forever fly?

3 There is a great physician near;
    Look up, my fainting soul! and live;
See,—in his heavenly smiles appear
    Such help as nature cannot give.

4 See,—in the Saviour's dying blood,
    Life, health, and bliss abundant flow:
'Tis only that dear sacred flood,
    Can ease thy pain and heal thy woe.

113   *Not ashamed of Christ.*   *L. M.*

1 JESUS! and shall it ever be,
  A mortal man ashamed of thee?
  Ashamed of thee, whom angels praise,
  Whose glories shine through endless days?

2 Ashamed of Jesus! sooner far
  Let evening blush to own a star;
  He sheds the beams of light divine,
  O'er this benighted soul of mine.

3 Ashamed of Jesus! that dear friend
  On whom my hopes of heaven depend?
  No;—when I blush, be this my shame,
  That I no more revere his name.

4 Ashamed of Jesus!—yes, I may,
  When I've no guilt to wash away,
  No tear to wipe,—no good to crave,—
  No fears to quell,—no soul to save.

5 Till then—nor is my boasting vain—
  Till then, I boast a Saviour slain!
  And oh! may this my glory be,
  That Christ is not ashamed of me.

---

114   *Christ Crowned.*   *C. M.*

1 All hail the power of Jesus' name!
    Let angels prostrate fall;
  Bring forth the royal diadem,
    And crown him Lord of all;

2 Crown him, ye morning stars of light!
   Who formed this floating ball;
Now hail the strength of Israel's might,
   And crown him, Lord of all.

3 Ye chosen seed of Adam's race,
   Ye ransomed from the fall!
Hail him, who saves you by his grace,
   And crown him, Lord of all.

4 Sinners! whose love can ne'er forget
   The wormwood and the gall,
Come, spread your trophies at his feet,
   And crown him, Lord of all.

5 Let every kindred, every tribe,
   On this terrestrial ball,
To him all majesty ascribe,
   And crown him, Lord of all.

---

115   *Christ Rejoiced in.*   **S. M.**

1 Awake and sing the song
   Of Moses and the Lamb;
Wake, every heart and every tongue!
   To praise the Saviour's name.

2 Sing of his dying love;
   Sing of his rising power;
Sing—how he intercedes above
   For those whose sins he bore.

3 Ye pilgrims! on the road
  To Zion's city, sing!
Rejoice ye in the Lamb of God,
  In Christ, the eternal King.

4 Soon shall we hear him say,
  "Ye blessed children! come!"
Soon will he call us hence away,
  And take his wanderers home.

5 There shall each raptured tongue
  His endless praise proclaim;
And sweeter voices tune the song
  Of Moses and the Lamb.

116   *Christ loved, although unseen.*   *S. M.*

1 Not with our mortal eyes
  Have we beheld the Lord;
Yet we rejoice to hear his name,
  And love him in his word.

2 On earth, we want the sight
  Of our Redeemer's face;
Yet, Lord! our inmost thoughts delight
  To dwell upon thy grace.

3 And, when we taste thy love,
  Our joys divinely grow
Unspeakable, like those above,
  And heaven begins below.

117 *Christ Supplicated.* **8s & 7s.**

1 LOVE divine, all love excelling,
   Joy of heaven to earth come down!
Fix in us thy humble dwelling,
   All thy faithful mercies crown;
Jesus! thou art all compassion,
   Pure, unbounded love thou art;
Visit us with thy salvation,
   Enter every trembling heart.

2 Breathe, oh! breathe thy loving Spirit
   Into every troubled breast;
Let us all thy grace inherit,
   Let us find thy promised rest:
Take away the love of sinning,
   Take our load of guilt away;
End the work of thy beginning,
   Bring us to eternal day.

3 Carry on thy new creation,
   Pure and holy may we be;
Let us see our whole salvation,
   Perfectly secured by thee;
Change from glory into glory,
   Till in heaven we take our place;
Till we cast our crowns before thee,
   Lost in wonder, love, and praise.

118 *Christ, a Friend.* *8s & 7s.*

1 ONE there is, above all others,
    Well deserves the name of Friend;
His is love beyond a brother's,
    Costly, free, and knows no end.

2 Which, of all our friends, to save us,
    Could, or would have shed his blood?
But this Jesus died to have us
    Reconciled in him to God.

3 When he lived on earth abased,
    Friend of sinners was his name;
Now, above all glory raised,
    He rejoices in the same.

4 Oh! for grace our hearts to soften!
    Teach us, Lord, at length to love;
We, alas! forget too often
    What a friend we have above.

119 *Christ's Free Grace.* *12s.*

1 THE voice of free grace cries, "Escape to the
    mountain!"
For Adam's lost race Christ hath opened a
    fountain;
For sin and uncleanness, and ev'ry transgres-
    sion,
His blood flows most freely in streams of
    salvation.

Chorus.—Hallelujah to the Lamb! he hath
purchased our pardon,
We'll praise him again when we pass
over Jordan.
His blood flows most freely in streams
of salvation,
We'll praise him again when we pass
over Jordan.

2 Ye souls that are wounded! oh! flee to the
Saviour!
He calls you in mercy,—'tis infinite favor;
Your sins are increasing,—escape to the
mountain,
His blood can remove them, it flows from
the fountain.

3 O Jesus! ride onward, triumphantly glorious,
O'er sin, death and hell thou art more than
victorious;
Thy name is the theme of the great congregation,
While angels and saints raise the shout of
salvation.

4 With joy shall we stand, when escaped to the
shore;
With harps in our hands, we'll praise him
the more;
We'll range the sweet plains on the bank
of the river,
And sing of salvation forever and ever!

120 *Christ's Full Salvation.* *C. M.*

1 MAJESTIC sweetness sits enthroned
    Upon the Saviour's brow;
His head with radiant glories crowned,
    His lips with grace o'erflow.

2 No mortal can with him compare,
    Among the sons of men;
Fairer is he than all the fair
    Who fill the heavenly train.

3 He saw me plung'd in deep distress,
    And flew to my relief;
For me he bore the shameful cross,
    And carried all my grief.

4 To him I owe my life and breath,
    And all the joys I have;
He makes me triumph over death,
    And saves me from the grave.

5 To heaven, the place of his abode,
    He brings my weary feet;
Shows me the glories of my God,
    And makes my joys complete.

6 Since from thy bounty I receive
    Such proofs of love divine,
Had I a thousand hearts to give,
    Lord! they should all be thine.

121   *Christ's Compassion.*   *C. M.*

1 WITH joy we meditate the grace
   Of our High-Priest above;
His heart is made of tenderness,
   His bowels melt with love.

2 Touched with a sympathy within,
   He knows our feeble frame;
He knows what sore temptations mean,
   For he has felt the same.

3 But spotless, innocent, and pure,
   The great Redeemer stood;
While Satan's fiery darts he bore,
   And did resist to blood.

4 He, in the days of feeble flesh,
   Poured out his cries and tears;
And, in his measure, feels afresh
   What every member bears.

5 Then let our humble faith address
   His mercy and his power;
We shall obtain delivering grace,
   In the distressing hour.

122   *Christ's Human Name.*

1 THERE is no name so sweet on earth,
   No name so sweet in heaven,
The name before his wondrous birth,
   To Christ, the Saviour given.

Chorus.—We love to sing around our King,
    And hail him blessed Jesus:
For there's no word ear ever heard,
    So dear, so sweet as Jesus.

2 His human name they did proclaim,
    When Abram's son they sealed him,
The name that still by God's good will,
    Deliverer revealed him.

3 And when he hung upon the tree,
    They wrote his name above him,
That all might see the reason we
    For evermore must love him.

4 So now upon his Father's throne,
    Almighty to release us
From sin and pains, he gladly reigns,
    The Prince and Saviour Jesus.

---

123   *Christ's Glory Proclaimed.*   *C. M.*

1 COME, let us join our cheerful songs,
    With angels round the throne,
Ten thousand thousand are their tongues,
    But all their joys are one.

2 "Worthy the Lamb that died," they cry,
    "To be exalted thus!"
"Worthy the Lamb," our lips reply,
    "For he was slain for us!"

3 Jesus is worthy to receive
    Honor and power divine;
And blessings, more than we can give,
    Be, Lord! forever thine.

4 Let all who dwell above the sky,
    And air, and earth, and seas,
Conspire to lift thy glories high,
    And speak thine endless praise.

5 The whole creation join in one,
    To bless the sacred name
Of Him who sits upon the throne,
    And to adore the Lamb.

———◆———

124   *Christ's Love Celebrated.*   *C. M.*

1 To our Redeemer's glorious name,
    Awake the sacred song!
Oh! may his love—immortal flame—
    Tune every heart and tongue!

2 His love what mortal thought can reach?
    What mortal tongue display?
Imagination's utmost stretch,
    In wonder dies away.

3 Dear Lord! while we adoring pay
    Our humble thanks to thee,
May every heart with rapture say,
    "The Saviour died for me!

4 Oh! may the sweet, the blissful theme,
   Fill every heart and tongue,
Till strangers love thy charming name,
   And join the sacred song.

125   *Christ's Cross and Crown.*   C. M.

1 MUST Jesus bear the cross alone,
   And all the world go free?
No, there's a cross for ev'ry one.
   And there's a cross for me.

2 The consecrated cross I'll bear,
   Till death shall set me free,
And then go home my crown to wear,
   For there's a crown for me.

3 Upon the crystal pavement, down
   At Jesus' pierced feet,
Joyful, I'll cast my golden crown,
   And his dear name repeat.

4 And palms shall wave, and harps shall ring,
   Beneath heaven's arches high;
The Lord that lives, the ransomed sing,
   That lives no more to die.

5 O precious cross! O glorious crown!
   O resurrection day!
Ye angels, from the stars come down,
   And bear my soul away.

9 *

1 FROM thee, my God! my joys shall rise
　　And run eternal rounds
Beyond the limits of the skies,
　　And all created bounds.

2 The holy triumphs of my soul
　　Shall death itself out-brave,
Leave dull mortality behind,
　　And fly beyond the grave.

3 There, where my blessed Jesus reigns,
　　In heaven's unmeasured space,
I'll spend a long eternity
　　In pleasure and in praise.

4 Blest Jesus! every smile of thine
　　Shall fresh endearments bring,
And thousand tastes of new delight
　　From all thy graces spring.

127　　　*Christ Worshiped in Heaven.*　　8s.

1 YE angels! who stand round the throne,
　　And view my Immanuel's face,—
In rapturous songs make him known,
　　Tune—tune your soft harps to his praise:
He formed you the spirits you are,
　　So happy, so noble, so good;

When others sunk down in despair,
  Confirmed by his power ye stood.

2 Ye saints! who stand nearer than they,
    And cast your bright crowns at his feet,
  His grace and his glory display,
    And all his rich mercies repeat:
  He snatched you from hell and the grave,
    He ransomed from death and despair:
  For you he was mighty to save,
    Almighty to bring you safe there.

3 Oh! when will the moment appear
    When I shall unite in your song!
  I'm weary of lingering here,
    And I to your Saviour belong:
  I'm fettered and chained here in clay,
    I struggle and pant to be free;
  I long to be soaring away,
    My God and my Saviour to see.

4 I long to put on my attire,
    Washed white in the blood of the Lamb;
  I long to be one of your choir,
    And tune my sweet harp to his name:
  I long—oh! I long to be there,
    Where sorrow and sin bid adieu,
  Your joy and your friendship to share,
    To wonder and worship with you.

HOLY SPIRIT.

128 *The Loving Spirit.* *C. M.*

1 COME, Holy Spirit, heavenly Dove!
  With all thy quickening powers,
Kindle a flame of sacred love,
  In these cold hearts of ours.

2 Look—how we grovel here below,
  Fond of these trifling toys!
Our souls can neither fly nor go,
  To reach eternal joys.

3 In vain we tune our formal songs,
  In vain we strive to rise;
Hosannas languish on our tongues,
  And our devotion dies.

4 Dear Lord! and shall we ever live,
  At this poor dying rate,
Our love so faint, so cold to thee,
  And thine to us so great?

5 Come, Holy Spirit, heavenly Dove!
  With all thy quickening powers:
Come, shed abroad a Saviour's love,
  And that shall kindle ours.

----

129 *The Renewing Spirit.* *C. M.*

1 How helpless guilty nature lies,
  Unconscious of its load!
The heart, unchanged, can never rise
  To happiness and God.

2 Can aught beneath a power divine,
  The stubborn will subdue?
'Tis thine, eternal Spirit! thine,
  To form the heart anew.

3 'Tis thine, the passions to recall,
  And upward bid them rise;
To make the scales of error fall,
  From reason's darkened eyes;

4 To chase the shades of death away,
  And bid the sinner live;
A beam of heaven, a vital ray,
  'Tis thine alone to give.

5 Oh! change these wretched hearts of ours,
  And give them life divine;
Then shall our passions and our powers,
  Almighty Lord! be thine.

---

130   *The Guiding Spirit.*   L. M.

1 COME, gracious Spirit, heavenly Dove!
  With light and comfort from above:
  Be thou our guardian, thou our guide,
  O'er every thought and step preside.

2 To us the light of truth display,
  And make us know and choose thy way;
  Plant holy fear in every heart,
  That we from God may ne'er depart.

3 Lead us to holiness—the road
  That we must take to dwell with God;
  Lead us to Christ, the living way,
  Nor let us from his precepts stray.

4 Lead us to God, our final rest,
  To be with him forever blessed;
  Lead us to heaven, its bliss to share,
  And drink of life's clear river there.

---

131   *The Uplifting Spirit.*   **L. M.**

1 DESCEND from heaven, immortal Dove!
  Stoop down, and take us on thy wings,
And mount, and bear us far above
  The reach of these inferior things;

2 Beyond—beyond this lower sky
  Up where eternal ages roll,
Where solid pleasures never die,
  And fruits immortal feast the soul.

3 Oh! for a sight, a blissful sight,
  Of our almighty Father's throne!
There sits the Saviour crowned with light,
  Clothed in a body like our own.

4 Adoring saints around him stand,
  And thrones and powers before him fall;
The God shines gracious through the man,
  And sheds sweet glories on them all.

5 Oh! what amazing joys they feel,
    While to their golden harps they sing,
  And sit on every heavenly hill,
    And spread the triumph of their King!

<hr>

132   *The Quickening Spirit.*   *C. M.*

1 ENTHRONED on high, almighty Lord!
    The Holy Ghost send down:
  Fulfill in us thy faithful word,
    And all thy mercies crown.

2 Though, on our heads, no tongues of fire
    Their wondrous powers impart,
  Grant, Saviour! what we more desire,
    Thy Spirit in our heart.

3 Spirit of life, and light, and love!
    Thy heavenly influence give;
  Quicken our souls, born from above,
    In Christ, that we may live.

4 To our benighted minds reveal
    The glories of his grace,
  And bring us, where no clouds conceal
    The brightness of his face.

5 His love within us shed abroad,
    Life's ever-springing well,
  Till God in us, and we in God,
    In love eternal dwell.

133　　*The Spirit Sought.*　　*C. M.*

1 GREAT Father of each perfect gift!
　　Behold, thy servants wait;
With longing eyes and lifted hands
　　We flock around thy gate.

2 Oh! shed abroad that choicest gift,
　　Thy Spirit from above,
To cheer our eyes with sacred light,
　　And fire our hearts with love.

3 Blest Earnest of eternal joy!
　　Declare our sins forgiven,
And bear, with energy divine,
　　Our raptured thoughts to heaven.

4 Diffuse, O God! thy copious showers,
　　That earth its fruit may yield,
And change the barren wilderness,
　　To Carmel's flowery field.

———◦◇◦———

134　　*The Spirit Promised.*　　*H. M.*

1 O THOU that hearest pray'r!
　　Attend our humble cry;
And let thy servants share
　　Thy blessing from on high!
We plead the promise of thy word;
Grant us thy Holy Spirit, Lord!

2 If earthly parents hear
　　Their children when they cry;

If they, with love sincere,
　Their varied wants supply;
Much more wilt thou thy love display,
And answer when thy children pray.

3 Our Heavenly Father, thou;
　We, children of thy grace;
Oh! let thy Spirit now
　Descend, and fill the place:
So shall we feel the heavenly flame,
And all unite to praise thy name.

135　　　*Prayer to the Spirit.*　　　S. M.

1 BLEST Comforter divine!
　Let rays of heavenly love
Amid our gloom and darkness shine,
　To guide our souls above.

2 Draw, with thy still small voice,
　From every sinful way;
And bid the mourning saint rejoice,
　Though earthly joys decay.

3 By thine inspiring breath,
　Make every cloud of care,
And e'en the gloomy vale of death,
　A smile of glory wear.

136　　　*The Spirit's Power.*　　　L. M.

1 ETERNAL Spirit! we confess,
And sing the wonders of thy grace;

Thy pow'r conveys our blessings down,
From God, the Father, and the Son.

2 Enlighten'd by thy heav'nly ray,
Our shades and darkness turn to day;
Thine inward teachings make us know
Our danger and our refuge too.

3 Thy power and glory work within,
And break the chains of reigning sin;
Do our imperious lusts subdue,
And form our wretched hearts anew.

4 The troubled conscience knows thy voice,
Thy cheering words awake our joys;
Thy words allay the stormy wind,
And calm the surges of the mind.

———◦◊◦———

137 *Prayer for Faith.* *L. M.*

1 COME, Holy Spirit! calm my mind,
And fit me to approach my God;
Remove each vain, each worldly thought,
And lead me to thy blest abode.

2 Hast thou imparted to my soul
A living spark of holy fire?
Oh! kindle now the sacred flame;
Make me to burn with pure desire.

3 A brighter faith and hope impart,
And let me now my Saviour see;
Oh! soothe and cheer my burdened heart,
And bid my spirit rest in thee.

138   *Prayer for Comfort.*   8s & 7s.

1 HOLY GHOST! dispel our sadness,
   Pierce the clouds of nature's night;
Come, thou Source of joy and gladness!
   Breathe thy life, and spread thy light.

2 Author of our new creation!
   Bid us all thine influence prove;
Make our souls thy habitation;
   Shed abroad the Saviour's love.

139   *Prayer for Grace.*   7s.

1 HOLY GHOST, with light divine,
   Shine upon this heart of mine;
   Chase the shades of night away,
   Turn my darkness into day.

2 Holy Ghost! with power divine,
   Cleanse this guilty heart of mine;
   Long hath sin, without control,
   Held dominion o'er my soul.

3 Holy Ghost! with joy divine,
   Cheer this saddened heart of mine;
   Bid my many woes depart,
   Heal my wounded, bleeding heart.

4 Holy Spirit! all-divine,
   Dwell within this heart of mine;
   Cast down every idol-throne,
   Reign supreme,—and reign alone.

140　　*Prayer for Life.*　　7s.

1 GRACIOUS Spirit! Love divine!
Let thy light within me shine;
All my guilty fears remove,
Fill me with thy heavenly love.

2 Speak thy pard'ning grace to me,
Set the burdened sinner free;
Lead me to the Lamb of God,
Wash me in his precious blood.

3 Life and peace to me impart,
Seal salvation on my heart;
Breathe thyself into my breast,
Earnest of immortal rest.

4 Let me never from thee stray,
Keep me in the narrow way;
Fill my soul with joy divine,
Keep me, Lord! forever thine.

----♦----

141　　*Regeneration.*　　C. M.

1 NOT all the outward forms on earth,
Nor rites that God has given,
Nor will of man, nor blood, nor birth,
Can raise a soul to heaven.

2 The sovereign will of God alone
Creates us heirs of grace,
Born in the image of his Son,
A new peculiar race.

3 The Spirit, like some heavenly wind,
   Breathes on the sons of flesh;
Creates anew the carnal mind,
   And forms the man afresh.

4 Our quickened souls awake, and rise,
   From the long sleep of death;
On heavenly things we fix our eyes,
   And praise employs our breath.

142   *Sealing.*   *C. M.*

1 WHY should the children of a king
   Go mourning all their days?
Great Comforter! descend, and bring
   Some tokens of thy grace.

2 Dost thou not dwell in all the saints,
   And seal the heirs of heaven?
When wilt thou banish my complaints,
   And show my sins forgiven?

3 Assure my conscience of her part
   In the Redeemer's blood;
And bear thy witness with my heart,
   That I am born of God.

4 Thou art the earnest of his love,
   The pledge of joys to come:
And thy soft wings, celestial Dove!
   Will safe convey me home.

10 *

143   *The Comforter.*   *L. M.*

1 SURE, the blest Comforter is nigh;
    'Tis he sustains my fainting heart·
Else would my hope forever die,
    And every cheering ray depart.·

2 Whene'er, to call the Saviour mine,
    With ardent wish my heart aspires,
Can it be less than power divine,
    That animates these strong desires?

3 And, when my cheerful hope can say,
    I love my God and taste his grace,
Lord! is it not thy blissful ray,
    That brings this dawn of sacred peace?

4 Let thy good Spirit in my heart
    Forever dwell, O God of love!
And light and heavenly peace impart,
    Sweet earnest of the joys above.

144   *The Spirit Entreated.*   *L. M.*

1 STAY, thou insulted Spirit! stay,
    Though I have done thee such despite;
Cast not a sinner quite away,
    Nor take thine everlasting flight.

2 Though I have most unfaithful been
    Of all who e'er thy grace received;
Ten thousand times thy goodness seen.
    Ten thousand times thy goodness grieved.

3 Yet, oh! the chief of sinners spare,
    In honor of my great High-Priest;
Nor, in thy righteous anger, swear
    I shall not see thy people's rest.

4 My weary soul, O God! release,
    Uphold me with thy gracious hand;
Guide me into thy perfect peace,
    And bring me to the promised land.

---

145   *The Spirit's Witness.*   7s & 6s.

1 SAVIOUR, I thy word believe,
    My unbelief remove;
Now thy quickening Spirit give,
    The unction from above:
Show me, Lord, how good thou art;
    Now thy gracious word fulfill;
Send the witness in my heart,
    The Holy Ghost reveal.

2 Blessed Comforter, come down,
    And live and move in me;
Make my ev'ry deed thine own,
    In all things led by thee:
Bid my sin and fear depart,
    And within, oh! deign to dwell:
Faithful Witness, in my heart,
    Thy perfect light reveal.

3 Whom the world cannot receive,
    O Lord, reveal in me;

Son of God, I cease to live,
　　Unless I live to thee:
Make me choose the better part;
　　Oh! do thou my pardon seal;
Send the witness to my heart,
　　The Holy Ghost reveal.

146   *The Spirit's Baptism.*   C. M.

1 OH! that in me the sacred fire
　　Might now begin to glow;
Burn up the dross of base desire,
　　And make the mountains flow.

2 Oh! that it now from heaven might fall,
　　And all my sins consume;
Come, Holy Ghost, for thee I call;
　　Spirit of burning, come.

3 Refining fire, go through my heart;
　　Illuminate my soul;
Scatter thy life through every part,
　　And sanctify the whole.

AWAKENING.

147   *Expostulation.*   *11s.*

1 OH! turn ye, oh! turn ye, for why will ye
　　die,
When God, in great mercy, is coming so nigh?
Now Jesus invites you, the Spirit says, Come,
And angels are waiting to welcome you home.

2 How vain the delusion, that while you delay,
Your hearts may grow better by staying away;
Come wretched, come guilty, come just as you
    are;
All helpless and dying, to Jesus repair.

3 Now Jesus is ready your souls to receive,
Oh! how can you question, if you will believe?
If sin be your burden, why will you not come?
'Tis you he makes welcome; he bids you come
    home.

---

148   *Delay not.*   *11s.*

1 DELAY not, delay not, O sinner—draw near;
    The waters of life are now flowing for thee:
No price is demanded, the Saviour is here,
    Redemption is purchased, salvation is free.

2 Delay not, delay not; why longer abuse
    The love and compassion of Jesus thy God?
A fountain is opened, how canst thou refuse
    To wash and be cleansed in his pardoning
        blood?

3 Delay not, delay not, O sinner, to come,
    For mercy still lingers, and calls thee to-day:
Her voice is not heard in the vale of the tomb;
    Her message, unheeded, will soon pass away.

4 Delay not, delay not—the Spirit of grace,
    Long grieved and resisted, may take its sad
        flight,

And leave thee in darkness to finish thy race,
  To sink in the gloom of eternity's night.

5 Delay not, delay not—the hour is at hand,
  The earth shall dissolve, and the heavens
      shall fade;
The dead, small and great, in the judgment
      shall stand;
  What power then, O sinner, shall lend thee
      its aid?

———•———

149   *The Way to Peace.*   *11s.*

1 ACQUAINT thee, O sinner, acquaint thee, with
      God,
And joy like the sunshine shall beam on thy
      road,
And peace like the dew-drop shall fall on thy
      head,
And sleep like an angel shall visit thy bed.

2 Acquaint thee, O sinner, acquaint thee, with
      God,
And he shall be with thee when fears are
      abroad;
Thy safeguard in danger that threatens thy
      path,
Thy joy in the valley and shadow of death.

150   *The Work of Life.*   **L. M.**

1 LIFE is the time to serve the Lord
The time to insure the great reward;
And, while the lamp holds out to burn,
The vilest sinner may return.

2 Life is the hour that God has given,
To escape from hell and fly to heaven;
The day of grace, and mortals may
Secure the blessings of the day.

3 The living know that they must die,
But all the dead forgotten lie;
Their mem'ry and their sense are gone,
Alike unknowing and unknown.

4 Then, what my thoughts design to do,
My hands! with all your might pursue;
Since no device, nor work is found,
Nor faith, nor hope, beneath the ground.

5 There are no acts of pardon past,
In the cold grave to which we haste;
But darkness, death, and long despair,
Reign in eternal silence there.

—◦—

151   *The Day of Grace.*   **L. M.**

1 WHILE life prolongs its precious light,
Mercy is found and peace is given:
But soon,—ah! soon,—approaching night
Shall blot out every hope of heaven.

2 While God invites, how blest the day!
   How sweet the gospel's charming sound!
Come, sinners! haste, oh! haste away,
   While yet a pard'ning God he's found.

3 Soon, borne on time's most rapid wing,
   Shall death command you to the grave,
Before his bar your spirits bring,
   And none be found to hear, or save.

4 In that lone land of deep despair,
   No Sabbath's heavenly light shall rise,
No God regard your bitter prayer,
   No Saviour call you to the skies.

------

152   *To-morrow not ours.*   *S. M.*

1 TO-MORROW, Lord! is thine,
   Lodged in thy sovereign hand;
And, if its sun arise and shine,
   It shines by thy command.

2 The present moment flies,
   And bears our life away;
Oh! make thy servants truly wise,
   That they may live to-day.

3 Since, on this fleeting hour,
   Eternity is hung,
Awaken, by thy mighty power,
   The aged and the young.

4 One thing demands our care;
  Be that one thing pursued;
Lest, slighted once, the season fair
  Should never be renewed.

5 To Jesus may we fly,
  Swift as the morning light,
Lest life's young golden beams should die,
  In sudden, endless night.

———•◦•———

153   *Man Condemned.*   *S. M.*

1 Ah! how shall fallen man
  Be just before his God?
If he contend in righteousness,
  We fall beneath his rod.

2 If he our ways should mark,
  With strict inquiring eyes,
Could we, for one of thousand faults,
  A just excuse devise?

3 All-seeing, powerful God!
  Who can with thee contend?
Or who, that tries the unequal strife,
  Shall prosper in the end?

4 The mountains, in thy wrath,
  Their ancient seats forsake;
The trembling earth deserts her place,
  Her rooted pillars shake.

11

5 Ah! how shall guilty man
  Contend with such a God?
None—none can meet him, and escape,
  But through the Saviour's blood.

---

154 *The Spirit's Call.* L. M.

1 Say, sinner! hath a voice within
  Oft whispered to thy secret soul,
Urged thee to leave the ways of sin,
  And yield thy heart to God's control?

2 Sinner! it was a heavenly voice,
  It was the Spirit's gracious call;
It bade thee make the better choice,
  And haste to seek in Christ thine all.

3 Spurn not the call to life and light;
  Regard, in time, the warning kind;
That call thou may'st not always slight,
  And yet the gate of mercy find.

4 God's Spirit will not always strive
  With hardened, self-destroying man;
Ye, who persist his love to grieve,
  May never hear his voice again.

5 Sinner! perhaps, this very day,
  Thy last accepted time may be:
Oh! should'st thou grieve him now away,
  Then hope may never beam on thee.

155   *Life and Death.*   L. M.

1 BROAD is the road that leads to death,
    And thousands walk together there;
But wisdom shows a narrow path,
    With here and there a traveler.

2 "Deny thyself and take thy cross,"
    Is the Redeemer's great command:
Nature must count her gold but dross,
    If she would gain this heavenly land.

3 The fearful soul that tires and faints,
    And walks the ways of God no more,
Is but esteemed almost a saint,
    And makes his own destruction sure.

4 Lord! let not all my hopes be vain;
    Create my heart entirely new,
Which hypocrites could ne'er attain,
    Which false apostates never knew.

156   *Heaven or Hell.*   C. P. M.

1 Lo! on a narrow neck of land,
Between two boundless seas I stand,
    Yet how insensible!
A point of time, a moment's space,
Removes me to yon heav'nly place,
    Or shuts me up in hell!

2 O God! my inmost soul convert,
And deeply on my thoughtless heart,

Eternal things impress;
Give me to feel their solemn weight,
And save me, ere it be too late;
Wake me to righteousness.

3 Before me place, in bright array,
The pomp of that tremendous day,
　　When thou with clouds shalt come,
To judge the nations at thy bar;
And tell me, Lord! shall I be there,
　　To meet a joyful doom!

4 Be this my one great business here,
With holy trembling, holy fear,
　　To make my calling sure!
Thine utmost counsel to fulfill,
To suffer all thy righteous will,
　　And to the end endure!

157　　　*The Great Question.*　　　*C. P. M.*

1 No room for mirth or trifling here,
For worldly hope, or worldly fear,
　　If life so soon is gone;
If now the Judge is at the door,
And all mankind must stand before
　　The inexorable throne!

2 Nothing is worth a thought beneath,
But how I may escape the death

That never, never dies!
How make mine own election sure.
And when I fail on earth, secure
A mansion in the skies.

3 Jesus, vouchsafe a pitying ray;
Be thou my Guide, be thou my Way
To glorious happiness!
Ah! write the pardon on my heart;
And whensoe'er I hence depart,
Let me depart in peace.

---

158   *Danger of Delay.*   7s.

1 HASTE, O sinner! to be wise,
Stay not for the morrow's sun;
Wisdom warns thee, from the skies,
All the paths of death to shun.

2 Haste, and mercy now implore;
Stay not for the morrow's sun;
Thy probation may be o'er
Ere this evening's work is done.

3 Haste, O sinner! now return;
Stay not for the morrow's sun;
Lest thy lamp should cease to burn
Ere salvation's work is done.

4 Haste, while yet thou canst be blest;
Stay not for the morrow's sun;
Death may thy poor soul arrest
Ere the morrow is begun.

11 *

159   *The Sinner Warned.*   7s.

1 SINNER! art thou still secure?
        Wilt thou still refuse to pray?
  Can thy heart or hand endure
        In the Lord's avenging day?

2 See,—his mighty arm is bared;
        Awful terrors clothe his brow!
  For his judgments stand prepared;
        Thou must either break or bow.

3 At his presence nature shakes,
        Earth affrighted hastes to flee,
  Solid mountains melt like wax:
        What will then become of thee?

4 Who his coming may abide?
        You that glory in your shame!
  Can you find a place to hide,
        When the world is wrapt in flame?

INVITING.

160   *The Gracious Call.*   C. M.

1 THE Saviour calls; let ev'ry ear
        Attend the heavenly sound;
  Ye doubting souls! dismiss your fear,
        Hope smiles reviving round.

2 For every thirsty, longing heart,
   Here streams of bounty flow,
And life, and health, and bliss impart,
   To banish mortal woe.

3 Ye sinners! come; 'tis mercy's voice;
   The gracious call obey;
Mercy invites to heavenly joys,
   And can you yet delay?

4 Dear Saviour! draw reluctant hearts;
   To thee let sinners fly,
And take the bliss thy love imparts,
   And drink, and never die.

---

161   *The Gospel Invitation.*   *C. M.*

1 YE wretched, hungry, starving poor!
   Behold a royal feast,
Where mercy spreads her bounteous store
   For every humble guest.

2 Here Jesus stands with open arms;
   He calls, he bids you come:
Guilt holds you back, and fear alarms;
   But see! there yet is room:

3 Room in the Saviour's bleeding heart;
   There love and pity meet;
Nor will he bid the soul depart,
   That trembles at his feet.

4 Oh! come, and with his children, taste
   The blessings of his love;
  While hope attends the sweet repast
   Of nobler joys above.

5 There, with united heart and voice,
   Before the eternal throne,
  Ten thousand thousand souls rejoice,
   In songs on earth unknown.

162   *Christ's Invitation.*   *L. M.*

1 "Come hither, all ye weary souls!
   Ye heavy-laden sinners! come;
  I'll give you rest from all your toils,
   And raise you to my heav'nly home.

2 "They shall find rest who learn of me,
   I'm of a meek and lowly mind;
  But passion rages like the sea,
   And pride is restless as the wind.

3 "Blessed is the man whose shoulders take
   My yoke, and bear it with delight;
  My yoke is easy to his neck,
   My grace shall make the burden light."

4 Jesus! we come at thy command;
   With faith, and hope, and humble zeal,
  Resign our spirits to thy hand,
   To mould and guide us at thy will.

163   *Rest for the Weary.*   *L. M.*

1 COME, weary souls! with sin distressed,
Come, and accept the promised rest;
The Saviour's gracious call obey,
And cast your gloomy fears away

2 Here, mercy's bourdless ocean flows,
To cleanse your guilt and heal your woes;
Pardon and life, and endless peace;
How rich the gift, how free the grace!

3 Lord! we accept, with thankful heart,
The hope thy gracious words impart;
We come with trembling,—yet rejoice,
And bless the kind inviting voice.

4 Dear Saviour! let thy powerful love
Confirm our faith,—our fears remove;
Oh! sweetly reign in every breast,
And guide us to eternal rest.

---

164   *The Gospel Feast.*   *C. M.*

1 LET every mortal ear attend,
And every heart rejoice;
The trumpet of the gospel sounds
With an inviting voice.

2 Ho! all ye hungry, starving souls,
That feed upon the wind,
And vainly strive, with earthly toils,
To fil' the immortal mind.

3 Eternal wisdom has prepared
    A soul-reviving feast,
And bids your longing appetites
    The rich provision taste.

4 Ho! ye that pant for living streams,
    And pine away and die!
Here you may quench your raging thirst
    With springs that never dry.

5 Rivers of love and mercy, here,
    In a rich ocean join;
Salvation in abundance flows,
    Like floods of milk and wine.

6 The happy gates of gospel grace
    Stand open night and day;
Lord! we are come to seek supplies,
    And drive our wants away.

---

165   *The Living Fountain.*   *C. M.*

1 OH! what amazing words of grace
    Are in the gospel found,
Suited to every sinner's case
    Who hears the joyful sound!

2 Come, then, with all your wants and wounds,
    Your every burden bring;
Here love, unchanging love abounds,
    A deep celestial spring.

3 This spring with living waters flows,
    And heavenly joys imparts;
Come, thirsty souls! your wants disclose,
    And drink with thankful hearts.

4 Millions of sinners, vile as you,
    Have here found life and peace;
Come, then, and prove its virtues too,
    And drink, adore, and bless.

---

166   *Come.*   *S. M.*

1 THE Spirit in our hearts
    Is whispering, Sinner, come;
The bride, the church of Christ, proclaims
    To all his children, Come.

2 Let him that heareth say
    To all about him, Come;
Let him that thirsts for righteousness
    To Christ, the fountain, come.

3 Yes, whosoever will,
    Oh! let him freely come
And freely drink the stream of life;
    'Tis Jesus bids him come.

4 Lo, Jesus, who invites,
    Declares, I quickly come:
Lord, even so! we wait thy hour:
    O blest Redeemer, come!

167   *The Sinner Called.*   S. M.

1 RETURN and come to God;
    Cast all your sins away;
  Seek ye the Saviour's cleansing blood;
    Repent, believe, obey.

2 Say not ye cannot come;
    For Jesus bled and died,
  That none who ask in humble faith
    Should ever be denied.

3 Say not ye will not come;
    'Tis God vouchsafes to call;
  And fearful will their end be found,
    On whom his wrath shall fall.

4 Come then, whoever will,
    Come while 'tis called to-day;
  Flee to the Saviour's cleansing blood;
    Repent, believe, obey.

168   *None but Jesus.*   8s, 7s & 4s.

1 COME, ye sinners! heavy-laden,
    Lost and ruined by the fall,
  If you wait till you are better,
    You will never come at all:
        Sinners only,
  Christ, the Saviour, came to call.

2 Let no sense of guilt prevent you,
    Nor of fitness fondly dream;
  All the fitness he requireth
    Is to feel your need of him:
      This he gives you;
  'Tis the Spirit's rising beam.

3 Agonizing in the garden,
    Lo! your Saviour prostrate lies;
  On the bloody tree behold him,
    There he groans, and bleeds, and dies:
      "It is finished,"
  Heaven accepts the sacrifice.

4 Lo! the incarnate God ascending
    Pleads the merit of his blood;
  Venture on him,—venture wholly
    Let no other trust intrude:
      None but Jesus
  Can do helpless sinners good.

------

169   *Glad Tidings.*   *8s, 7s & 4s.*

  1 SINNERS! will you scorn the message
      Coming from the courts above?
    Mercy speaks in every passage;
      Every line is full of love;
        Oh! believe it,
    Every line is full of love.

  2 Now, the heralds of salvation
      Joyful news from heaven proclaim;
    12

Sinners freed from condemnation,
Through the all-atoning Lamb!
Life receiving,
Through the all-atoning Lamb.

3 O ye angels! hovering round us,
Waiting spirits! speed your way,
Hasten to the court of heaven,
Tidings bear without delay,
Rebel sinners
Glad the message will obey.

———•◇•———

170 *Now the Accepted Time.* S. M.

1 Now is the accepted time,
Now is the day of grace;
O sinners! come, without delay,
And seek the Saviour's face.

2 Now is the accepted time,
The Saviour calls to-day;
To-morrow it may be too late;
Then why should you delay.

3 Now is the accepted time,
The Gospel bids you come;
And every promise in his word,
Declares there yet is room.

4 Lord! draw reluctant souls,
And melt them by thy love;
Then will the angels speed their way,
To bear the news above.

171 *Children Exhorted.* *8s, 7s, and 4s.*

1 CHILDREN! hear the melting story
 Of the Lamb that once was slain;
'Tis the Lord of life and glory;
 Shall he plead with you in vain?
  Oh! receive him,
And salvation now obtain.

2 Yield no more to sin and folly,
 So displeasing in his sight;
Jesus loves the pure and holy,
 They alone are his delight;
  Seek his favor,
And your hearts to him unite.

3 All your sins to him confessing
 Who is ready to forgive,
Seek the Saviour's richest blessing,
 On his precious name believe;
  He is waiting,
Will you not his grace receive?

---

172 *Mercy's Voice.* C. M.

1 SINNERS! the voice of God regard;
 'Tis Mercy speaks to-day;
He calls you by his sovereign word,
 From sin's destructive way.

2 Like the rough sea that cannot rest,
 You live devoid of peace:

A thousand stings, within your breast,
  Deprive your souls of ease.

3 Your way is dark, and leads to hell;
    And will you onward go?
  Can you in endless burnings dwell,
    Or bear eternal woe?

4 Lo! he who turns to God, shall live,
    Through his abounding grace;
  His mercy will the guilt forgive
    Of those who seek his face.

5 Bow to the sceptre of his word,
    Renouncing every sin;
  Submit to him, your sovereign Lord,
    And learn his will divine.

6 His love exceeds your highest thoughts;
    He pardons like a God;
  He will forgive your numerous faults,
    Through Christ's atoning blood.

---

173   *Pardon in Christ.*   C. M.

1 How sad our state by nature is!
    Our sin—how deep it stains!
  And Satan binds our captive minds,
    Fast in his slavish chains.

2 But there's a voice of sovereign grace,
    Sounds from the sacred word:
  "Ho! ye despairing sinners! come,
    And trust upon the Lord."

3 My soul obeys the almighty call
   And runs to this relief;
I would believe thy promise, Lord!
   Oh! help my unbelief.

4 To the dear fountain of thy blood,
   Incarnate God! I fly;
Here let me wash my spotted soul,
   From stains of deepest dye.

5 A guilty, weak, and helpless worm,
   On thy kind arms I fall;
Be thou my strength and righteousness,
   My Jesus, and my all.

------

174 *Why will ye Die?* 7s.

1 SINNERS! turn; why will ye die?
God, your Maker, asks you—Why?
God, who did your being give,
Made you with himself to live,
He the fatal cause demands,
Asks the work of his own hands,
Why, ye thankless creatures! why,
Will ye cross his love, and die?

2 Sinners! turn; why will ye die?
God, your Saviour, asks you—Why?
He, who did your souls retrieve,
Died himself that ye might live:
12 *

Will ye let him die in vain ?
Crucify your Lord again?
Why, ye ransomed sinners ! why
Will ye slight his grace, and die ?

3 Sinners ! turn ; why will ye die?
God, the Spirit, asks you—Why?
Many a time with you he strove,
Wooed you to embrace his love :
Will ye not his grace receive ?
Will ye still refuse to live ?
Oh ! ye guilty sinners ! why,
Why will ye forever die ?

175   *The Young Exhorted.*   C. M.

1 YE hearts with youthful vigor warm!
    In smiling crowds draw near ;
And turn from every mortal charm,
    A Saviour's voice to hear.

2 He, Lord of all the worlds on high,
    Stoops to converse with you :
And lays his radiant glories by,
    Your friendship to pursue.

3 The soul, that longs to see his face,
    Is sure his love to gain,
And they, who early seek his grace,
    Shall never seek in vain.

176 *Christ at the Door.* L. M.

1 BEHOLD a stranger at the door!
He gently knocks, has knock'd before;
Has waited long, is waiting still:
You treat no other friend so ill.

2 Oh! lovely attitude—he stands
With melting heart and loaded hands:
Oh! matchless kindness—and he shows
This matchless kindness to his foes.

3 But will he prove a friend indeed?
He will—the very friend you need:
The friend of sinners—yes, 'tis he,
With garments dyed on Calvary.

4 Rise, touched with gratitude divine,
Turn out his enemy and thine,
That soul-destroying monster, sin,
And let the heavenly stranger in.

5 Admit him, ere his anger burn,
His feet departed, ne'er return;
Admit him,—or the hour 's at hand,
You'll at his door rejected stand.

———◦◇◦———

177 *The Sinner Entreated.* L. M.

1 RETURN, O wanderer! now return,
And seek thine injured Father's face;
Those new desires that in thee burn,
Were kindled by reclaiming grace.

2 Return, O wanderer! now return,
  He hears thy deep repentant sigh;
He hears thy softened spirit mourn,
  When no intruding ear is nigh.

3 Return, O wanderer! now return,
  Thy Saviour bids thy spirit live:
Go to his bleeding feet, and learn
  How freely Jesus can forgive.

4 Return, O wanderer! now return,
  And wipe away the falling tear;
Thy Father calls—"No longer mourn!"
  'Tis mercy's voice invites thee near.

178   *Peace at the Cross.*   **7s. 6 lines.**

1 YE! who in his courts are found,
  List'ning to the joyful sound,
  Lost and helpless as ye are,
  Sons of sorrow, sin, and care,
  Glorify the King of kings,
  Take the peace the gospel brings.

2 Turn to Christ your longing eyes,
  View this bleeding sacrifice;
  See in him your sins forgiven,
  Pardon, holiness, and heaven;
  Glorify the King of kings,
  Take the peace the gospel brings.

179 *Life at the Cross.* *7s. 6 lines.*

1 WEARY souls, that wander wide
　　From the central point of bliss,
Turn to Jesus crucified,
　　Fly to those dear wounds of his;
Sink into the purple flood;
Rise into the life of God.

2 Oh, believe the record true,
　　God to you his Son hath given;
Ye may now be happy too,
　　Find on earth the life of heaven,
Live the life of heaven above,
All the life of glorious love.

---

180 *Come and Welcome.* *7s. 6 lines.*

1 FROM the cross uplifted high,
Where the Saviour deigns to die,
What melodious sounds we hear,
Bursting on the ravished ear!
"Love's redeeming work is done,
Come and welcome, sinner, come!

2 "Sprinkled now with blood the throne,
Why beneath thy burdens groan?
On my piercéd body laid,
Justice owns the ransom paid;
Bow the knee, and kiss the Son;
Come and welcome, sinner, come!"

181 *Christ Pleading.* 8s & 7s.

1 Now the Saviour standeth pleading
  At the sinner's bolted heart;
Now in heaven he 's interceding,
  Taking there the sinner's part.

2 Sinner! can you hate this Saviour?
  Will you thrust him from your arms?
Once he died through your behaviour,
  Now he calls you by his charms.

3 Sinner! hear your God and Saviour,
  Hear his gracious voice to-day,
Turn from all your vain behaviour,
  Oh! repent, return, and pray!

4 Now he 's waiting to be gracious,
  Now he stands and looks on thee:
See what kindness, love, and pity,
  Shine around on you and me.

182 *The World Unsatisfying.* 8s & 7s.

1 Tell us, wanderer! wildly roving
  From the path that leads to peace,
Pleasure's false enchantment loving,
  When will thy delusion cease?

2 Once, like thee, by joys surrounded,
  We could kneel at pleasure's shrine,
Then our brightest hopes were bounded,
  By delights as false as thine.

3 But those visions never blessed us,
    Soon their fleeting day was o'er;
Then the world, that had caressed us,
    Charmed us with its smiles no more.

4 Such is pleasure's transient story;
    Lasting happiness is known
Only in the path to glory,
    In the Saviour's love alone.

183　　　*Child of Sin and Sorrow.*

1 CHILD of sin and sorrow,
    Fill'd with dismay,
Wait not for to-morrow,
    Yield thee to-day;
Heav'n bids thee come,
While yet there 's room;
Child of sin and sorrow,
    Hear and obey.

2 Child of sin and sorrow,
    Why wilt thou die?
Come while thou canst borrow
    Help from on high:
Grieve not that love
Which from above;
Child of sin and sorrow,
    Would bring thee nigh.

3 Child of sin and sorrow,
  Thy moments glide,
Like the flitting arrow,
  Or the rushing tide;
Ere time is o'er,
Heaven's grace implore;
Child of sin and sorrow,
  In Christ confide.

---

184   *" Come to Me."*   *(Chant.)*

1 With tearful eyes I look around,
  Life seems a dark and | stormy | sea;
Yet, 'midst the gloom, I hear a sound,
  A heavenly | whisper, | Come to | me.

2 It tells me of a place of rest,
  It tells me where my | soul may | flee;
Oh! to the weary, faint, opprest,
  How sweet the | bidding, | Come to | me.

3 When nature shudders, loth to part
  From all I love, en- | joy, and | see;
When a faint chill steals o'er my heart,
  A sweet voice | utters | Come to | me.

4 Come, for all else must fall and die,
  Earth is no resting | place for | thee;
Heavenward direct thy weeping eye,
  I am thy | portion, | Come to | me.

5 O voice of mercy! voice of love!
In conflict, grief, and | ago- | ny,
Support me, cheer me from above!
And gently | whisper, | Come to | me.

---

185   *Children Called.*

1 LIKE mist on the mountain,
  Like ships on the sea,
So swiftly the years
  Of our pilgrimage flee;
In the grave of our fathers
  How soon we shall lie!
Dear children, to-day
  To the Saviour fly.

2 How sweet are the flow'rets
  In April and May!
But often the frost
  Makes them wither away.
Like flowers you may fade;
  Are you ready to die?
While "yet there is room,"
  To the Saviour fly.

3 When Samuel was young,
  He first knew the Lord;
He slept in his smile,
  And rejoiced in his word;
So most of God's children
  Are early brought nigh:

13

Oh seek him in youth;
To the Saviour fly.

4 Do you ask me for pleasure?
Then lean on his breast,
For there the sin-laden
And weary find rest.
In the valley of death
You will triumphing cry,
"If this be called dying,
'Tis pleasant to die."

---

186 *Come, ye Disconsolate.* *11s & 10s.*

1 COME, ye disconsolate! where'er ye languish,
Come to the mercy-seat, fervently kneel:
Here bring your wounded hearts, here tell your
anguish;
Earth has no sorrow that heaven cannot heal.

2 Joy of the desolate, light of the straying,
Hope of the penitent, fadeless and pure!
Here speaks the Comforter, tenderly saying,
Earth has no sorrow that heaven cannot cure.

3 Here see the bread of life; see waters flow-
ing,
Forth from the throne of God, pure from
above:
Come to the feast of love; come, ever knowing,
Earth has no sorrow, but heaven can remove.

187 *Come to Jesus.*

1 COME to Jesus, Come to Jesus,
  Come to Jesus just now;
Just now come to Jesus,
  Come to Jesus just now.

2 He will save you, he will save you,
  He will save you just now;
Just now he will save you,
  He will save you just now.

3 Oh believe him, Oh believe him,
  Oh believe him just now,
Just now, Oh believe him,
  Oh believe him, just now.

4 He is able, he is able,
  He is able just now,
Just now he is able,
  He is able just now.

5 He is willing, he is willing,
  He is willing just now,
Just now he is willing,
  He is willing just now.

6 He'll receive you, he'll receive you,
  He'll receive you just now,
Just now he'll receive you,
  He'll receive you just now.

7 He'll forgive you, he'll forgive you,
  He'll forgive you just now,
Just now he'll forgive you,
  He'll forgive you just now.

8 He will cleanse you, he will cleanse you,
  He will cleanse you just now,
Just now he will cleanse you,
  He will cleanse you just now.

9 He'll renew you, he'll renew you,
  He'll renew you just now,
Just now he'll renew you,
  He'll renew you just now,

10 Jesus loves you, Jesus loves you,
  Jesus loves you just now,
Just now Jesus loves you,
  Jesus loves you just now,

11 Don't reject him, don't reject him,
  Don't reject him just now,
Just now don't reject him,
  Don't reject him just now.

12 Only trust him, only trust him
  Only trust him just now,
Just now only trust him,
  Only trust him just now.

13 You will praise him, you will praise him,
  You will praise him just now,
Just now you will praise him,
  You will praise him just now.

PENITENTIAL.

188   *Sorrow at the Cross.   C. M. Double.*

1 ALAS! and did my Saviour bleed?
    And did my Sovereign die?
  Would he devote that sacred head,
    For such a worm as I?

Chorus.—Remember me, remember me,
      O Lord, remember me;
    Remember all thy dying groans,
      And then remember me.

2 Was it for crimes that I had done,
    He groaned upon the tree?
  Amazing pity! grace unknown!
    And love beyond degree.

3 Well might the sun in darkness hide,
    And shut his glories in,
  When Christ, the mighty Maker, died,
    For man the creature's sin.

4 Thus might I hide my blushing face,
    While his dear cross appears;
  Dissolve my heart in thankfulness,
    And melt mine eyes to tears.

5 But floods of tears can ne'er repay
    The debt of love I owe;
  Here, Lord! I give myself away;
    'Tis all that I can do.

13 *

189 *Contrition.* *C. M.*

1 O THOU! whose tender mercy heais
    Contrition's humble sigh :
Whose hand, indulgent, wipes the tears
    From sorrow's weeping eye ;

2 See, low before thy throne of grace,
    A wretched wanderer mourn ;
Hast thou not bid me seek thy face?
    Hast thou not said—"Return?"

3 And shall my guilty fears prevail
    To drive me from thy feet?
Oh! let not this dear refuge fail,
    This only safe retreat.

4 Oh! shine on this benighted heart,
    With beams of mercy shine ;
And let thy healing voice impart
    A taste of joys divine.

————◇————

190 *Penitent.* *L. M.*

1 SHOW pity, Lord! O Lord! forgive ;
Let a repenting rebel live ;
Are not thy mercies large and free?
May not a sinner trust in thee?

2 Oh! wash my soul from every sin,
And make my guilty conscience clean ;
Here on my heart the burden lies,
And past offences pain mine eyes.

3 My lips with shame my sins confess,
Against thy law, against thy grace:
Lord! should thy judgment grow severe,
I am condemned, but thou art clear.

4 Should sudden vengeance seize my breath,
I must pronounce thee just in death.
And, if my soul were sent to hell,
Thy righteous law approves it well.

5 Yet save a trembling sinner, Lord!
Whose hope, still hovering round thy word,
Would light on some sweet promise there,
Some sure support against despair.

————◦◆◦————

191   *Supplication.*   **L. M.**

1 O THOU that hearest when sinners cry!
Though all my crimes before thee lie,
Behold them not with angry look,
But blot their mem'ry from thy book.

2 Create my nature pure within,
And form my soul averse to sin;
Let thy good Spirit ne'er depart,
Nor hide thy presence from my heart.

3 I cannot live without thy light,
Cast out and banished from thy sight:
Thy holy joys, my God! restore,
And guard me, that I fall no more.

4 Though I have grieved thy Spirit, Lord!
His help and comfort still afford;
' And let a wretch come near thy throne,
To plead the merits of thy Son.

192   *Heart-broken at the Cross. 7s. 6 lines.*

1 HEART of stone! relent, relent,
    Break, by Jesus' cross subdued;
See his body, mangled, rent,
    Cover'd with a gore of blood!
Sinful soul! what hast thou done?
Crucified God's only Son!

2 Yes, thy sins have done the deed,
    Driven the nails that fixed him there,
Crown'd with thorns his sacred head,
    Pierced him with the bloody spear,
Made his soul a sacrifice,
While for sinful man he dies.

3 Wilt thou let him bleed in vain,
    Still to death thy Lord pursue?
Open all his wounds again,
    And the shameful cross renew?
No; with all my sins I'll part:
Break, oh! break, my bleeding heart!

193   *Looking unto Jesus. 7s. 6 lines.*

1 WEEPING soul, no longer mourn,
    Jesus all thy griefs hath borne,

View him bleeding on the tree,
Pouring out his life for thee;
There thine every sin he bore,
Weeping soul, lament no more.

2 Cast thy guilty soul on him,
Find him mighty to redeem;
At his feet thy burden lay,
Look thy doubts and fears away;
Now by faith the Son embrace,
Plead his promise, trust his grace.

194   *Approaching the Mercy-Seat.*   C. M.

1 APPROACH, my soul! the mercy-seat,
Where Jesus answers prayer;
There humbly fall before his feet,
For none can perish there.

2 Thy promise is my only plea,
With this I venture nigh:
Thou callest burdened souls to thee,
And such, O Lord! am I.

3 Bowed down beneath a load of sin,
By Satan sorely pressed,
By wars without and fears within,
I come to thee for rest.

4 Be thou my shield and hiding-place,
That, sheltered near thy side,
I may my fierce accuser face,
And tell him—"Thou hast died."

5 Oh! wondrous love,—to bleed and die,
　　To bear the cross and shame,
That guilty sinners such as I,
　　Might plead thy gracious name.

————•◦•————

195　　　　*The Sinner's Friend.*　　　C. M

1 JESUS! thou art the sinner's Friend;
　　As such I look to thee;
Now in the fullness of thy love,
　　O Lord! remember me.

2 Remember thy pure word of grace,
　　Remember Calvary;
Remember all thy dying groans,
　　And then remember me.

3 Thou wondrous Advocate with God!
　　I yield myself to thee;
While thou art sitting on thy throne,
　　Dear Lord! remember me.

4 Lord! I am guilty—I am vile,
　　But thy salvation 's free;
Then, in thine all-abounding grace,
　　Dear Lord! remember me.

5 And when I close my eyes in death,
　　When creature-helps all flee,
Then, O my dear Redeemer God!
　　I pray remember me.

196   *Confession and Prayer.*   **7s.**

1 SOVEREIGN Ruler, Lord of all!
Prostrate at thy feet I fall;
Hear, oh! hear my earnest cry,
Frown not, lest I faint and die.

2 Vilest of the sons of men,
Chief of sinners I have been;
Oft abused thee to thy face,
Trampled on thy richest grace.

3 Justly might thy righteous dart
Pierce this bleeding, broken heart;
Justly might thine angry breath
Blast me in eternal death.

4 But with thee there's mercy found,
Balm to heal my every wound:
Soothe, oh! soothe the troubled breast,
Give the weary wanderer rest.

---

197   *Mercy Implored.*   **7s.**

1 DEPTH of mercy! can there be
Mercy still reserved for me?
Can my God his wrath forbear,
Me, the chief of sinners, spare?

2 I have long withstood his grace,
Long provoked him to his face,
Would not hear his gracious calls,
Grieved him by a thousand falls.

3 There for me the Saviour stands,
  Shows his wounds, and spreads his hands:
  God is love! I know, I feel,
  Jesus weeps and loves me still.

4 Lord, incline me to repent,
  Let me now my fall lament,
  Deeply my revolt deplore,
  Weep, believe, and sin no more.

198   *Pleading in Jesus' Name. L. M. 6 lines.*

1 FATHER of mercies, God of love!
    Oh! hear an humble suppliant's cry;
  Bend from thy lofty seat above,
    Thy throne of glorious majesty;
  Oh! deign to hear my mournful voice,
  And bid my drooping heart rejoice.

2 I urge no merit of my own,
    No worth to claim thy gracious smile;
  No,—when I come before thy throne,
    Dare to converse with God a while,
  Thy name, blest Jesus! is my plea,
  Dearest and sweetest name to me.

3 Father of mercies, God of love!
    Then hear thy humble suppliant's cry;
  Bend from thy lofty seat above,
    Thy throne of glorious majesty;
  One pardoning word can make me whole.
  And soothe the anguish of my soul.

199 *Backslider's Return. L. M. 6 lines.*

1 WEARY of wandering from my God,
  And now made willing to return.
I hear, and bow beneath the rod;
  To him with penitence, I mourn:
I have an Advocate above,
A friend before the throne of love.

2 O Jesus! full of truth and grace,
  More full of grace than I of sin,
Yet once again I seek thy face,
  Open thine arms and take me in;
Oh! freely my backslidings heal,
And love the dying sinner still.

3 Ah! give me, Lord! the tender heart,
  That trembles at the approach of sin;
A godly fear of sin impart,
  Implant and root it deep within;
That I may fear thy gracious power,
And never dare to offend thee more.

———•◦•———

200 *Searching the Heart.* **S. M.**

1 AH! whither should I go,
  Burdened, and sick, and faint?
To whom should I my troubles show,
  And pour out my complaint?

2 My Saviour bids me come,
  Ah! why do I delay?

14

He calls the weary sinner home,
  And yet from him I stay.

3 What is it keeps me back,
    From which I cannot part;
  Which will not let my Saviour take
    Possession of my heart?

4 Some cursed thing unknown
    Must surely lurk within;
  Some idol which I will not own,
    Some secret bosom sin.

5 Jesus, the hindrance show,
    Which I have feared to see;
  And let me now consent to know
    What keeps me back from thee. ●

201   *Weeping with Christ.*   S. M.

1 Did Christ o'er sinners weep?
    And shall our cheeks be dry?
  Let floods of penitential grief
    Burst forth from every eye.

2 The Son of God in tears
    The angels wondering see;
  Be thou astonished, O my soul!
    He shed those tears for thee.

3 He wept, that we might weep;
    Each sin demands a tear;
  In heaven alone no sin is found,
    And there's no weeping there.

202 *Offering a Broken Heart.* **L. M.**

1 A BROKEN heart, my God! my King!
Is all the sacrifice I bring;
The God of grace will ne'er despise
A broken heart for sacrifice.

2 My soul lies humbled in the dust,
And owns thy dreadful sentence just;
Look down, O Lord! with pitying eye,
And save a soul condemned to die.

3 Then I will teach the world thy ways;
Sinners shall learn thy sovereign grace;
I'll lead them to my Saviour's blood,
And they shall praise the pardoning God.

4 Oh! may thy love inspire my tongue;
Salvation shall be all my song;
And all my powers shall join to bless
The Lord, my strength and righteousness.

203 *Returning to Christ.* **C. M.**

1 How oft, alas! this wretched heart
Has wandered from the Lord!
How oft my roving thoughts depart,
Forgetful of his word!

2 Yet sovereign mercy calls—"Return!"
Dear Lord! and may I come?
My vile ingratitude I mourn;
Oh! take the wanderer home.

3 And canst thou, wilt thou, yet forgive,
   And bid my crimes remove?
And shall a pardoned rebel live,
   To speak thy wondrous love?

4 Almighty grace! thy healing power,
   How glorious—how divine!
That can, to life and bliss, restore
   A heart so vile as mine!

5 Thy pardoning love—so free, so sweet,
   Dear Saviour! I adore;
Oh! keep me at thy sacred feet,
   And let me rove no more.

204   *Even Me.*

1 LORD, I hear of showers of blessings,
   Thou art scattering full and free.
Showers the thirsty land refreshing,
   Let some droppings fall on me.
     Even me, even me,
Let some droppings fall on me.

2 Pass me not, O God, my Father,
   Sinful though my heart may be;
Thou might'st leave me, but the rather
   Let thy mercy light on me:
     Even me, Even me.
Let thy mercy light on me.

3 Pass me not, O gracious Saviour,
    Let me live and cling to thee;
I am longing for thy favor;
    Whilst thou'rt calling, call for me:
        Even me.

4 Pass me not, O mighty Spirit,
    Thou canst make the blind to see;
Testify of Jesus' merit,
    Speak the word of power to me:
        Even me.

5 Have I long in sin been sleeping,
    Long been slighting, grieving thee?
Has the world my heart been keeping?
    Oh, forgive and rescue me!
        Even me.

6 Love of God, so pure and changeless;
    Blood of Christ, so rich and free;
Grace of God, so rich and boundless;
    Magnify it all in me:
        Even me.

7 Pass me not; thy lost one bringing,
    Bind my heart, O Lord, to thee;
Whilst the streams of life are springing,
    Blessing others, oh, bless me:
        Even me.

14 *

CONVERSION.

205   *Blind Bartimeus.*   **8s and 7s.**

1 "Mercy, O thou Son of David!"
    Thus blind Bartimeus prayed;
"Others by thy word are saved,
    Now to me afford thine aid."

2 Many for his crying chid him,
    But he called the louder still;
Till the gracious Saviour bid him,
    "Come, and ask me what you will."

3 Money was not what he wanted,
    Though by begging used to live;
But he asked and Jesus granted
    Alms which none but he could give.

4 "Lord, remove this grievous blindness,
    Let my eyes behold the day:"
Straight he saw, and won by kindness,
    Followed Jesus in the way.

5 Oh! methinks I hear him praising,
    Publishing to all around,
"Friends, is not my case amazing?
    What a Saviour I have found!"

6 "Oh that all the blind but knew him,
    And would be advised by me;
Surely they would hasten to him,
    He would cause them all to see."

206   *Turning to Jesus.*   *C. M.*

1 WELCOME, O Saviour! to my heart;
    Possess thy humble throne;
  Bid every rival hence depart,
    And claim me for thine own.

2 The world and Satan I forsake,
    To thee I all resign;
  My longing heart, O Jesus! take,
    And fill with love divine.

3 Oh! may I never turn aside,
    Nor from thy bosom flee;
  Let nothing here my heart divide,
    I give it all to thee.

207   *Just as I am.*   *L. M.*

1 JUST as I am, without one plea,
  But that thy blood was shed for me,
  And that thou bidd'st me come to thee,
    O Lamb of God, I come!

2 Just as I am, and waiting not
  To rid my soul of one dark blot,
  To thee, whose blood can cleanse each spot,
    O Lamb of God, I come!

3 Just as I am, though tossed about
  With many a conflict, many a doubt,
  With fears within and wars without,
    O Lamb of God, I come!

4 Just as I am, poor, wretched, blind,
  Sight, riches, healing of the mind,
  Yea, all I need, in thee to find,
    O Lamb of God, I come!

5 Just as I am—thou wilt receive.
  Wilt welcome, pardon, cleanse, relieve,
  Because thy promise I believe,
    O Lamb of God, I come!

6 Just as I am—thy love unknown
  Has broken every barrier down;
  Now, to be thine, yea, thine alone,
    O Lamb of God, I come!

—————◦◇◦—————

208   *Yielding to Jesus.*   *S. M.*

1 AND can I yet delay
    My little all to give?
  To tear my soul from earth away,
    My Jesus to receive?

2 Nay, but I yield, I yield!
    I can hold out no more:
  I sink, by dying love compelled,
    And own thee conqueror!

3 Though late, I all forsake,
    My friends, my all resigu;
  Gracious Redeemer, take, oh, take,
    And seal me ever thine!

209 *Singing Redeeming Love.* *C. P. M.*

1 AWAKED by Sinai's awful sound,
My soul in bonds of guilt I found,
  And knew not where to go:
One solemn truth increased my pain,
The sinner "must be born again,"
  Or sink to endless woe.

2 I heard the law its thunders roll,
While guilt lay heavy on my soul,
  A vast oppressive load:
All creature aid I saw was vain!
The sinner "must be born again,"
  Or drink the wrath of God.

3 The saints I heard with rapture tell
How Jesus conquered death and hell,
  To bring salvation near:
Yet still I found this truth remain,
The sinner "must be born again,"
  Or sink in deep despair.

4 But, while I thus in anguish lay,
The bleeding Saviour passed that way,
  My bondage to remove:
The sinner, once by justice slain,
Now by his grace is born again.
  And sings redeeming love.

210 *Choosing God's Service.* 7s

1 PEOPLE of the living God!
  I have sought the world around,
Paths of sin and sorrow trod,
  Peace and comfort no where found;
Now to you my spirit turns,
  Turns, a fugitive unblest;
Brethren! where your altar burns,
  Oh! receive me into rest.

2 Lonely, I no longer roam,
  Like the cloud, the wind, the wave;
Where you dwell shall be my home,
  Where you die shall be my grave:
Mine the God whom you adore,
  Your Redeemer shall be mine;
Earth can fill my soul no more,
  Every idol I resign.

211 *Following Jesus.* 8s & 7s.

1 JESUS! I my cross have taken,
  All to leave, and follow thee;
Naked, poor, despised, forsaken,
  Thou, from hence, my all shalt be;
Perish every fond ambition,
  All I've sought, or hoped, or known!
Yet how rich is my condition,
  God and heaven are still my own!

2 Let the world despise and leave me ;
    They have left my Saviour, too.
  Human hearts and looks deceive me:
    Thou art not like them untrue:
  Oh! while thou dost smile upon me,
    God of wisdom, love, and might!
  Foes may hate, and friends disown me;
    Show thy face, and all is bright.

3 Perish, earthly fame and treasure!
    Come, disaster, scorn, and pain!
  In thy service, pain is pleasure!
    With thy favor, life is gain:
  Oh! 'tis not in grief to harm me,
    While thy love is left to me;
  Oh! 'twere not in joy to charm me,
    Were that joy unmixed with thee.

---

212   *Renouncing the World.*   **H. M.**

1 COME, my fond fluttering heart,
    Come, struggle to be free;
  Thou and the world must part,
    However hard it be:
  My trembling spirit owns it just,
  But cleaves yet closer to the dust.

2 Ye fair enchanting throng,
    Ye golden dreams, farewell;
  Earth has prevailed too long,
    And now I break the spell:

Ye cherished joys of early years—
Jesus, forgive these parting tears!

213   *Crying Abba, Father.*   H. M.

1 ARISE, my soul, arise,
      Shake off thy guilty fears;
The bleeding sacrifice
      In my behalf appears:
Before the throne my surety stands;
My name is written on his hands.

2 He ever lives above,
      For me to intercede,
His all redeeming love,
      His precious blood to plead;
His blood atoned for all our race,
And sprinkles now the throne of grace.

3 My God is reconciled;
      His pardoning voice I hear:
He owns me for his child,
      I can no longer fear;
With confidence I now draw nigh,
And Father, Abba, Father, cry.

214   *Surrendering the Heart.* 8s, 7s & 4s.

1 WELCOME, welcome, dear Redeemer!
      Welcome to this heart of mine;

Lord! I make a full surrender,
　　Every power and thought be thine;
　　Thine entirely,
Through eternal ages thine.

2 Known to all to be thy mansion,
　　Earth and hell will disappear;
Or in vain attempt possession,
　　When they find the Lord is near:
　　Shout, O Zion!
Shout, ye saints! the Lord is here.

215　　　*Before the Cross.*　　　*8s & 7s.*

1 SWEET the moments, rich in blessing,
　　Which before the cross I spend!
Life, and health, and peace possessing,
　　From the sinner's dying friend.

2 Here I'll sit, forever viewing
　　Mercy streaming in his blood;
Precious drops! my soul bedewing,
　　Plead and claim my peace with God.

3 Here it is I find my heaven,
　　While upon the cross I gaze;
Love I much?—I've much forgiven,
　　I'm a miracle of grace.

4 Love and grief my heart dividing,
　　Gazing here I'd spend my breath,
Constant still in faith abiding,
　　Life deriving from his death.

15

5 Lord! in ceaseless contemplation,
    Fix my heart and eyes on thine,
Till I taste thy whole salvation,
    Where, unveiled, thy glories shine.

216　　　*Joy over the Penitent.*　　　C. M.

1 Oh! how divine, how sweet the joy
    When but one sinner turns,
And, with a humble, broken heart,
    His sin and error mourns!

2 Pleased with the news, the saints below
    In songs their tongues employ;
Beyond the skies the tidings go,
    And heaven is filled with joy.

3 Well-pleased, the Father sees and hears
    The conscious sinner's moan;
Jesus receives him in his arms,
    And claims him for his own.

4 Nor angels can their joys contain,
    But kindle with new fire:
"The sinner lost is found!" they sing,
    And strike the sounding lyre.

217　　　*Renouncing the World.*　　　L. M.

1 I send the joys of earth away,
    Away, ye tempters of the mind!
False as the smooth, deceitful sea,
    And empty as the whistling wind.

2 Your streams were floating me along,
  Down to the gulf of black despair:
And, while I listened to your song,
  Your streams had e'en conveyed me there.

3 Lord! I adore thy matchless grace,
  That warned me of that dark abyss;
That drew me from those treacherous seas,
  And bade me seek superior bliss.

4 Now, to the shining realms above,
  I stretch my hands, and glance mine eyes;
Oh! for the pinions of a dove,
  To bear me to the upper skies.

5 There, from the bosom of my God,
  Oceans of endless pleasure roll;
There would I fix my last abode,
  And drown the sorrows of my soul.

---

218   *Joy in Heaven.*   **L. M.**

1 Who can describe the joys that rise,
  Through all the courts of Paradise,
To see a prodigal return,
To see an heir of glory born?

2 With joy the Father doth approve
  The fruit of his eternal love;
The Son with joy looks down, and sees
The purchase of his agonies.

3 The Spirit takes delight to view
　The holy soul he formed anew,
　And saints and angels join to sing
　The growing empire of their King.

<hr>

219　　　*Marching to Zion.*　　　C. M.

1 SING, all ye ransomed of the Lord!
　　Your great Deliverer sing:
　Ye pilgrims! now for Zion bound,
　　Be joyful in your King.

2 See the fair way his hand hath made;
　　How peaceful and how plain!
　The simplest traveler need not err,
　　Nor seek the path in vain.

3 A hand divine shall lead you on,
　　Through all the blissful road;
　Till to the sacred mount you rise,
　　And see your smiling God.

4 Bright garlands of immortal joy
　　Shall bloom on every head;
　While sorrow, sighing, and distress,
　　Like shadows, all are fled.

5 March on in your Redeemer's strength;
　　Pursue his footsteps still;
　With joyful hope, still fix your eye
　　On Zion's heavenly hill.

220   *Forgiveness of Sins.*   *S. M.*

1 Oh! blesséd souls are they,
    Whose sins are covered o'er;
Divinely blessed, to whom the Lord
    Imputes their guilt no more.

2 They mourn their follies past,
    And keep their hearts with care;
Their lips and lives, without deceit,
    Shall prove their faith sincere.

3 While I concealed my guilt,
    I felt the festering wound;
Till I confessed my sins to thee,
    And ready pardon found.

4 Let sinners learn to pray,
    Let saints keep near the throne;
Our help in times of deep distress,
    Is found in God alone.

221   *Abiding by the Cross.*   *7s & 6s.*

1 God of my salvation, hear,
    And help me to believe;
Now to thee do I draw near,
    Thy blessing to receive:
Full of sin, alas, I am,
    But to thee for refuge flee;
Friend of sinners, spotless Lamb,
    Thy blood was shed for me.

15 *

2 No good word, or work, or thought,
  I bring to gain thy grace;
Pardon I accept unbought;
  Thy proffer I embrace:
Needy, guilty, vile I am,
  Yet I know thy love is free;
Friend of sinners, spotless Lamb,
  Thy blood was shed for me.

3 Saviour, from thy wounded side
  I never will depart;
At thy cross will I abide,
  With humble, trusting heart:
When my place above I claim,
  This shall be my only plea:
Friend of sinners, spotless Lamb,
  Thy blood was shed for me.

222   *Pleading at the Cross.*   *7s & 6s.*

1 LAMB of God! whose bleeding love
  We now recall to mind,
Send the answer from above,
  And let us mercy find:
Think on us who think on thee;
  Every burdened soul release;
Oh! remember Calvary,
  And bid us go in peace.

2 Let thy blood, by faith applied,
  The sinner's pardon seal;

Speak us freely justified,
  And all our sickness heal:
By thy passion on the tree,
  Let our griefs and troubles cease;
Oh! remember Calvary,
  And bid us go in peace.

3 Can we ever hence depart,
  Till thou our wants relieve?
Write forgiveness on our heart,
  And all thine image give:
Still our souls shall cry to thee,
  Till renewed by holiness;
Oh! remember Calvary,
  And bid us go in peace.

---

223   *Fleeing to the Cross.*   C. P. M.

1 O THOU who hearest the prayer of faith,
Wilt thou not save a soul from death,
  That casts itself on thee?
I have no refuge of my own,
But fly to what my Lord hath done,
  And suffered once for me.

2 Slain in the guilty sinner's stead,
Thy spotless righteousness I plead,
  And thine atoning blood:
Thy righteousness my robe shall be,
Thy merit shall atone for me,
  And bring me near to God.

3 Then snatch me from eternal death,
　The spirit of adoption breathe,
　　His consolation send:
　By him some word of life impart,
　And sweetly whisper to my heart,
　"Thy Maker is thy friend."

224　　　　*Subdued by the Cross.*　　　*C. M.*

1 I SAW one hanging on a tree,
　　In agonies and blood;
　He fixed his languid eyes on me,
　　As near his cross I stood.

2 Oh! never, till my latest breath,
　　Shall I forget that look;
　It seemed to charge me with his death,
　　Though not a word he spoke.

3 My conscience felt and owned the guilt,
　　It plunged me in despair:
　I saw my sins his blood had spilt,
　　And helped to nail him there.

4 A second look he gave, that said,
　　"I freely all forgive;
　This blood is for thy ransom paid,
　　I die that thou may'st live."

5 Thus, while his death my sin displays,
　　In all its blackest hue,
　Such is the mystery of grace,
　　It seals my pardon too.

225 *Loving Jesus.* *8s & 7s.*

1 COME, thou Fount of ev'ry blessing!
   Tune my heart to grateful lays;
Streams of mercy, never ceasing,
   Call for songs of loudest praise.

Chorus.—I love Jesus, Hallelujah,
   I love Jesus, yes, I do,
   I do love Jesus, He's my Saviour,
   Jesus smiles and loves me too.

2 Teach me some melodious measure,
   Sung by raptured saints above;
Fill my soul with sacred pleasure,
   While I sing redeeming love.

3 Jesus sought me, when a stranger,
   Wandering from the fold of God;
He to save my soul from danger,
   Interposed his precious blood.

4 Oh! to grace how great a debtor,
   Daily I'm constrained to be!
Let thy grace, Lord! like a fetter,
   Bind my wandering heart to thee.

5 Prone to wander, Lord! I feel it;
   Prone to leave the God I love:
Here's my heart, oh! take and seal it,
   Seal it from thy courts above.

226   *Joyful Hope.*   *8s & 7s.*

1 KNOW, my soul! thy full salvation;
  Rise o'er sin, and fear, and care,
Joy to find, in every station,
  Something still to do or bear:
Think what Spirit dwells within thee;
  Think what Father's smiles are thine;
Think what Jesus did to win thee;
  Child of heaven! canst thou repine?

2 Haste thee on from grace to glory,
  Armed with faith and winged with prayer;
Heaven's eternal day 's before thee,
  God's own hand shall guide thee there:
Soon shall close thine earthly mission,
  Soon shall pass thy pilgrim-days;
Hope shall change to glad fruition,
  Faith to sight, and prayer to praise.

227   *Jesus is Mine.*

1 FADE, fade each earthly joy,
  Jesus is mine;
Break every tender tie,
  Jesus is mine;
Dark is the wilderness,
Earth has no resting-place,
Jesus alone can bless,
  Jesus is mine.

2 Tempt not my soul away,
    Jesus is mine;
Here would I ever stay,
    Jesus is mine;
Perishing things of clay,
Born for but one brief day,
Pass from my heart away,
    Jesus is mine.

3 Farewell, ye dreams of night,
    Jesus is mine;
Lost in this dawning light,
    Jesus is mine;
All that my soul has tried,
Left but a dismal void,
Jesus has satisfied,
    Jesus is mine.

4 Farewell mortality,
    Jesus is mine;
Welcome eternity,
    Jesus is mine;
Welcome, O loved and blest,
Welcome, sweet scenes of rest,
Welcome, my Saviour's breast,
    Jesus is mine.

CHRISTIAN LIFE.

228 *First Love.*

1　How happy are they
　Who the Saviour obey,
And have laid up their treasure above!
　Oh, what tongue can express,
　The sweet comfort and peace
Of a soul in its earliest love!

2　That comfort was mine,
　When compassion divine
To my soul in its misery came;
　When first I believed,
　And salvation received,
And rejoiced in Immanuel's name.

3　My remnant of days
　Would I spend to his praise,
Who hath died my lost soul to redeem;
　Whether many or few,
　All my years are his due;
May they all be devoted to him.

———◦◇◦———

229 *Joy in God.*　　　　C. M.

1 UNITE, my roving thoughts, unite,
　In silence soft and sweet;
And thou, my soul, sit gently down
　At thy great Sov'reign's feet.

2 Jehovah's awful voice is heard,
   Yet gladly I attend;
For lo! the everlasting God
   Proclaims himself my Friend.

3 Harmonious accents to my soul,
   The sounds of peace convey;
The tempest at his word subsides,
   And winds and seas obey.

4 By all its joys, I charge my heart
   To grieve his love no more;
But, charmed by melody divine.
   To give its follies o'er.

230   *Triumphing in Jesus.*   *7s.*

1 Now begin the heavenly theme,
Sing aloud in Jesus' name;
Ye, who his salvation prove,
Triumph in redeeming love.

2 Ye, who see the Father's grace
Beaming in the Saviour's face,
As to Canaan on ye move,
Praise, and bless redeeming love.

3 Mourning souls! dry up your tears;
Banish all your sinful fears;
See your guilt and curse remove,
Cancelled by redeeming love.
  16

4 Welcome all, by sin oppressed,
    Welcome to his sacred rest!
    Nothing brought him from above,
    Nothing but redeeming love.

5 Hither, then, your music bring;
    Strike aloud each joyful string;
    Mortals! join the hosts above,
    Join to praise redeeming love.

6 When his Spirit leads us home,
    When we to his glory come,
    We shall all the fullness prove
    Of the Lord's redeeming love.

----⋄----

231   *Communing with Jesus.*   *L. M.*

1 JESUS, our best beloved friend,
      Draw out our souls in sweet desire;
    Jesus, in love to us descend,
      Baptize us with thy Spirit's fire.

2 Our souls and bodies we resign,
      To fear and follow thy commands;
    Oh! take our hearts, our hearts are thine,
      Accept the service of our hands.

3 Firm, faithful, watching unto prayer,
      Our Master's voice will we obey,
    Toil in the vineyard here, and bear
      The heat and burden of the day.

4 Yet Lord, for us a resting-place,
   In heaven, at thy right hand, prepare;
And till we see thee face to face,
   Be all our conversation there.

232   *Running for the Prize.*   C. M.

1 AWAKE, my soul! stretch every nerve,
   And press with vigor on;
A heavenly race demands thy zeal,
   And an immortal crown.

2 'Tis God's all-animating voice,
   That calls thee from on high;
'Tis he, whose hand presents the prize,
   To thine aspiring eye.

3 A cloud of witnesses around
   Hold thee in full survey;
Forget the steps already trod,
   And onward urge thy way,

4 Blest Saviour! introduced by thee,
   Our race have we begun;
And, crowned with vict'ry, at thy feet,
   We'll lay our trophies down.

233   *The Men of Faith.*   C. M.

1 RISE, O my soul! pursue the path,
   By ancient worthies trod;
Aspiring, view those holy men,
   Who lived and walked with God.

2 Though dead, they speak in reason's ear,
 And in example live;
Their faith, and hope, and mighty deeds,
 Still fresh instruction give.

3 'T was through the Lamb's most precious
  blood,
 They conquered every foe;
And, to his power and matchless grace,
 Their crowns of life they owe.

4 Lord! may I ever keep in view
 The patterns thou hast given;
And ne'er forsake the blessed road,
 That led them safe to heaven.

———◆◆◆———

234 *The Heavenly Race.* **L. M.**

1 AWAKE, our souls! away, our fears!
 Let ev'ry trembling thought be gone;
Awake, and run the heavenly race,
 And put a cheerful courage on.

2 True, 'tis a strait and thorny road,
 And mortal spirits tire and faint;
But they forget the mighty God,
 Who feeds the strength of ev'ry saint.

3 The mighty God, whose matchless power
 Is ever new, and ever young,
And firm endures, while endless years
 Their everlasting circles run

4 From thee, the overflowing spring,
    Our souls shall drink a full supply;
While such as trust their native strength,
    Shall melt away, and droop, and die.

5 Swift as an eagle cuts the air,
    We'll mount aloft to thine abode;
On wings of love our souls shall fly,
    Nor tire amid the heavenly road.

235　　*The Christian Warfare.*　　L. M.

1 STAND up, my soul! shake off thy fears,
    And gird the gospel armor on;
March to the gates of endless joy,
    Where Jesus, thy great Captain, 's gone.

2 Hell and thy sins resist thy course;
    But hell and sin are vanquished foes;
Thy Jesus nailed them to the cross,
    And sung the triumph when he rose.

3 Then let my soul march boldly on,
    Press forward to the heavenly gate;
There peace and joy eternal reign,
    And glittering robes for conquerors wait.

4 There shall I wear a starry crown,
    And triumph in almighty grace;
While all the armies of the sky
    Join in my glorious Leader's praise.
    16 *

236 *The Christian Soldier.* C. M.

1 Am I a soldier of the cross,
  A follower of the Lamb?
And shall I fear to own his cause,
  Or blush to speak his name?

2 Are there no foes for me to face?
  Must I not stem the flood?
Is this vile world a friend of grace,
  To help me on to God?

3 Sure, I must fight if I would reign;
  Increase my courage, Lord!
I'll bear the toil, endure the pain,
  Supported by thy word.

4 Thy saints, in all this glorious war,
  Shall conquer, though they die;
They see the triumph from afar,
  And seize it with their eye.

5 When that illustrious day shall rise,
  And all thine armies shine,
In robes of victory, through the skies,
  The glory shall be thine.

237 *Christian Assurance.* C. M.

1 I'm not ashamed to own my Lord,
  Or to defend his cause;
Maintain the honor of his word,
  The glory of his cross.

2 Jesus, my God! I know his name;
    His name is all my trust;
Nor will he put my soul to shame,
    Nor let my hope be lost.

3 Firm as his throne, his promise stands;
    And he can well secure
What I've committed to his hands,
    Till the decisive hour.

4 Then will he own my worthless name,
    Before his Father's face,
And, in the New-Jerusalem,
    Appoint my soul a place.

238　　　　　*The fight of Faith.*　　　　*S. M.*

1 My soul! be on thy guard,
    Ten thousand foes arise;
And hosts of sins are pressing hard,
    To draw thee from the skies.

2 Oh! watch, and fight, and pray;
    The battle ne'er give o'er;
Renew it boldly every day,
    And help divine implore.

3 Ne'er think the vict'ry won,
    Nor lay thine armor down;
Thine arduous work will not be done,
    Till thou obtain thy crown.

239 *Watchfulness.* S. M.

1 A CHARGE to keep I have,
  A God to glorify;
A never-dying soul to save,
  And fit it for the sky.

2 To serve the present age,
  My calling to fulfill,
Oh! may it all my powers engage,
  To do my Master's will.

3 Arm me with jealous care,
  As in thy sight to live;
And oh! thy servant, Lord! prepare
  A strict account to give.

4 Help me to watch and pray,
  And on thyself rely,
Assured, if I my trust betray,
  I shall forever die.

240 *The Child-like Temper.* 7s.

1 Quiet, Lord! my froward heart;
  Make me teachable and mild;
Upright, simple, free from art;
  Make me as a weaned child:
From distrust and envy free,
Pleased with all that pleases thee.

2 What thou shalt to-day provide,
  Let me as a child receive;

What to-morrow may betide,
  Calmly to thy wisdom leave:
'Tis enough that thou wilt care;
Why should I the burden bear?

3 As a little child relies
  On a care beyond his own,
Knows he's neither strong nor wise,
  Fears to move one step alone;
Let me thus with thee abide,
As my Father, guard, and guide.

241　　　　　*The Mind of Christ.*　　　　*7s.*

1 FATHER of eternal grace!
  Glorify thyself in me;
Meekly beaming in my face,
  May the world thine image see.

2 Happy only in thy love,
  Poor, unfriended, or unknown;
Fix my thoughts on things above,
  Stay my heart on thee alone.

3 Humble, holy, all-resigned
  To thy will: thy will be done!
Give me, Lord! the perfect mind
  Of thy well-beloved Son.

4 Counting gain and glory loss,
  May I tread the path he trod;
Die with Jesus on the cross,
  Rise with him, to thee, my God!

242 *Faint, yet Pursuing* *11s.*

1 THOUGH faint, yet pursuing, we g♪ on our
    way;
The Lord is our leader, his word is our stay;
Though suff'ring, and sorrow, and trial be
    near,
The Lord is our refuge, and whom can we
    fear?

2 He raiseth the fallen, he cheereth the faint;
The weak and oppressed, he will hear their
    complaint;
The way may be weary, and thorny the road,
But how can we falter? our help is in God!

3 Though clouds may surround us, our God is
    our light;
Though storms rage around us, our God is
    our might:
So faint, yet pursuing, still onward we come;
The Lord is our Leader, and heaven is our
    home.

------

243 *Pilgrim's Song.* *7s & 6s.*

1 RISE, my soul! and stretch thy wings,
    Thy better portion trace;
Rise from transitory things,
    Toward heaven, thy native place:

Sun, and moon, and stars decay,
  Time shall soon this earth remove;
Rise, my soul! and haste away,
  To seats prepared above.

2 Rivers to the ocean run,
  Nor stay in all their course;
Fire ascending seeks the sun,
  Both speed them to their source:
So a soul, that's born of God,
  Pants to view his glorious face;
Upward tends to his abode,
  To rest in his embrace.

3 Cease, ye pilgrims! cease to mourn,
  Press onward to the prize:
Soon the Saviour will return,
  Triumphant in the skies:
Yet a season, and you know
  Happy entrance will be given;
All our sorrows left below,
  And earth exchanged for heaven.

---

244   *Salvation Welcomed.*   *C. M.*

1 SALVATION! oh! the joyful sound,
  'Tis pleasure to our ears;
A sov'reign balm for every wound,
  A cordial for our fears.

2 Buried in sorrow and in sin,
   At hell's dark door we lay;
But we arise, by grace divine,
   To see a heavenly day.

3 Salvation! let the echo fly
   The spacious earth around;
While all the armies of the sky
   Conspire to raise the sound.

---

245   *Salvation Sure.*   *C. M.*

1 COME, let us join our songs of praise
   To our ascended Priest;
He entered heaven, with all our names
   Engraven on his breast.

2 Below, he washed our guilt away,
   By his atoning blood;
Now he appears before the throne,
   And pleads our cause with God.

3 Clothed with our nature still, he knows
   The weakness of our frame.
And how to shield us from the foes
   Whom he himself o'ercame.

4 Nor time, nor distance, e'er shall quench
   The fervor of his love;
For us he died in kindness here,
   For us he lives above.

5 Oh! may we ne'er forget his grace,
　　Nor blush to bear his name;
　Still may our hearts hold fast his faith,
　　Our lips his praise proclaim.

246　　　*The Debt all Paid.*

1 NOTHING, either great or small,
　　Remains for me to do;
　Jesus died, and paid it all,
　　Yes, all the debt I owe.
Chorus.—Jesus paid it all,
　　　　All the debt I owe.
　　　Jesus died and paid it all,
　　　　Yes, all the debt I owe.

2 When he from his lofty throne,
　　Stooped down to do and die,
　Everything was fully done;
　　"'Tis finished!" was his cry.

3 Weary, working, plodding one,
　　Oh, wherefore toil you so?
　Cease your doing, all was done;
　　Yes, ages long ago.

4 Till to Jesus' work you cling,
　　Alone by simple faith,
　"Doing" is a deadly thing,
　　Your "doing" ends in death.
　17

5 Cast your deadly "doing" down,
  Down at Jesus' feet;
Stand in him, in him alone,
  All glorious and complete.

---

247 *My Saviour Died for Me.* C. M.

1 THOU art my hiding-place, O Lord!
    In thee I put my trust;
Encouraged by thy holy word,
    A feeble child of dust:
I have no argument beside,
    I urge no other plea;
And 'tis enough, my Saviour died,
    My Saviour died for me!

2 When storms of fierce temptation beat,
    And furious foes assail,
My refuge is the mercy-seat,
    My hope within the vail:
From strife of tongues, and bitter words,
    My spirit flies to thee;
Joy to my heart the thought affords,
    My Saviour died for me!

---

248 *Heaven on Earth.* S. M.

1 COME, ye who love the Lord!
    And let your joys be known;
Join in a song of sweet accord,
    And thus surround the throne.

2 Let those refuse to sing,
    Who never knew our God;
  But children of the heavenly King,
    May speak their joys abroad.

3 The men of grace have found
    Glory begun below;
  Celestial fruits on earthly ground
    From faith and hope may grow.

4 The hill of Zion yields
    A thousand sacred sweets,
  Before we reach the heavenly fields,
    Or walk the golden streets.

5 Then let our songs abound,
    And every tear be dry;
  We're marching through Immanuel's ground,
    To fairer worlds on high.

-----

249   *Salvation by Grace.*   *S. M.*

1 GRACE! 'tis a charming sound,
    Harmonious to the ear;
  Heaven with the echo shall resound,
    And all the earth shall hear.

2 Grace first contrived the way
    To save rebellious man;
  And all the steps that grace display,
    Which drew the wondrous plan.

3 Grace led my roving feet
   To tread the heavenly road;
And new supplies each hour I meet,
   While pressing on to God.

4 Grace all the work shall crown,
   Through everlasting days;
It lays in heaven the topmost stone,
   And well deserves the praise.

---

250   *Delight in God.*   *C. M.*

1 O LORD, I would delight in thee,
   And on thy care depend;
To thee in every trouble flee,
   My best my only friend.

2 When all created streams are dried,
   Thy fullness is the same;
May I with this be satisfied,
   And glory in thy name.

3 Oh that I had a stronger faith
   To look within the vail,
To credit what my Saviour saith,
   Whose word can never fail.

4 He who has made my heaven secure
   Will here all food provide;
While Christ is rich can I be poor?
   What can I want beside?

5 O Lord, I cast my care on thee;
   I triumph and adore;
Henceforth my great concern shall be
   To love and praise thee more.

251   *Breathing after Holiness.*   C. M.

1 Oh! that the Lord would guide my ways
   To keep his statutes still;
Oh! that my God would grant me grace
   To know and do his will.

2 Oh! send thy Spirit down, to write
   Thy law upon my heart;
Nor let my tongue indulge deceit,
   Or act the liar's part.

3 Order my footsteps by thy word,
   And make my heart sincere;
Let sin have no dominion, Lord!
   But keep my conscience clear.

4 My soul hath gone too far astray,
   My feet too often slip;
Yet, since I've not forgot thy way,
   Restore thy wandering sheep.

5 Make me to walk in thy commands,
   'Tis a delightful road;
Nor let my head, or heart, or hands,
   Offend against my God.
   17 *

252   *Searching the Heart.*   **L. M.**

1 RETURN, my roving heart! return,
     And chase those shadowy forms no more;
Now seek, in solitude to mourn,
     And thy forsaken God implore.

2 O thou great God! whose piercing eye
     Distinctly marks each deep recess;
In these sequestered hours draw nigh,
     And with thy presence fill the place.

3 Through all the windings of my heart,
     My search let heavenly wisdom guide,
And still its radiant beams impart,
     Till all be cleansed and purified.

4 Oh! with the visits of thy love,
     Vouchsafe my inmost soul to cheer,
Till every grace shall join to prove,
     That God has fixed his dwelling here.

---

253   *All in God.*   **L. M.**

1 WHEN, gracious Lord, when shall it be
That I shall find my all in thee,
The fullness of thy promise prove,
The seal of thine eternal love?

2 Ah! wherefore did I ever doubt?
Thou wilt in no wise cast me out,
A helpless soul that comes to thee
With only sin and misery.

3 Lord, I am blind, be thou my sight
  Lord, I am weak, be thou my migh ;
  A helper of the helpless be;
  And let me find my all in thee!

254　　*Trust in God's Care.*　　C. M.

1 My God! my Father! blissful name!
    Oh! may I call thee mine?
  May I with sweet assurance claim
    A portion so divine?

2 This only can my fears control,
    And bid my sorrows fly;
  What harm can ever reach my soul
    Beneath my Father's eye?

3 Whate'er thy providence denies,
    I calmly would resign;
  For thou art good, and just, and wise;
    Oh! bend my will to thine.

4 Whate'er thy sacred will ordains,
    Oh! give me strength to bear;
  Let me but know my Father reigns,
    And trust his tender care.

255　　*Trust and Praise.*　　C. M.

1 Through all the changing scenes of life,
    In trouble, and in joy,
  The praises of my God shall still
    My heart and tongue employ.

2 Of his deliverance I will boast,
　Till all, who are distressed,
From my example comfort take,
　And charm their griefs to rest.

3 Oh! magnify the Lord with me,
　With me exalt his name;
When in distress to him I called,
　He to my rescue came.

4 The hosts of God encamp around
　The dwellings of the just;
Deliverance he affords to all
　Who on his succor trust.

5 Oh! make but trial of his love;
　Experience will decide,
How blest are they, and only they,
　Who in his truth confide.

6 Fear him, ye saints! and ye will then
　Have nothing else to fear:
Make ye his service your delight,
　He'll make your wants his care.

—————

256　　　*A Contrite Heart.*　　　C. M.

1 OH! for a heart to praise my God!
　A heart from sin set free;
A heart that always feels thy blood,
　So freely shed for me.

2 A heart resigned, submissive, meek,
  My great Redeemer's throne;
Where only Christ is heard to speak,
  Where Jesus reigns alone.

3 A humble, lowly, contrite heart,
  Believing, true, and clean;
Which neither life nor death can part
  From him that dwells within!

4 A heart in every thought renewed,
  And full of love divine;
Perfect, and right, and pure, and good,
  A copy, Lord, of thine.

5 Thy nature, gracious Lord, impart;
  Come quickly from above;
Write thy new name upon my heart,
  Thy new, best name of love.

— · ◆ · —

257   *Reconciliation with God.*   *C. M.*

1 ETERNAL Sun of Righteousness,
  Display thy beams divine,
And cause the glories of thy face
  Upon my heart to shine.

2 Light, in thy light, oh! may I see,
  Thy grace and mercy prove;
Revived, and cheered, and blest by thee,
  The God of pardoning love.

3 Lift up thy countenance serene,
    And let thy happy child
Behold, without a cloud between,
    The Godhead reconciled.

---

258   *God's Guidance Sought.* *8s, 7s & 4s.*

1 GUIDE me, O thou great Jehovah!
    Pilgrim through this barren land;
I am weak, but thou art mighty;
    Hold me with thy powerful hand:
        Bread of heaven!
Feed me till I want no more.

2 Open, Lord! the crystal fountain,
    Whence the healing waters flow;
Let the fiery, cloudy pillar,
    Lead me all my journey through:
        Strong deliverer!
Be thou still my strength and shield.

3 When I tread the verge of Jordan,
    Bid my anxious fears subside;
Death of death, and hell's destruction!
    Land me safe on Canaan's side:
        Songs of praises
I will ever give to thee.

---

259   *Hope Encouraged.* *8s, 7s & 4s.*

1 O MY soul! what means this sadness?
    Wherefore art thou thus cast down?

Let thy grief be turned to gladness,
Bid thy restless fear be gone;
Look to Jesus,
And rejoice in his dear name.

2 Though ten thousand ills beset thee,
Though thy heart is stained with sin,
Jesus lives, he'll ne'er forget thee,
He will make thee pure within;
He is faithful
To perform his gracious word.

3 Though distresses now attend thee,
And thou treadest the thorny road;
His right hand shall still defend thee,
Soon he'll bring thee home to God;
Thou shalt praise him,
Praise the great Redeemer's name.

4 Oh! that I could now adore him,
Like the heavenly host above,
Who forever bow before him,
And unceasing sing his love!
Happy spirits!
When shall I your chorus join?

———◦◦◦———

260　　*Watching and Praying.*　　*C. M.*

1 ALAS! what hourly dangers rise,
What snares beset my way!
To heaven, oh! let me lift mine eyes,
And hourly watch and pray.

2 How oft my mournful thoughts complain,
  And melt in flowing tears!
I strive against my foes in vain,
  I sink amid my fears.

3 O Lord! increase my faith and hope,
  When foes and fears prevail;
And bear my fainting spirit up,
  Or soon my strength will fail.

4 Oh! keep me in tny heavenly way,
  And bid the tempter flee;
And never, never let me stray
  From happiness and thee.

----

261   *Spiritual Sloth.*   *C. M.*

1 MY drowsy powers! why sleep ye so?
  Awake, my sluggish soul!
Nothing has half thy work to do,
  Yet nothing's half so dull.

2 The little ants, for one poor grain,
  Labor, and tug, and strive;
Yet we, who have a heaven to obtain,
  How negligent we live !

3 We, for whose sake all nature stands,
  And stars their courses move;
We, for whose guard the angel-bands
  Come flying from above;

4 We, for whom God, the Son, came down,
  And labored for our good;
How careless to secure that crown
He purchased with his blood!

5 Lord! shall we lie so sluggish still,
  And never act our parts?
Come, holy Dove! from th' heavenly hill,
  And sit and warm our hearts.

6 Then shall our active spirits move,
  Upward our souls shall rise;
With hands of faith, and wings of love,
  We'll fly and take the prize.

262 *Unbelief Banished.* 5s & 6s.

1 BEGONE, unbelief,
    My Saviour is near,
  And for my relief
    Will surely appear:
  By prayer let me wrestle,
    And he will perform;
  With Christ in the vessel,
    I smile at the storm.

2 Though dark be my way,
    Since he is my guide,
  'Tis mine to obey,
    'Tis his to provide;

18

His way was much rougher
　　And darker than mine;
Did Jesus thus suffer,
　　And shall I repine?

3 Determined to save,
　　He watched o'er my path,
When, Satan's blind slave,
　　I sported with death:
And can he have taught me
　　To trust in his name,
And thus far have brought me,
　　To put me to shame?

4 Why should I complain
　　Of want or distress,
Temptation or pain?
　　He told me no less:
The heirs of salvation,
　　I know from his word,
Through much tribulation
　　Must follow their Lord.

5 His love, in time past,
　　Forbids me to think
He'll leave me at last
　　In trouble to sink:
Though painful at present,
　　'Twill cease before long,
And then, oh how pleasant
　　The conqueror's song!

263 *Confidence in God.* C. M.

1 AUTHOR of good, we rest on thee.
   Thine ever watchful eye
Alone our real wants can see,
   Thine hand alone supply.

2 In thine all gracious providence
   Our cheerful hopes confide;
Oh let thy power be our defence,
   Thy love our footsteps guide.

3 Not what we wish, but what we want,
   Thy mercy still supply!
The good unasked, O Father, grant;
   The ill, though asked, deny.

264 *Rest in God.* S. M.

1 OH! cease, my wandering soul,
   On restless wing to roam;
All this wide world, to either pole,
   Has not for thee a home.

2 Behold the ark of God;
   Behold the open door;
Oh! haste to gain that dear abode,
   And rove, my soul, no more.

3 There safe shalt thou abide,
   There sweet shall be thy rest,
And every longing satisfied,
   With full salvation blest.

265 *Resting on God.* S. M.

1 My spirit on thy care,
  Blest Saviour, I recline;
Thou wilt not leave me to despair,
  For thou art love divine.

2 In thee I place my trust,
  On thee I calmly rest;
I know thee good, I know thee just,
  And count thy choice the best.

3 Let good or ill befall,
  It must be good for me;
Secure of having thee in all,
  Of having all in thee.

266 *Burdens cast on God.* S. M.

1 How gentle God's commands!
  How kind his precepts are!
Come, cast your burdens on the Lord,
  And trust his constant care.

2 Beneath his powerful sway
  His saints securely dwell;
That hand which bears all nature up
  Will guide his children well.

3 Why should this anxious load
  Press down your weary mind?
Haste to your heavenly Father's throne,
  And sweet refreshment find.

4 His goodness stands approved,
    Renewed from day to day;
  I'll drop my burden at his feet,
    And bear a song away.

267   *Faith Founded on Promises.*   11s.

1 How firm a foundation, ye saints of the Lord!
  Is laid for your faith in his excellent word!
  What more can he say, than to you he hath
        said,
  You, who unto Jesus for refuge have fled?

2 "Fear not, I am with thee, oh! be not dis-
        mayed,
  I, I am thy God, and will still give thee aid;
  I'll strengthen thee, help thee, and cause
        thee to stand,
  Upheld by my righteous, omnipotent hand.

3 "When through the deep waters I call thee
        to go,
  The rivers of sorrow shall not thee overflow;
  For I will be with thee, thy troubles to bless,
  And sanctify to thee thy deepest distress.

4 "When through fiery trials thy pathway shall
        lie,
  My grace all sufficient shall be thy supply;
  The flame shall not hurt thee, I only design
  Thy dross to consume, and thy gold to refine.
    18 *

5 "E'en down to old age, all my people shall
　　　prove
My sovereign, eternal, unchangeable love;
And, when hoary hairs shall their temples
　　　adorn,
Like lambs they shall still in my bosom be
　　　borne.

6 "The soul that on Jesus hath leaned for
　　　repose,
I will not, I cannot, desert to his foes;
That soul, though all hell should endeavor to
　　　shake,
I'll never,—no, never,—no, never forsake."

268　　　*Mercy in Affliction.*　　　*C. M.*

1 O THOU whose mercy guides my way!
　　Though now it seems severe,
Forbid my unbelief to say,
　　There is no mercy here.

2 Oh! grant me to desire the pain,
　　That comes in kindness down,
More than the world's alluring gain,
　　Succeeded by a frown.

3 Then, though thou bend my spirit low,
　　Love only shall I see;
The very hand that strikes the blow
　　Was wounded once for me.

269   *Hope in the Covenant.*   *L. M.*

1 How oft have sin and Satan strove
    To rend my soul from thee, my God!
But everlasting is thy love,
    And Jesus seals it with his blood.

2 The oath and promise of the Lord
    Join to confirm the wondrous grace;
Eternal power performs the word,
    And fills all heaven with endless praise.

3 Amid temptations, sharp and long,
    My soul to this dear refuge flies;
Hope is my anchor, firm and strong,
    While tempests blow, and billows rise.

4 The gospel bears my spirit up;
    A faithful and unchanging God
Lays the foundation for my hope,
    In oaths, and promises, and blood.

———◆———

270   *Adoption.*   *L. M.*

1 GREAT God! indulge my humble claim,
    Thou art my hope, my joy, my rest;
The glories, that compose thy name,
    Stand all engaged to make me blest.

2 Thou great and good, thou just and wise!
    Thou art my Father, and my God;
And I am thine, by sacred ties,
    Thy son, thy servant, bought with blood.

3 With early feet I love to appear
　　Among thy saints, and seek thy face;
Oft have I seen thy glory there.
　　And felt the power of sovereign grace.

4 I'll lift my hands, I'll raise my voice,
　　While I have breath to pray or praise;
This work shall make my heart rejoice,
　　And spend the remnant of my days.

271　　*Prayer for Repentance.*　　*7s & 6s.*

1 JESUS, let thy pitying eye
　　Call back a wandering sheep;
False to thee like Peter, I
　　Would fain like Peter weep;
Let me be by grace restored,
　　And to me thy mercy shown;
Turn, and look upon me, Lord,
　　And break my heart of stone.

2 Saviour, Prince, enthroned above,
　　Repentance to impart,
Give me, through thy dying love,
　　The humble, contrite heart;
This I should have long implored,
　　For thou all my sin hast known;
Turn, and look upon me, Lord,
　　And break my heart of stone.

3 See me, Saviour, from above,
   Nor suffer me to die;
Life, and happiness, and love,
   Fall from thy gracious eye:
Speak the reconciling word,
   Let thy mercy melt me down;
Turn, and look upon me, Lord,
   And break my heart of stone.

272   *Prayer for Strength.*   *7s & 6s.*

1 NEAR me, O my Saviour, stand,
   In sore temptation's hour;
Save me with thine outstretched hand,
   And show forth all thy power;
Oh! be mindful of thy word;
   All-sufficient grace bestow;
Keep me, keep me, gracious Lord,
   And never let me go.

2 Give me, Lord, a holy fear,
   And fix it in my heart;
That I may from evil near
   With timely care depart;
Sin be more than hell abhorred,
   Faith resist the tyrant foe;
Keep me, keep me, gracious Lord,
   And never let me go.

3 Never let me leave thy breast,
   From thee, my Saviour, stray;

Thou art my support and rest,
  My true and living way;
My exceeding great reward,
  Mine above, and mine below;
Keep me, keep me, gracious Lord,
  And never let me go.

273   *Appropriating Christ.*   **7s & 6s.**

1 O SACRED Head, now wounded,
  With grief and shame weighed down,
Now scornfully surrounded
  With thorns, thine only crown;
O sacred Head, what glory,
  What bliss till now was thine!
Yet though despised and gory,
  I joy to call thee mine.

2 How art thou pale with anguish,
  With sore abuse and scorn!
How does that visage languish,
  Which once was bright as morn!
Thy grief, and thy compassion,
  Were all for sinners' gain;
Mine, mine was the transgression,
  But thine the deadly pain.

3 What language shall I borrow,
  To praise thee, heavenly Friend:
For this, thy dying sorrow,
  Thy pity without end?

Lord, make me thine forever,
  Nor let me faithless prove:
Oh! let me never, never,
  Abuse such dying love.

4 Forbid that I should leave thee;
    O Jesus, leave not me;
  By faith I would receive thee;
    Thy blood can make me free:
  When strength and comfort languish,
    And I must hence depart,
  Release me then from anguish,
    By thine own wounded heart.

5 Be near when I am dying,
    Oh! show thy cross to me!
  And for my succor flying,
    Come, Lord, to set me free:
  These eyes new faith receiving,
    From Jesus shall not move;
  For he who dies believing,
    Dies safely—through thy love.

274   *Unfruitfulness Deplored.*   *C. M.*

1 Long have I sat beneath the sound
    Of thy salvation, Lord!
  But still, how weak my faith is found,
    And knowledge of thy word.

2 Oft I frequent thy holy place,
   And hear almost in vain;
How small a portion of thy grace
   My memory can retain.

3 How cold and feeble is my love!
   How negligent my fear!
How low my hope of joys above!
   How few affections there!

4 Great God! thy sovereign power impart,
   To give thy word success;
Write thy salvation in my heart,
   And make me learn thy grace.

5 Show my forgetful feet the way,
   That leads to joys on high;
There knowledge grows without decay,
   And love shall never die.

275   *Submission.*   *C. M.*

1 O Lord! my best desires fulfill,
   And help me to resign
Life, health, and comfort to thy will,
   And make thy pleasure mine.

2 Why should I shrink at thy command?
   Thy love forbids my fears;
Why tremble at the gracious hand
   That wipes away my tears?

3 No, let me rather freely yield
    What most I prize to thee;
  Thou never hast a good withheld,
    Nor wilt withhold from me.

4 Thy favor, all my journey through,
    Shall be my rich supply;
  What more I want, or think I do,
    Let wisdom still deny.

276   *In Darkness.*   7s.

1 ONCE I thought my mountain strong,
    Firmly fixed no more to move;   .
  Then my Saviour was my song,
    Then my soul was filled with love:
  Those were happy, golden days,
  Sweetly spent in prayer and praise.

2 Little, then, myself I knew,
    Little thought of Satan's power;
  Now I feel my sins renew,
    Now I feel the stormy hour;
  Sin has put my joys to flight,
  Sin has turned my day to night.

3 Saviour! shine, and cheer my soul,
    Bid my dying hopes revive,
  Make my wounded spirit whole,
    Far away the tempter drive;
  Speak the word and set me free,
  Let me live alone to thee.

19

277 *The Fearful Encouraged.* *S. M.*

1 GIVE to the winds thy fears;
  Hope, and be undismayed;
God hears thy sighs, and counts thy tears,
  God shall lift up thy head.

2 Through waves, and clouds, and storms,
  He gently clears thy way;
Wait thou his time, so shall thy night
  Soon end in joyous day.

3 Still heavy is thy heart?
  Still sink thy spirits down?
Cast off the weight, let fear depart,
  And every care be gone.

4 What though thou rulest not;
  Yet heaven, and earth, and hell,
Proclaim God sitteth on the throne,
  And ruleth all things well.

5 Leave to his sovereign sway
  To choose and to command:
So shalt thou, wondering, own his way
  How wise, how strong his hand.

---

278 *Confidence Strengthened.* *S. M.*

1 YOUR harps, ye trembling saints!
  Down from the willows take;
Loud to the praise of love divine,
  Bid every string awake.

2 Though in a foreign land,
    We are not far from home;
And, nearer to our house above,
    We every moment come.

3 His grace will, to the end,
    Stronger and brighter shine;
Nor present things, nor things to come,
    Shall quench this spark divine.

4 When we in darkness walk,
    Nor feel the heavenly flame;
Then will we trust our gracious God,
    And rest upon his name.

5 Soon shall our doubts and fears
    Subside at his control;
His loving-kindness shall break through
    The midnight of the soul.

6 Blest is the man, O God!
    That stays himself on thee:
Who waits for thy salvation, Lord!
    Shall thy salvation see.

279　　*Working for the Master.*　　S. M.

1 WORK for the Master, work!
    At home and by the way;
Where'er thy Lord appoints thy lot,
    Work, while 'tis called to-day.

2 Work for the Master, work!
    From early morn 'till even;
Put forth thine energies in hope
    Of winning souls for heaven.

3 Work for the Master, work!
    No longer plead delay;
With all thy powers at once engage,
    Go, work, and watch, and pray.

4 Work for the Master, work!
    Thy toil will soon be done,
And thou, with spirits of the just,
    Shalt shout the harvest home.

———⋄⋄⋄———

280   *Listening to Jesus.*   **7s.**

1 HARK! my soul! it is the Lord;
    'Tis thy Saviour, hear his word;
Jesus speaks, and speaks to thee,
    "Say, poor sinner! lovest thou me?

2 "I delivered thee when bound,
    And, when bleeding, healed thy wound;
Sought thee wandering, set thee right,
    Turned thy darkness into light.

3 "Can a woman's tender care
    Cease toward the child she bare?
Yes, she may forgetful be,
    Yet will I remember thee.

4 "Mine is an unchanging love,
   Higher than the heights above;
   Deeper than the depths beneath,
   Free and faithful—strong as death.

5 "Thou shalt see my glory soon,
   When the work of grace is done;
   Partner of my throne shalt be:
   Say, poor sinner! lovest thou me?"

6 Lord! it is my chief complaint,
   That my love is weak and faint;
   Yet I love thee, and adore;
   Oh! for grace to love thee more.

---

281   *Leaning on God.*   7s.

1 CAST thy burden on the Lord,
   Only lean upon his word;
   Thou wilt soon have cause to bless,
   His unchanging faithfulness.

2 He sustains thee by his hand,
   He enables thee to stand;
   Those whom Jesus once hath loved
   From his grace are never moved.

3 Heaven and earth may pass away,
   God's free grace shall not decay:
   He hath promised to fulfill
   All the pleasure of his will.
19 *

4 Jesus! guardian of thy flock,
　　Be thyself our constant rock,
　　Make us, by thy powerful hand,
　　Firm as Zion's mountain stand.

————◆————

282　　*Loving the Shepherd.*　　*S. M.*

1 I WAS a wandering sheep,
　　I did not love the fold;
　I did not love my shepherd's voice,
　　I would not be controlled;
　I was a wayward child,
　　I did not love my home,
　I did not love my Father's voice,
　　I loved afar to roam.

2 The Shepherd sought his sheep,
　　The Father sought his child;
　He followed me o'er vale and hill,
　　O'er deserts waste and wild;
　He found me nigh to death,
　　Famished, and faint, and lone,
　He bound me with the bands of love,
　　He saved the wandering one.

3 He spake in tender love,
　　He raised my drooping head;
　He gently closed my bleeding wounds,
　　My fainting soul he fed;

He washed my filth away,
 He made me clean and fair;
He brought me to my home in peace,
 The long-sought wanderer.

4 Jesus my Shepherd is,
 'Twas he that loved my soul;
'Twas he that washed me in his blood,
 'Twas he that made me whole:
'Twas he that sought the lost,
 That found the wandering sheep:
'Twas he that brought me to the fold;
 'Tis he that still doth keep.

5 No more a wandering sheep,
 I love to be controlled,
I love my tender Shepherd's voice,
 I love the peaceful fold:
No more a wayward child,
 I seek no more to roam,
I love my heavenly Father's voice,
 I love, I love his home.

---

283   *Walking with God.*   *C. M.*

1 OH! for a closer walk with God,
 A calm and heavenly frame,
A light to shine upon the road,
 That leads me to the Lamb!

2 Where is the blessedness I knew,
    When first I saw the Lord?
Where is the soul refreshing view
    Of Jesus, and his word?

3 What peaceful hours I once enjoyed,
    How sweet their mem'ry still!
But they have left an aching void,
    The world can never fill.

4 Return, O holy Dove! return,
    Sweet messenger of rest!
I hate the sins that made thee mourn,
    And drove thee from my breast.

5 The dearest idol I have known,
    Whate'er that idol be,
Help me to tear it from thy throne,
    And worship only thee.

6 So shall my walk be close with God,
    Calm and serene my frame;
So purer light shall mark the road
    That leads me to the Lamb.

————◦◦————

284   *Love to Christ.*   *C. M.*

1 Do not I love thee, O my Lord?
    Behold my heart, and see;
And turn each hateful idol out,
    That dares to rival thee.

2 Is not thy name melodious still,
    To mine attentive ear?
Doth not each pulse with pleasure beat,
    My Saviour's voice to hear?

3 Hast thou a lamb in all thy flock,
    I would disdain to feed?
Hast thou a foe, before whose face,
    I fear thy cause to plead?

4 Thou knowest I love thee, dearest Lord!
    But oh! I long to soar,
Far from the sphere of mortal joys,
    That I may love thee more.

2i5   *Depending on Grace.*   *C. M.*

1 AMAZING grace! how sweet the sound!
    That saved a wretch like me;
I once was lost, but now am found,
    Was blind, but now I see.

Chorus.—I'm bound for the promised land,
        I'm bound for the promised land,
        My Saviour calls me, I must go,
        I am bound for the promised land.

2 'Twas grace that taught my heart to fear,
    And grace my fears relieved;
How precious did that grace appear,
    The hour I first believed.

3 Through many dangers, toils, and snares,
   I have already come;
'Tis grace hath brought me safe thus far,
   And grace will lead me home.

4 Yea, when this flesh and heart shall fail,
   And mortal life shall cease,
I shall possess, within the vail,
   A life of joy and peace.

5 The earth shall soon dissolve like snow,
   The sun forbear to shine;
But God, who called me here below,
   Will be forever mine.

286   *Prospect of the Righteous.*   L. M.

1 WHAT sinners value I resign;
Lord! 'tis enough that thou art mine;
I shall behold thy blissful face,
And stand complete in righteousness.

2 This life's a dream—an empty show;
But the bright world, to which I go,
Hath joys substantial and sincere;
When shall I wake, and find me there?

3 Oh! glorious hour!—Oh! blest abode!
I shall be near and like my God;
And flesh and sin no more control
The sacred pleasures of the soul.

4 My flesh shall slumber in the ground,
  Till the last trumpet's joyful sound;
  Then burst the chains, with sweet surprise,
  And in my Saviour's image rise.

287 *Heaven Anticipated.* 7s & 6s,

1 Oh! when shall I see Jesus,
    And reign with him above;
  And from that flowing fountain
    Drink everlasting love?
  When shall I be delivered
    From this vain world of sin,
  And with my blessed Jesus,
    Drink endless pleasure in?

2 Through grace I am determined
    To conquer though I die;
  And then away to Jesus
    On wings of love I'll fly.
  Farewell to sin and sorrow,
    I bid you all adieu;
  Then, O my friends, prove faithful,
    And, on, your way pursue.

3 Whene'er you meet with troubles
    And trials in your way,
  Oh! cast your cares on Jesus,
    And don't forget to pray.

Gird on the heavenly armor
　　Of faith, and hope, and love;
Then, when the combat's ended,
　　He'll carry you above.

---

288   *Faith, our Guide.*   *L. M.*

1 'Tis by the faith of joys to come,
　　We walk through deserts dark as night;
Till we arrive at heaven, our home,
　　Faith is our guide, and faith our light.

2 The want of sight she well supplies;
　　She makes the pearly gates appear;
Far into distant worlds she pries,
　　And brings eternal glories near.

3 Cheerful we tread the desert through,
　　While faith inspires a heavenly ray;
Though lions roar, and tempests blow,
　　And rocks and dangers fill the way.

4 So Abr'am, by divine command,
　　Left his own home to walk with God;
His faith beheld the promised land,
　　And fired his zeal along the road.

---

289   *Trusting Jesus.*   *8s & 7s.*

1 Yes, for me, for me he careth,
　　With a brother's tender care;
Yes, with me, with me he shareth
　　Every burden, every fear.

2 Yes, for me he standeth pleading
    At the mercy-seat above;
Ever for me interceding,
    Constant in untiring love.

3 Yes, in me abroad he sheddeth
    Joys unearthly, love and light;
And to cover me he spreadeth
    His paternal wing of might.

4 Yes, in me, in me he dwelleth;
    I in him and he in me!
And my empty soul he filleth,
    Here and through eternity.

5 Thus I wait for his returning,
    Singing all the way to heaven;
Such the joyful song of morning,
    Such the tranquil song of even.

———◆———

290 *Renouncing Self-Righteousness.* **L. M.**

1 No more, my God! I boast no more,
    Of all the duties I have done;
I quit the hopes I held before,
    To trust the merits of thy Son.

2 Now, for the love I bear his name,
    What was my gain, I count my loss;
My former pride I call my shame,
    And nail my glory to his cross.

3 Yes, and I must, and will, esteem
    All things but loss for Jesus' sake;
Oh! may my soul be found in him,
    And of his righteousness partake.

4 The best obedience of my hands
    Dares not appear before thy throne;
But faith can answer thy demands,
    By pleading what my Lord has done.

291   *Faith's Power.*   *C. M.*

1 FAITH adds new charms to earthly bliss,
    And saves me from its snares;
Its aid, in every duty, brings,
    And softens all my cares.

2 The wounded conscience knows its power,
    The healing balm to give;
That balm the saddest heart can cheer,
    And make the dying live.

3 Wide it unveils celestial worlds,
    Where deathless pleasures reign;
And bids me seek my portion there,
    Nor bids me seek in vain.

4 It shows the precious promise, sealed
    With the Redeemer's blood;
And helps my feeble hope to rest
    Upon a faithful God.

5 There—there, unshaken would I rest,
    Till this vile body dies;
And then, on faith's triumphant wings
    To endless glory rise.

292   *Pleasures Unseen.*   *C. M.*

1 Oh! could our thoughts and wishes fly
    Above these gloomy shades,
To those bright worlds beyond the sky,
    Which sorrow ne'er invades!

2 There, joys, unseen by mortal eyes,
    Or reason's feeble ray,
In ever-blooming prospects rise,
    Unconscious of decay.

3 Lord! send a beam of light divine,
    To guide our upward aim;
With one reviving touch of thine,
    Our languid hearts inflame.

4 Oh! then, on faith's sublimest wing,
    Our ardent hopes shall rise
To those bright scenes, where pleasures spring
    Immortal, in the skies.

293   *Nearness to God.*   *C. M.*

1 Oh! could I find, from day to day,
    A nearness to my God,
Then should my hours glide sweet away,
    Nor sin, nor fear intrude.

2 Lord, I desire with thee to live
    Anew from day to day;
In joys the world can never give,
    Nor ever take away.

3 O Jesus! come and rule my heart,
    And make me wholly thine,
That I may never more depart,
    Nor grieve thy love divine.

---

294 *Contrition and Prayer.* *C. M.*

1 OH! for that tenderness of heart,
    That bows before the Lord;
That owns how just and good thou art,
    And trembles at thy word.

2 Oh! for those humble, contrite tears,
    Which from repentance flow;
That sense of guilt, which, trembling, fears
    The long-suspended blow!

3 Saviour! to me, in pity give,
    For sin, the deep distress;
The pledge thou wilt at last receive,
    And bid me die in peace.

4 Oh! fill my soul with faith and love,
    And strength to do thy will;
Raise my desires and hopes above,
    Thyself to me reveal

295   *Confiding in God.*   C. M.

1 SINCE all the varying scenes of time
    God's watchful eye surveys,
Oh! who so wise to choose our lot
    Or to appoint our ways?

2 Good, when he gives—supremely good;
    Nor less when he denies;
E'en crosses, from his sovereign hand,
    Are blessings in disguise.

3 Why should we doubt a Father's love,
    So constant and so kind?
To his unerring, gracious will,
    Be every wish resigned.

4 In thy fair book of life divine,
    My God! inscribe my name;
There let it fill some humble place,
    Beneath my Lord, the Lamb!

———◆———

296   *Thirsting after God.*   C. M.

1 As pants the hart for cooling streams,
    When heated in the chase,
So longs my soul, O God! for thee,
    And thy refreshing grace.

2 I sigh to think of happier days,
    When thou, O Lord! wast nigh;
When every heart was tuned to praise,
    And none more blessed than I.

20 *.

3 Why restless, why cast down, my soul?
 Trust God, and thou shalt sing
His praise again, and find him still
 Thy health's eternal spring.

297 *Hope Banishing Fear.* *C. M.*

1 WHEN I can read my title clear,
 To mansions in the skies,
I bid farewell to every fear,
 And wipe my weeping eyes.

2 Should earth against my soul engage,
 And fiery darts be hurled,
Then I can smile at Satan's rage,
 And face a frowning world.

3 Let cares, like a wild deluge, come,
 And storms of sorrow fall;
May I but safely reach my home,
 My God, my heaven, my all.

4 There shall I bathe my weary soul,
 In seas of heavenly rest;
And not a wave of trouble roll,
 Across my peaceful breast.

298 *The Church's Safety.* *L. M.*

1 GOD is the refuge of his saints,
 When storms of sharp distress invade;
Ere we can offer our complaints,
 Behold him present with his aid.

2 Let mountains from their seats be hurled,
 Down to the deep and buried there ·
Convulsions shake the solid world;
 Our faith shall never yield to fear.

3 There is a stream, whose gentle flow
 Supplies the city of our God;
Life, love, and joy still gliding through,
 And watering our divine abode.

4 That sacred stream, thy holy word,
 Our grief allays, our fear controls:
Sweet peace thy promises afford,
 And give new strength to fainting souls.

5 Zion enjoys her monarch's love,
 Secure against a threatening hour;
Nor can her firm foundations move,
 Built on his truth, and armed with power.

---

299   *Believers One.*   *S. M.*

1 BLEST be the tie, that binds
 Our hearts in Christian love;
The fellowship of kindred minds
 Is like to that above.

2 Before our Father's throne,
 We pour our ardent prayers;
Our fears, our hopes, our aims, are one,
 Our comforts and our cares.

3 We share our mutual woes,
   Our mutual burdens bear;
And often, for each other, flows,
   The sympathizing tear.

4 When we asunder part,
   It gives us inward pain;
But we shall still be joined in heart,
   And hope to meet again.

5 This glorious hope revives
   Our courage, by the way;
While each, in expectation, lives,
   And longs to see the day.

6 From sorrow, toil, and pain,
   And sin, we shall be free;
And perfect love and friendship reign,
   Through all eternity.

---

300   *Adoption.*   *S. M.*

1 BEHOLD! what wondrous grace
   The Father has bestowed,
On sinners of a mortal race,
   To call them sons of God.

2 'Tis no surprising thing,
   That we should be unknown;
The Jewish world knew not their King,
   God's everlasting Son.

3 Nor doth it yet appear,
    How great we must be made ;
But, when we see our Saviour here,
    We shall be like our Head.

4 A hope, so much divine,
    May trials well endure ;
May purge our souls from sense and sin,
    As Christ, the Lord, is pure.

5 If, in my Father's love,
    I share a filial part,
Send down thy Spirit, like a dove,
    To rest upon my heart.

6 We would no longer lie,
    Like slaves, beneath the throne ;
Our faith shall—"Abba, Father !"—cry,
    And thou the kindred own.

301   *Brotherly Love.*   C. M.

1 How sweet and heavenly is the sight,
    When those, who love the Lord,
In one another's peace delight,
    And so fulfill his word !

2 Oh ! may we feel each brother's sigh,
    And with him bear a part ;
May sorrows flow from eye to eye,
    And joy from heart to heart.

3 Let love, in one delightful stream,
    Through every bosom flow;
Let union sweet, and dear esteem,
    In every action, glow.

4 Love is the golden chain, that binds
    The happy souls above;
And he's an heir of heaven, who finds
    His bosom glow with love.

302   *Parting.*   7s.

1 FOR a season called to part,
    Let us now ourselves commend,
To the gracious eye and heart
    Of our ever-present Friend.

2 Jesus! hear our humble prayer;
    Tender Shepherd of thy sheep!
Let thy mercy and thy care
    All our souls in safety keep.

3 In thy strength may we be strong;
    Sweeten every cross and pain;
Grant that, if we live, ere long
    We may meet in peace again.

4 Then, if thou thy help afford,
    Joyful songs to thee shall rise,
And our souls shall praise the Lord,
    Who regards our humble cries.

303   *Nearing Home.*   S. M.

1 ONE sweetly solemn thought
      Comes to me o'er and o'er:
  Nearer my home I am to-day,
      Than e'er I've been before.

2 Nearer my Father's house,
      Where many mansions be;
  Nearer my Saviour's great white throne,
      Nearer the jasper sea!

3 Nearer my bound of life,
      My laying burdens down,
  My dropping the long-borne, heavy cross,
      My wearing the starry crown.

4 But, lying dark between
      And winding through the night,
  Is that deep stream which I must pass
      Before I reach the light.

5 Dear Saviour, leave me not;
      Confirm my feeble faith;
  And make me fearless when I stand
      Upon the shore of Death.

304   *Singing of Heaven.*   S. M.

1 OH sing to me of heaven,
      When I am called to die;
  Sing songs of holy ecstacy,
      To waft my soul on high.

2 When cold and sluggish drops
   Roll off my marble brow,
Break forth in songs of joyfulness;
   Let heaven begin below.

3 When the last moments come,
   Oh, watch my dying face,
To catch the bright seraphic gleam
   Which o'er my features plays.

4 Then to my raptured ear
   Let one sweet song be given;
Let music charm me last on earth,
   And greet me first in heaven.

----

305 *Nearer, my God, to Thee.* **6s & 4s.**

1 NEARER, my God, to thee,
   Nearer to thee:
E'en though it be a cross
   That raiseth me,
Still all my song shall be,
Nearer, my God, to thee,
   Nearer to thee.

2 Though like a wanderer,
   Daylight all gone,
Darkness be over me,
   My rest a stone,
Yet in my dreams I'd be
Nearer, my God, to thee,
   Nearer to thee.

3 There let the way appear,
   Steps up to heaven;
All that thou sendest me,
   In mercy given,
Angels to beckon me
Nearer, my God, to thee,
   Nearer to thee.

4 Then, with my waking thoughts,
   Bright with thy praise,
Out of my stony griefs,
   Bethel I'll raise;
So by my woes to be
Nearer, my God, to thee,
   Nearer to thee.

5 Or if on joyful wing,
   Cleaving the sky,
Sun, moon, and stars forgot,
   Upward I fly,
Still all my song shall be,
Nearer, my God, to thee,
   Nearer to thee.

---

306   *Closer Walk.*   *6s & 4s.*

1 Saviour! I follow on,
   Guided by thee,
Seeing not yet the hand
   That leadeth me;

Hushed be my heart and still,
Fear I no further ill,
Only to meet thy will
My will shall be.

2 Saviour! I long to walk
  Closer with thee;
Led by thy guiding hand,
  Ever to be;
Constantly near thy side,
Quickened and purified,
Living for him who died
  Freely for me!

---

307   *Pressing on.*   *S. M.*

1 A FEW more years shall roll,
  A few more seasons come;
And we shall be with those that rest,
  Asleep within the tomb:
Then, O my Lord, prepare
  My soul for that great day;
Oh, wash me in thy precious blood,
  And take my sins away!

2 A few more storms shall beat
  On this wild, rocky shore;
And we shall be where tempests cease,
  And surges swell no more;

Then, O my Lord, prepare
My soul for that calm day,
Oh, wash me in thy precious blood,
And take my sins away!

3 A few more struggles here,
A few more partings o'er,
A few more toils, a few more tears,
And we shall weep no more:
Then, O my Lord, prepare
My soul for that blest day;
Oh, wash me in thy precious blood,
And take my sins away.

4 A few more Sabbaths here
Shall cheer us on our way;
And we shall reach the endless rest,
The eternal Sabbath day:
Then, O my Lord, prepare
My soul for that sweet day;
Oh, wash me in thy precious blood,
And take my sins away!

5 'Tis but a little while,
And he shall come again,
Who died that we might live, who lives
That we with him may reign:
Then, O my Lord, prepare
My soul for that glad day;
Oh, wash me in thy precious blood,
And take my sins away!

308   *Seeking the Shepherd.   8s, 7s & 4s.*

1 SAVIOUR, like a Shepherd lead us,
    Much we need thy tenderest care;
In thy pleasant pastures feed us,
    For our use thy folds prepare.
        Blessed Jesus,
    Thou hast bought us, thine we are.

2 We are thine, do thou befriend us,
    Be the Guardian of our way;
Keep thy flock, from sin defend us,
    Seek us when we go astray.
        Blessed Jesus,
    Hear us when to thee we pray.

3 Thou hast promised to receive us,
    Poor and sinful though we be;
Thou hast mercy to relieve us,
    Grace to cleanse, and power to free.
        Blessed Jesus,
    We will early turn to thee,

4 Early will we seek thy favor,
    Early will we do thy will;
Blessed Lord and only Saviour,
    With thy love our bosoms fill.
        Blessed Jesus,
    Thou hast loved us, love us still.

309 *Following the Shepherd.* *C. M.*

1 To thee, my Shepherd, and my Lord,
    A grateful song I'll raise:
Oh let the humblest of thy flock
    Attempt to speak thy praise.

2 My life, my joy, my hope, I owe
    To thine amazing love:
Ten thousand thousand comforts here,
    And nobler bliss above.

3 To thee my trembling spirit flies,
    With sin and grief oppressed;
Thy gentle voice dispels my fears,
    And lulls my cares to rest.

4 Lead on, dear Shepherd!—led by thee,
    No evil shall I fear;
Soon shall I reach thy fold above,
    And praise thee better there.

310 *Gentle Leading.* *8s & 7s. Double.*

1 GENTLY, Lord! oh! gently lead us,
    Through this lonely vale of tears;
Through the changes thou'st decreed us,
    Till our last great change appears;
When temptation's darts assail us,
    When in devious paths we stray.
Let thy goodness never fail us,
    Lead us in thy perfect way.

21 *

2 In the hour of pain and anguish,
    In the hour when death draws near,
  Suffer not our hearts to languish,
    Suffer not our souls to fear:
  And, when mortal life is ended,
    Bid us on thy bosom rest,
  Till, by angel bands attended,
    We awake among the blest.

311   *Thy Will be Done.*   **L. M.**

1 My God! my Father! while I stray,
  Far from my home on life's rough way
  Oh! teach me from my heart to say,
    Thy will be done! Thy will be done!

2 Though dark my path, and sad my lot,
  Let me be still and murmur not,
  But breathe the prayer divinely taught,
    Thy will be done!

3 If thou shouldst call me to resign
  What most I prize—it ne'er was mine;
  I only yield thee what was thine:
    Thy will be done!

4 Renew my will from day to day,
  Blend it with thine, and take away
  All that now makes it hard to say,
    Thy will be done!

5 If but my fainting heart be blest
With thy sweet Spirit for its guest,
My God, to thee I leave the rest,
    Thy will be done!

312   *The Lord Providing.*   5s & 6s.

1 THOUGH troubles assail,
    And dangers affright;
Though friends should all fail,
    And foes all unite;
Yet one thing secures us,
    Whatever betide;
The Scripture assures us
    The Lord will provide.

2 We may, like the ships,
    By tempests be tossed
On perilous deeps,
    But cannot be lost;
Though Satan enrages
    The wind and the tide,
The promise engages
    The Lord will provide.

3 No strength of our own,
    Or goodness we claim;
Yet since we have known
    The Saviour's great name,
In this our strong tower
    For safety we hide,

The Lord is our power,
    The Lord will provide.

4 When life sinks apace,
    And death is in view,
This word of his grace
    Shall comfort us through :
No fearing or doubting,
    With Christ on our side,
We hope to die shouting,
    The Lord will provide.

---

313   *God's Infinite Grace.*   C. M.

1 How rich thy favors, God of grace !
    How various and divine !
Full as the ocean they are poured,
    And bright as heaven they shine.

2 He to eternal glory calls,
    And leads the wondrous way
To his own palace where he reigns
    In uncreated day.

3 The songs of everlasting years
    That mercy shall attend,
Which leads through sufferings of an hour,
    To joys that never end.

314 *Looking Home.*

1 Ah! this heart is void and chill,
 'Mid earth's noisy thronging;
For my Father's mansions still
 Earnestly 'tis longing.

Chorus.—Looking home, Looking home,
  Toward the heavenly mansions
 Jesus hath prepared for me,
  In his Father's kingdom.

2 Soon the glorious day will dawn,
 Heavenly pleasures bringing;
Night will be exchanged for morn,
 Sighs give place to singing.

3 Oh! to be at home again,
 All for which we're sighing,
From all earthly want and pain
 To be swiftly flying.

4 With this load of sin and care,
 Then no longer bending,
But with waiting angels there
 On our soul attending.

5 Blessed home, oh! blessed home,
 All for which we're sighing,
Soon our Lord will bid us come
 To our Father's kingdom.

315   *Sweet Land of Rest.*

1 SWEET land of rest! for thee I sigh,
     When will the moment come?
When I shall lay my armor by,
     And dwell with Christ at home.

Chorus.—Home, home, sweet, sweet home,
       And dwell with Christ at home, home.

2 No tranquil joys on earth I know,
     No peaceful sheltering home,
This world's a wilderness of woe,
     This world is not my home.

3 To Jesus Christ I sought for rest,
     He bade me cease to roam,
But fly for succor to his breast,
     And he'd conduct me home.

4 When, by affliction sharply tried,
     I view the gaping tomb,
Although I dread death's chilling tide,
     Yet still I sigh for home.

5 Weary of wandering round and round,
     This vale of sin and gloom,
I long to leave the unhallowed ground,
     And dwell with Christ at home.

---

316   *The Bright Crown.*   C. M.

1 Ye valiant soldiers of the cross,
     Ye happy, praying band;

Though in this world you suffer loss,
You'll reach fair Canaan's land.

Chorus.—Let us never mind the scoffs nor the
frowns of the world,
For we all have the cross to bear;
It will only make the crown the
brighter to shine,
When we have the crown to wear.

2 All earthly pleasures we'll forsake,
When heaven appears in view,
In Jesus' strength we'll undertake
To fight our passage through.

3 Oh what a glorious shout there'll be,
When we arrive at home,
Our friends and Jesus we shall see,
And God shall say, " Well done."

---

317   *The Starry Crown.*   *C. M.*

1 I STAND on Zion's mount,
And view my starry crown;
No power on earth my hope can shake,
Nor hell can thrust me down.

2 The lofty hills and towers,
That lift their heads on high,
Shall all be leveled low in dust,
Their very names shall die.

3 The vaulted heavens shall fall,
　　Built by Jehovah's hands;
　　But firmer than the heavens, the Rock
　　Of my salvation stands.

318　　*Home.*　　*11s.*

1 'MID scenes of confusion and creature com-
　　　　plaints,
　How sweet to my soul is communion with
　　　　saints;
　To find at the banquet of mercy there's room,
　And feel, in the presence of Jesus, at home.

Chorus.—Home, home, sweet, sweet home;
　　　　Prepare me, dear Saviour, for glory,
　　　　my home.

2 Sweet bonds that unite all the children of
　　　　peace!
　And thrice precious Jesus, whose love can-
　　　　not cease,
　Though oft from thy presence in sadness I
　　　　roam,
　I long to behold thee in glory, at home.

3 I sigh from this body of sin to be free,
　Which hinders my joy and communion with
　　　　thee;
　Though now my temptations like billows may
　　　　foam,
　All, all will be peace, when I'm with thee at
　　　　home.

4 While here in the valley of conflict I stay,
   Oh give me submission, and strength as my
      day;
   In all my afflictions to thee would I come,
   Rejoicing in hope of my glorious home.

5 Whate'er thou deniest, oh give me thy grace,
   The Spirit's sure witness, and smiles of thy
      face;
   Endue me with patience to wait at thy
      throne,
   And find, even now, a sweet foretaste of
      home.

6 I long, dearest Lord, in thy beauties to shine;
   No more, as an exile, in sorrow to pine;
   And, in thy dear image, arise from the tomb,
   With glorified millions to praise thee, at
      home.

319　　　*The Soul's Home.*　　　**11s.**

1 O WHERE can the soul find relief from its
      foes?
   A shelter of safety, a home of repose?
   Can earth's highest summit, or deepest hid
      vale,
   Give a refuge, nor sorrow nor sin can assail?
      No, no! there's no home!
   There's no home on earth—the soul has no
      home.

22

2 Shall it leave the low earth, and soar to the
　　sky,
And seek for a home in the mansions on
　　high?
In the bright realms of bliss will a dwelling
　　be given,
And the soul find a home in the glory of
　　heaven?
　　Yes, yes! there's a home!
There's a home in high heaven—the soul has
　　a home.

———◦◦◦———

PRAYER.

320　　　　　*Prayer.*　　　　　*C. M.*

1 PRAYER is the soul's sincere desire,
　　Unuttered or expressed:
The motion of a hidden fire
　　That trembles in the breast.

2 Prayer is the burden of a sigh,
　　The falling of a tear,
The upward glancing of an eye,
　　When none but God is near.

3 Prayer is the simplest form of speech
　　That infant lips can try;
Prayer, the sublimest strains that reach
　　The majesty on high.

4 Prayer is the Christian's vital breath,
  The Christian's native air;
His watchword at the gates of death,
  He enters heaven with prayer.

5 Prayer is the contrite sinner's voice,
  Returning from his ways;
While angels, in their songs, rejoice,
  And cry,—"Behold he prays!"

6 O thou! by whom we come to God,
  The life, the truth, the way,
The path of prayer thyself hast trod:
  Lord! teach us how to pray.

321　　　*Prayer for Sincerity.*　　　*C. M.*

1 LORD! when we bend before thy throne,
  And our confessions pour,
Oh! may we feel the sins we own,
  And hate what we deplore.

2 Our contrite spirits pitying see;
  True penitence impart;
And let a healing ray, from thee,
  Beam hope on every heart.

3 When we disclose our wants in prayer,
  Oh! let our wills resign:
And not a thought our bosom share,
  Which is not wholly thine.

4 Let faith each meek petition fill,
    And waft it to the skies;
And teach our hearts—'tis goodness still
    That grants it, or denies.

322   *Prevalent Prayer.*   *S. M.*

1 BEHOLD the throne of grace!
    The promise calls us near;
There Jesus shows a smiling face,
    And waits to answer prayer.

2 The rich atoning blood,
    Which sprinkled round we see,
Provides, for those who come to God,
    An all-prevailing plea.

3 Thine image, Lord! bestow,
    Thy presence and thy love;
We ask to serve thee here below,
    And reign with thee above.

4 Teach us to live by faith,
    Conform our will to thine;
Let us victorious be in death,
    And, then, in glory shine.

5 If thou these blessings give,
    And wilt our portion be,
All worldly joys we'll cheerful leave,
    And find our heaven in thee.

323   *Importunate Prayer.*   S. M.

1 JESUS, who knows full well
   The heart of every saint,
Invites us all our griefs to tell,
   To pray and never faint.

2 He bows his gracious ear,
   We never plead in vain;
Then let us wait till he appear,
   And pray, and pray again.

3 Jesus, the Lord, will hear
   His chosen when they cry;
Yes, though he may a while forbear,
   He'll help them from on high.

4 Then let us earnest cry,
   And never faint in prayer;
He sees, he hears, and, from on high,
   Will make our cause his care.

324   *Habitual Devotion.*   C. M.

1 WHILE thee I seek, protecting Power!
   Be my vain wishes stilled;
And may this consecrated hour
   With better hopes be filled.

2 Thy love the power of thought bestowed;
   To thee my thoughts would soar;
Thy mercy o'er my life has flowed,
   That mercy I adore.

22 *

3 In each event of life, how clear
    Thy ruling hand I see!
Each blessing to my soul more dear,
    Because conferred by thee.

4 In every joy that crowns my days,
    In every pain I bear,
My heart shall find delight in praise,
    Or seek relief in prayer.

5 When gladness wings my favored hour
    Thy love my breast shall fill;
Resigned, when storms of sorrow lower,
    My soul shall meet thy will.

6 My lifted eye, without a tear,
    The gathering storm shall see;
My steadfast heart shall know no fear,
    That heart shall rest on thee.

---

325   *The Mercy-Seat.*   **L. M.**

1 FROM every stormy wind that blows,
From every swelling tide of woes,
There is a calm, a sure retreat,
'Tis found beneath the mercy-seat.

2 There is a place where Jesus sheds
The oil of gladness on our heads;
A place than all beside more sweet,
It is the blood-bought mercy-seat.

3 There is a scene where spirits blend,
  Where friend holds fellowship with friend;
  Though sundered far, by faith they meet
  Around one common mercy-seat.

4 There, there, on eagle wings we soar,
  And sense and sin becloud no more,
  And heaven comes down, our souls to greet,
  And glory crowns the mercy-seat.

---

326   *Prayer for Thankfulness.*   *C. M.*

1 FATHER! whate'er of earthly bliss,
    Thy sovereign will denies,
  Accepted, at thy throne of grace,
    Let this petition rise:

2 "Give me a calm, a thankful heart,
    From every murmur free;
  The blessings of thy grace impart,
    And make me live to thee.

3 "Let the sweet hope, that I am thine,
    My life and death attend;
  Thy presence through my journey shine
    And crown my journey's end.

---

327   *Prayer for Rest.*   *7s.*

1 COME, my soul! thy suit prepare,
    Jesus lives to answer prayer;

He himself has bid thee pray;
Rise, and ask without delay.

2 With my burden I begin;
Lord! remove this load of sin;
Let thy blood, for sinners spilt,
Set my conscience free from guilt.

3 Lord! I come to thee for rest,
Take possession of my breast;
There, thy sovereign right maintain,
And, without a rival, reign.

4 While I am a pilgrim here,
Let thy love my spirit cheer,
Be my guide, my guard, my friend;
Lead me to my journey's end.

5 Show me what I have to do,
Every hour my strength renew;
Let me live a life of faith,
Let me die thy people's death.

---

328   *Prayer for Blessing.*   **7s.**

1 LORD! we come before thee now;
At thy feet we humbly bow;
Oh! do not our suit disdain;
Shall we seek thee, Lord! in vain?

2 Lord! on thee our souls depend,
In compassion, now descend;
Fill our hearts with thy rich grace,
Tune our lips to sing thy praise.

3 In thine own appointed way,
  Now we seek thee, here we stay,
  Lord! we know not how to go,
  Till a blessing thou bestow.

4 Send some message, from thy word,
  That may joy and peace afford;
  Let thy Spirit now impart
  Full salvation to each heart.

5 Comfort those who weep and mourn,
  Let the time of joy return;
  Those, who are cast down, lift up,
  Make them strong in faith and hope.

6 Grant, that all may seek and find
  Thee, a God supremely kind:
  Heal the sick, the captive free,
  Let us all rejoice in thee.

329   *Prayer to Christ.*   7s.

1 LIGHT of life!—seraphic Fire!
    Love divine!—thyself impart;
  Every fainting soul inspire;
    Shine in every drooping heart.

2 Every mourning sinner cheer;
    Scatter all our guilty gloom:
  Saviour—Son of God! appear;
    To thy living temples come.

3 Come, in this accepted hour,
　　Bring thy heavenly kingdom in;
　Fill us with thy glorious power,
　　Rooting out the love of sin.

4 Nothing more can we require,
　　We will covet nothing less;
　Be thou all our heart's desire,
　　All our joy and all our peace.

330　　*Sweet Hour of Prayer.*

1 SWEET hour of prayer! sweet hour of prayer!
　That calls me from a world of care,
　And bids me at my Father's throne,
　Make all my wants and wishes known:
　In seasons of distress and grief,
　My soul has often found relief;
　And oft escaped the tempter's snare
　By thy return, sweet hour of prayer,

2 Sweet hour of prayer! sweet hour of prayer!
　Thy wings shall my petition bear,
　To him whose truth and faithfulness,
　Engage the waiting soul to bless;
　And since he bids me seek his face,
　Believe his word, and trust his grace,
　I'll cast on him my every care,
　And wait for thee, sweet hour of prayer.

3 Sweet hour of prayer! sweet hour of prayer!
May I thy consolation share;
Till from Mount Pisgah's lofty height,
I view my home, and take my flight:
This robe of flesh I'll drop, and rise
To seize the everlasting prize;
And shout, while passing through the air,
Farewell, farewell, sweet hour of prayer.

------

331   *Thy Will be Done.*   *L. M.*

1 O LOVE divine, that stooped to share
Our sharpest pang, our bitterest tear,
On thee we cast each earth-born care,
We smile at pain when thou art near!

2 Though long the weary way we tread,
And sorrow crown each lingering year,
No pain we shun, no darkness dread,
Our hearts still whispering, thou art near!

3 When drooping pleasure turns to grief,
And trembling faith is changed to fear,
The murmuring wind, the quivering leaf
Shall softly tell us, thou art near!

REVIVAL.

332 *Source of Revival.* **L. M.**

1 O Sun of righteousness! arise,
With gentle beams on Zion shine;
Dispel the darkness from our eyes,
And souls awake to life divine.

2 On all around, let grace descend,
Like heavenly dew, or copious showers;
That we may call our God our friend,
That we may hail salvation ours.

333 *Year of Jubilee.* **H. M.**

1 Blow ye the trumpet! blow,
The gladly solemn sound!
Let all the nations know,
To earth's remotest bound:
The year of jubilee is come;
Return, ye ransomed sinners! home.

2 Exalt the Lamb of God,
The sin-atoning Lamb;
Redemption by his blood,
Through all the world, proclaim;
The year of jubilee is come;
Return, ye ransomed sinners! home.

3 Ye slaves of sin and hell!
Your liberty receive;

And safe in Jesus dwell,
    And blest in Jesus live:
The year of jubilee is come;
Return, ye ransomed sinners! home.

4 The gospel trumpet hear,
    The news of pardoning grace:
Ye happy souls! draw near,
    Behold your Saviour's face:
The year of jubilee is come;
Return, ye ransomed sinners! home.

5 Jesus, our great High-Priest,
    Has full atonement made:
Ye weary spirits! rest,
    Ye mourning souls be glad:
The year of jubilee is come;
Return, ye ransomed sinners! home.

---

334   *Need of Revival.*   **S. M.**

1 O Lord! thy work revive
    In Zion's gloomy hour;
And let our dying graces live,
    By thy restoring power.

2 Oh! let thy chosen few
    Awake to earnest prayer;
Their solemn vows again renew,
    And walk in filial fear.

3 Thy Spirit then will speak,
    Through lips of humble clay,
  Till hearts of adamant shall break,
    Till rebels shall obey.

4 Now lend thy gracious ear,
    Now listen to our cry;
  Oh! come, and bring salvation near:
    Our souls on thee rely.

335   *Prayer for Revival.*   *S. M.*

1 Oh for the happy hour
    When God will hear our cry,
  And send, with a reviving power,
    His Spirit from on high.

2 Our prayers are faint and dull,
    And languid all our songs;
  Where once with joy our hearts were full,
    And rapture tuned our tongues.

3 Thou, thou alone canst give
    Thy gospel sure success;
  Canst bid the dying sinner live
    Anew in holiness.

4 Come, then, with power divine,
    Spirit of life and love;
  Then shall our people all be thine,
    Our church like that above.

336   *Effect of Revival.*   8s, 7s & 4s.

1 SEE, from Zion's sacred mountain,
    Streams of living water flow!
God has opened there a fountain,
    That supplies the plains below:
        They are blessed,
    Who its sovereign virtues know.

2 Through ten thousand channels flowing,
    Streams of mercy find their way;
Life, and health, and joy bestowing,
    Making all around look gay:
        O ye nations!
    Hail the long-expected day.

3 Gladdened by the flowing treasure,
    All-enriching as it goes;
Lo, the desert smiles with pleasure,
    Buds and blossoms as the rose:
        Every object
    Sings for joy where'er it flows.

4 Trees of life, the banks adorning,
    Yield their fruit to all around;
Those who eat are saved from mourning,
    Pleasure comes, and hopes abound;
        Fair their portion!
    Endless life, with glory crowned.

337 *Rejoicing in Revival.* **H. M.**

1 O ZION! tune thy voice,
    And raise thy hands on high;
  Tell all the earth thy joys,
    And boast salvation nigh;
Cheerful in God, | While rays divine
Arise and shine, | Stream all abroad.

2 He gilds thy mourning face
    With beams that cannot fade;
  His all-resplendent grace
    He pours around thy head;
The nations round | With lustre new,
Thy form shall view, | Divinely crowned.

3 In honor to his name,
    Reflect that sacred light;
  And loud that grace proclaim,
    Which makes thy darkness bright;
Pursue his praise, | In worlds above,
Till sovereign love, | The glory raise.

—————

338 *Beginning of Revival.* **7s.**

1 SAW ye not the cloud arise,
    Little as the human hand?
  Now it spreads along the skies,
    Hangs o'er all the thirsty land.

2 Lo, the promise of a shower
    Drops already from above;
  But the Lord will shortly pour
    All the blessings of his love.

3 When he first the work begun,
    Small and feeble was the day;
  Now the word doth swiftly run,
    Now it wins its widening way.

4 More and more it spreads and grows,
    Ever mighty to prevail;
  Sin's strongholds it now o'erthrows,
    Shakes the trembling gates of hell.

5 Sons of God! your Saviour praise;
    He the door hath opened wide;
  He hath given the word of grace;
    Jesus' word is glorified.

---

339   *The Vision of Dry Bones.*   *L. M.*

1 Look down, O Lord! with pitying eye,
  See Adam's race in ruin lie;
  Sin spreads its trophies o'er the ground,
  And scatters slaughtered heaps around.

2 And can these dead awake and live?
  And can these perished bones revive?
  That, mighty God! to thee is known;
  That wondrous work is all thine own.

23 *

3 Thy ministers are sent in vain,
To prophesy upon the slain;
In vain they call, in vain they cry,
Till thine almighty aid is nigh.

4 But if thy Spirit deign to breathe,
Life spreads through all the realms of death;
Dry bones obey thy powerful voice,
They move, they waken, they rejoice.

5 So, when the trumpet's awful sound
Shall shake the heavens, and rend the ground,
Dead saints shall from their tombs arise,
And spring to life beyond the skies.

---

340 *Revival Sought.* **8s, 7s & 4s.**

1 SAVIOUR! visit thy plantation;
Grant us, Lord! a gracious rain;
All will come to desolation,
Unless thou return again.

Chorus.—Lord revive us, Lord revive us,
All our help must come from **thee.**

2 Keep no longer at a distance;
Shine upon us from on high,
Lest, for want of thine assistance,
Every plant should droop and die.

3 Let our mutual love be fervent,
Make us prevalent in prayers;
Let each one, esteemed thy servant,
Shun the world's enticing snares.

4 Break the tempter's fatal power;
   Turn the stony heart to flesh;
   And begin, from this good hour,
   To revive thy work afresh.

---

341   *Declension Lamented.*   8s & 7s.

1 ONCE, O Lord, thy garden flourished,
   Every part looked gay and green;
   Then thy word our spirits nourished,
   Happy seasons we have seen!

2 But a drought has since succeeded,
   And a sad decline we see:
   Lord, thy help is greatly needed,
   Help can only come from thee.

3 Some, in whom we once delighted,
   We shall meet no more below;
   Some, alas! we fear are blighted,
   Scarce a single leaf they show.

4 Dearest Saviour, hasten hither;
   Thou canst make them bloom again;
   Oh! permit them not to wither,
   Let not all our hopes be vain.

SPREAD OF THE GOSPEL.

342   *Thy Kingdom Come.*   L. M.

1 JESUS! we bow before thy throne,
   We lift our eyes to seek thy face;

To bleeding hearts thy love make known,
  On contrite souls bestow thy grace.

2 See, spread beneath thy gracious eye,
  A world o'erwhelmed in guilt and tears,
Where deathless souls in ruin lie,
  And no kind voice dispels their fears!

3 Lord! arm thy truth with power divine,
  Its conquests spread from shore to shore,
Till sun and stars forget to shine,
  And earth and skies shall be no more.

4 Oh! rise, ye ransomed captives! rise,
  Peal the loud anthem here below;
Let earth reflect it to the skies,
  And heaven with new-born rapture glow.

543   *Prayer for Zion.*   L. M.

1 INDULGENT Sovereign of the skies!
  And wilt thou bow thy gracious ear?
While feeble mortals raise their cries,
  Wilt thou, the great Jehovah, hear?

2 How shall thy servants give thee rest,
  Till Zion's mouldering walls thou raise?
Till thine own power shall stand confessed,
  And make Jerusalem a praise?

3 Look down, O God! with pitying eye,
  And view the desolations round;
See what wide realms in darkness lie,
  What scenes of woe and crime abound!

4 Loud let the gospel trumpet blow,
    And call the nations from afar;
Let all the isles their Saviour know,
    And earth's remotest ends draw near.

<hr>

344   *Prayer for Gospel Success.*   *S. M.*

1 O LORD, our God! arise,
    The cause of truth maintain;
And, wide o'er all the peopled world,
    Extend her blessed reign.

2 Thou Prince of life! arise,
    Nor let thy glory cease:
Far spread the conquests of thy grace,
    And bless the earth with peace.

3 Thou Holy Ghost! arise,
    Expand thy quickening wing,
And, o'er a dark and ruined world,
    Let light and order spring.

4 All on the earth! arise,
    To God, the Saviour, sing;
From shore to shore, from earth to heaven,
    Let echoing anthems ring.

<hr>

345   *Prayer for Inebriates.*   *C. M.*

1 LIFE from the dead, Almighty God,
    'Tis thine alone to give;
To lift the poor inebriate up,
    And bid the helpless live.

2 Life from the dead!   For those we plead
    Fast bound in passion's chain,
  That, from their iron fetters freed,
    They wake to life again.

3 Life from the dead!   Quickened by thee,
    Be all their powers inclined
  To temperance, truth, and piety,
    And pleasures pure, refined.

4 And may they by thy help abide,
    The tempter's power withstand,
  By grace restored and purified,
    In Christ accepted stand.

<hr>

346   *Prayer for Gospel Triumph.*   L. M.

  1 ARM of the Lord! awake, awake,
    Put on thy strength, the nations shake,
    And let the world, adoring, see
    Triumphs of mercy wrought by thee.

  2 Say to the heathen, from thy throne,
    "I am Jehovah—God alone!"
    Thy voice their idols shall confound,
    And cast their altars to the ground.

  3 Almighty God! thy grace proclaim,
    In every land of every name;
    Let Zion's time of favor come;
    Oh! bring the tribes of Israel home.

4 Arm of the Lord! awake, awake!
Put on thy strength, the nations shake;
Let hostile powers before thee fall,
And crown the Saviour—Lord of all.

347   *Time to Favor Zion.*

1 SOVEREIGN of worlds! display thy power,
Be this thy Zion's favored hour;
Bid the bright morning-star arise,
And point the nations to the skies,

2 Set up thy throne where Satan reigns,
On Afric's shore, on India's plains;
Far let the gospel's sound be known,
And claim the nations for thine own.

3 Speak,—and the world shall hear thy voice,
Speak,—and the desert shall rejoice:
Scatter the gloom of heathen night;
Bid every nation hail the light.

348   *Prayer for the World. 8s, 7s & 4s.*

1 O'ER the gloomy hills of darkness,
Cheered by no celestial ray,
Sun of righteousness! arising,
Bring the bright, the glorious day;
Send the gospel
To the earth's remotest bound.

2 Kingdoms wide that sit in darkness,
    Grant them, Lord! the glorious light;
And, from eastern coast to western,
    May the morning chase the night;
        And redemption,
    Freely purchased, win the day.

3 Fly abroad, thou mighty gospel!
    Win and conquer, never cease;
May thy lasting, wide dominions,
    Multiply, and still increase:
        Sway thy sceptre,
    Saviour! all the world around.

------

349   *Prayer for the Heathen.*   *8s, 7s & 4s.*

1 O'ER the realms of pagan darkness
    Let the eye of pity gaze;
See the kindreds of the people,
    Lost in sin's bewildering maze:
        Darkness brooding
    On the face of all the earth!

2 Light of them who sit in error!
    Rise and shine—thy blessings bring;
Light—to lighten all the Gentiles!
    Rise with healing in thy wing:
        To thy brightness,
    Let all kings and nations come.

3 Let the heathen, now adoring
    Idol gods of wood and stone,

Come, and worshiping before him,
  Serve the living God alone;
    Let thy glory
Fill the earth, as floods the sea.

4 Thou! to whom all power is given,
    Speak the word; at thy command,
Let the company of heralds,
    Spread thy name from land to land:
      Lord! be with them,
  Always till time's latest end.

———— ·◇· ————

350   *The World's Conversion.*   L. M.

1 O SPIRIT of the living God!
    In all thy plenitude of grace,
Where'er the foot of man hath trod,
    Descend on our apostate race.

2 Give tongues of fire, and hearts of love,
    To preach the reconciling word;
Give power and unction from above,
    Where'er the joyful sound is heard.

3 Be darkness, at thy coming, light,
    Confusion—order, in thy path:
Souls without strength, inspire with might;
    Bid mercy triumph over wrath.

4 O Spirit of the Lord! prepare
    A sinful world their God to meet:
Breathe thou abroad, like morning-air,
    Till hearts of stone begin to beat.

24

5 Baptize the nations; far and nigh
    The triumphs of the cross record;
The name of Jesus glorify,
    Till every kindred call him—Lord.

351   *Christ's Coming Reign.*   L. M.

1 ASCEND thy throne, almighty King!
    And spread thy glories all abroad;
Let thine own arm salvation bring,
    And be thou known the gracious God.

2 Let millions bow before thy seat,
    Let humble mourners seek thy face;
Bring daring rebels to thy feet,
    Subdued by thy victorious grace.

3 Oh! let the kingdoms of the world
    Become the kingdoms of the Lord;
Let saints and angels praise thy name,
    Be thou through heaven and earth adored.

352   *Messiah's Rule.*   7s. Double.

1 HASTEN, Lord! the glorious time,
    When, beneath Messiah's sway;
Every nation, every clime,
    Shall the gospel-call obey.

2 Mightiest kings his power shall own,
    Heathen tribes his name adore;
Satan and his host, o'erthrown,
    Bound in chains, shall hurt no more.

3 Then shall wars and tumults cease,
  Then be banished grief and pain;
Righteousness, and joy, and peace,
  Undisturbed shall ever reign.

4 Bless we, then, our gracious Lord;
  Ever praise his glorious name;
All his mighty acts record,
  All his wondrous love proclaim.

353   *Prayer for all Lands.*   S. M.

1 O God of sovereign grace!
  We bow before thy throne;
And plead for all the human race,
  The merits of thy Son.

2 Spread through the earth, O Lord!
  The knowledge of thy ways;
And let all lands, with joy, record
  The great Redeemer's praise.

354   *Prayer for Christ's Triumph.*   L. M.

1 Soon may the last glad song arise
Through all the millions of the skies,
That song of triumph which records
That all the earth is now the Lord's!

2 Let thrones and powers and kingdoms be
Obedient, mighty God, to thee!
And, over land and stream and main,
Wave thou the sceptre of thy reign!

3 Oh, let that glorious anthem swell,
Let host to host the triumph tell,
That not one rebel heart remains,
But over all the Saviour reigns!

---

355 *Christ's Kingdom.* L. M.

1 JESUS shall reign, where'er the sun
Does his successive journeys run;
His kingdom stretch from shore to shore,
Till moons shall wax and wane no more.

2 For him shall endless prayer be made,
And endless praises crown his head;
His name, like sweet perfume, shall rise
With every morning sacrifice.

3 People and realms of every tongue,
Dwell on his love with sweetest song;
And infant voices shall proclaim
Their early blessings on his name.

4 Blessings abound where'er he reigns;
The prisoner leaps to lose his chains;
The weary find eternal rest;
And all the sons of want are blest.

5 Let every creature rise and bring
Peculiar honors to our King;
Angels descend with songs again,
And earth repeat the loud Amen.

356　　*Universal Praise.*　　L. M.

1 FROM all that dwell below the skies,
　Let the Creator's praise arise;
　Let the Redeemer's name be sung,
　Through every land, by every tongue.

2 Eternal are thy mercies, Lord!
　Eternal truth attends thy word;
　Thy praise shall sound from shore to shore,
　Till suns shall rise and set no more.

357　　*Christ's Beneficent Reign.*　　7s & 6s.

1 HAIL to the Lord's anointed,
　　Great David's greater Son!
　Hail, in the time appointed,
　　His reign on earth begun!
　He comes to break oppression,
　　To set the captive free,
　To take away transgression,
　　And rule in equity.

2 He comes, with succor speedy,
　　To those who suffer wrong;
　To help the poor and needy,
　　And bid the weak be strong;
　To give them songs for sighing,
　　Their darkness turn to light,
　Whose souls, condemned and dying,
　　Were precious in his sight.

24 *

3 He shall come down, like showers
   Upon the fruitful earth,
And love, and joy, like flowers,
   Spring in his path to birth:
Before him, on the mountains,
   Shall peace, the herald go;
And righteousness, in fountains,
   From hill to valley flow.

4 For him shall prayer unceasing
   And daily vows ascend;
His kingdom still increasing,
   A kingdom without end:
The tide of time shall never
   His covenant remove;
His name shall stand forever;
   That name to us is—Love.

358   *Prayer for Israel.*   **L. M.**

1 ARISE, great God! and let thy grace
Shed its glad beams on Israel's race;
Restore the long-lost, scattered band,
Recall them to their native land.

2 Their misery let thy mercy heal;
Their trespass hide, their pardon seal;
O God of Israel! hear our prayer,
And grant them still thy love to share.

3 Thy quickening Spirit now impart,
  And wake to joy each grateful heart;
  While Israel's rescued tribes, in thee,
  Their bliss and full salvation see.

359   *Morning-light Breaking.*   *7s & 6s.*

1 THE morning light is breaking,
    The darkness disappears;
  The sons of earth are waking
    To penitential tears:
  Each breeze that sweeps the ocean,
    Brings tidings from afar,
  Of nations in commotion,
    Prepared for Zion's war.

2 See heathen nations bending
    Before the God we love,
  And thousand hearts ascending
    In gratitude above;
  While sinners, now confessing,
    The gospel-call obey,
  And seek the Saviour's blessing,
    A nation in a day.

3 Blest river of salvation,
    Pursue thine onward way;
  Flow thou to every nation,
    Nor in thy richness stay;

Stay not till all the lowly
   Triumphant reach their home;
Stay not till all the holy
   Proclaim, "The Lord is come!"

------

360   . *Christ's Final Victory.*   *7s & 6s.*

1 WHEN shall the voice of singing
   Flow joyfully along?
When hill and valley, ringing
   With one triumphant song,
Proclaim the contest ended,
   And him, who once was slain,
Again to earth descended,
   In righteousness to reign.

2 Then, from the craggy mountains,
   The sacred shout shall fly;
And shady vales and fountains
   Shall echo the reply:
High tower and lowly dwelling
   Shall send the chorus round,
All hallelujah swelling
   In one eternal sound.

------

361   *Captivity Ending.*   *8s, 7s & 4s.*

1 ON the mountain tops appearing,
   Lo! the sacred herald stands,
Welcome news to Zion bearing,
   Zion long in hostile lands:

Mourning captive!
God himself will loose thy bands.

2 Has thy night been long and mournful,
  All thy friends unfaithful proved?
Have thy foes been proud and scornful,
  By thy sighs and tears unmoved?
    Cease thy mourning:
Zion still is well-beloved.

3 God, thy God, will now restore thee,
  He himself appears thy Friend;
All thy foes shall flee before thee,
  Here their boasts and triumphs end:
    Great deliverance
Zion's King will quickly send.

4 Peace and joy shall now attend thee,
  All thy warfare now is past,
God, thy Saviour, shall defend thee,
  Peace and joy are come at last:
    All thy conflicts
End in everlasting rest.

---

362   *The Latter Day.*   8s, 7s & 4s.

1 Look, ye saints! the day is breaking;
  Joyful times are near at hand;
God, the mighty God, is speaking
  By his word in every land;
    Day advances,
Darkness flies, at his command.

2 While the foe becomes more daring,
  While he enters like a flood,
God, the Saviour, is preparing
  Means to spread his truth abroad:
    Every language
  Soon shall tell the love of God.

3 God of Jacob, high and glorious!
  Let thy people see thy power;
Let the gospel be victorious,
  Through the world for evermore;
    Then shall idols
  Perish, while thy saints adore.

———◇———

363   *A Brighter Day.*

1 "Lift your heads" with faith; the morrow
  Dawneth brighter than to-day;
Angel hands will lift the shadows,
  Chase the gathering gloom away.

Chorus.—"Lift your heads," the day is break-
      ing,
    Soon the morning will appear;
  See the earth from slumber waking.
    "Lift your heads," the day draws
      near.

2 Art thou lonely, sad, and weary,
  Watching through the silent night?
Dry thy tears, the orient glistens
  Like a thread of silver light.

3 Does the night seem long and weary,
    Dangers threatening 'long the way?
  Joy will soon return to bless thee,
    Soon will dawn a brighter day.

4 What, though wars and earth's commotions
    Try your faith, and cause dismay;
  God, your Father, rules the nations,
    He will send a brighter day.

5 Let the heart be cheered with gladness,
    Though the sun is veiled from sight;
  See, the stars are brightly beaming
    Through the shadows of the night.

Chorus.—Look! e'en now the morn is break-
              ing,
      See the shadows flee away;
      See! the earth from slumber waking,
      "Lift your heads!" behold the day!

------

364   *Missionary Hymn.*   *7s & 6s.*

  1 From Greenland's icy mountains,
      From India's coral strand,
    Where Afric's sunny fountains
      Roll down their golden sand;
    From many an ancient river,
      From many a palmy plain,
    They call us to deliver
      Their land from error's chain.

2 What, though the spicy breezes
    Blow soft o'er Ceylon's isle,
  Though every prospect pleases,
    And only man is vile?
  In vain, with lavish kindness,
    The gifts of God are strown;
  The heathen, in his blindness,
    Bows down to wood and stone.

3 Shall we, whose souls are lighted
    With wisdom from on high,
  Shall we, to men benighted,
    The lamp of life deny?
  Salvation! O Salvation!
    The joyful sound proclaim,
  Till earth's remotest nation
    Has learned Messiah's name.

4 Waft—waft, ye winds! his story,
    And you, ye waters! roll,
  Till, like a sea of glory,
    It spreads from pole to pole;
  Till, o'er our ransomed nature,
    The Lamb for sinners slain,
  Redeemer, King, Creator,
    In bliss returns to reign.

* * *

365   *Christian Effort.*   H. M.

1 RISE, gracious God! and shine
    In all thy saving might;

And prosper each design,
    To spread thy glorious light.
Let healing streams of mercy flow,
That all the earth thy truth may know.

2 Put forth thy glorious power!
    The nations then will see,
And earth present her store,
    In converts born of thee;
God, our own God, his church will bless,
And earth shall yield her full increase.

<hr>

366   *Waiting for Christ.*   **L. M.**

1 JESUS! thy church with longing eyes
    For thine expected coming waits:
When will the promised light arise,
    And glory beam on Zion's gates?

2 E'en now, when tempests round us fall,
    And wintry clouds o'ercast the sky,
Thy words with pleasure we recall,
    And deem that our redemption's nigh.

3 Oh! come and reign o'er every land;
    Let Satan from his throne be hurled,
All nations bow to thy command,
    And grace revive a dying world.

4 Teach us, in watchfulness and prayer
    To wait for thine appointed hour;
And fit us, by thy grace, to share
    The triumphs of thy conquering power.

367   *The Gospel Banner.*   7s & 6s.

1 Now be the gospel banner,
    In every land, unfurled;
And be the shout,—" Hosanna !"
    Re-echoed through the world.
Till every isle and nation,
    Till every tribe and tongue,
Receive the great salvation,
    And join the happy throng.

2 What, though the embattled legions
    Of earth and hell combine?
His arm, throughout their regions,
    Shall soon resplendent shine :
Ride on, O Lord ! victorious,
    Immanuel, Prince of Peace !
Thy triumph shall be glorious,
    Thy empire still increase.

3 Yes,—thou shalt reign forever,
    O Jesus, King of kings !
Thy light, thy love, thy favor,
    Each ransomed captive sings :
The isles for thee are waiting,
    The deserts learn thy praise,
The hills and valleys greeting,
    The song responsive raise.

368   *Gospel Labors.*   C. M.

1 GREAT God! the nations of the earth
    Are by creation thine;
And in thy works, from nature's birth,
    Thy radiant glories shine.

2 But, Lord! thy greater love hath sent
    Thy gospel to our race;
Unveiling thy divine intent
    Of rich redeeming grace.

3 Soon may these gracious tidings roll
    The spacious earth around,
Till every tribe and every soul
    Shall hear the joyful sound.

4 Then, to her sable sons conveyed,
    Shall Afric learn thy word,
And vassals, long enslaved, become
    The freemen of the Lord.

5 When shall the scattered wanderers meet,
    That now in darkness rove,
And, gathered round Immanuel's feet,
    Sing of his saving love?

6 O Lord! each faithful effort own,
    To spread the gospel rays;
And rear, on sin's demolished throne,
    The temples of thy praise.

369 *Charities.* C. M.

1 JESUS, our Lord! how rich thy grace!
   Thy bounties—how complete!
How shall we count the wondrous sum,
   Or pay the mighty debt?

2 High on a throne of radiant light,
   Dost thou exalted shine;
What can our poverty bestow,
   Since all the world is thine?

3 But thou hast brethren here below,
   The children of thy grace,
Whose humble names thou wilt confess,
   Before thy Father's face.

4 In them may'st thou be clothed and fed,
   Be visited and cheered;
And, in their accents of distress,
   The Saviour's voice be heard.

5 Whate'er our willing hands can give,
   Lord! at thy feet we lay;
Grace will the humble gift receive,
   And grace at length repay.

---

370 *Morning Star.* 7s. Double.

1 WATCHMAN! tell us of the night,
   What its signs of promise are?
Traveler! o'er yon mountain's height!
   See that glory-beaming star:

Watchman! does its beauteous ray
  Aught of hope or joy foretell?
Traveler! yes; it brings the day,
  Promised day of Israel.

2 Watchman! tell us of the night;
  Higher yet that star ascends;
Traveler! blessedness and light,
  Peace and truth, its course portends:
Watchman! will its beams alone
  Gild the spot that gave them birth?
Traveler! ages are its own,
  See, it bursts o'er all the earth.

3 Watchman! tell us of the night,
  For the morning seems to dawn;
Traveler! darkness takes its flight,
  Doubt and terror are withdrawn:
Watchman! let thy wanderings cease,
  Hie thee to thy quiet home:
Traveler! lo! the Prince of peace,
  Lo! the Son of God is come!

---

371   *Love to the Church.*   S. M.

1 I LOVE thy kingdom, Lord!
  The house of thine abode,
The church our blest Redeemer saved
  With his own precious blood.

2 I love thy church, O God!
  Her walls before thee stand,

25 *

Dear as the apple of thine eye,
   And graven on thy hand.

3 For her my my tears shall fall;
   For her my prayers ascend;
To her my cares and toils be given,
   Till toils and cares shall end.

4 Beyond my highest joy,
   I prize her heavenly ways,
Her sweet communion, solemn vows,
   Her hymns of love and praise.

5 Sure as thy truth shall last,
   To Zion shall be given
The brightest glories earth can yield
   And brighter bliss of heaven.

---

372   *The Church's Glory.*   *8s & 7s.*

1 GLORIOUS things of thee are spoken,
   Zion, city of our God!
He, whose word cannot be broken,
   Formed thee for his own abode:
On the rock of ages founded,
   What can shake thy sure repose?
With salvation's walls surrounded,
   Thou may'st smile at all thy foes.

2 See the streams of living waters,
   Springing from eternal love,
To supply thy sons and daughters,
   And all fear of want remove!

Who can faint, while such a river
　　Ever flows his thirst t' assuage?
Grace, which, like the Lord, the giver,
　　Never fails from age to age.

3 Round each habitation, hovering,
　　See the cloud and fire appear,
For a glory and a covering,
　　Showing that the Lord is near!
Glorious things of thee are spoken,
　　Zion, city of our God!
He, whose word cannot be broken,
　　Formed thee for his own abode.

373　　　　　*Zion's God.*　　　　*8s, 7s & 4s.*

1 ZION stands with hills surrounded,
　　Zion, kept by power divine;
All her foes shall be confounded,
　　Though the world in arms combine:
　　　　Happy Zion;
What a favored lot is thine.

2 Every human tie may perish,
　　Friend to friend unfaithful prove,
Mothers cease their own to cherish,
　　Heaven and earth at last remove;
　　　　But no changes
Can attend Jehovah's love.

3 In the furnace God may prove thee,
    Thence to bring thee forth more bright;
But can never cease to love thee;
    Thou art precious in his sight:
        God is with thee:
        God, thine everlasting light.

* * *

ORDINANCES.

374   *Consecrating Children.*   C. M.

1 SEE Israel's gentle Shepherd stand,
    With all engaging charms!
Hark! how he calls the tender lambs,
    And folds them in his arms!

2 "Permit them to approach," he cries,
    "Nor scorn their humble name;
For 'twas to bless such souls as these,
    The Lord of angels came."

3 We bring them, Lord! in thankful hands,
    And yield them up to thee;
Joyful that we ourselves are thine,
    Thine let our offspring be.

4 Ye little flock! with pleasure hear,
    Ye children seek his face;
And fly, with transports, to receive
    The blessings of his grace.

5 If orphans they are left behind,
    Thy guardian care we trust;
That care shall heal our bleeding hearts,
    If weeping o'er their dust.

—◆—

375   *The Gospel Feast.*   C. M.

1 How sweet and awful is the place,
    With Christ within the doors,
While everlasting love displays
    The choicest of her stores!

2 While all our hearts, in praise and song,
    Join to admire the feast,
Each of us cries with thankful tongue,
    "Lord! why was I a guest?

3 "Why was I made to hear thy voice,
    And enter while there's room,
When thousands make a wretched choice,
    And rather starve than come?"

4 'Twas the same love that spread the feast,
    That sweetly forced us in;
Else we had still refused to taste,
    And perished in our sin.

5 Pity the nations, O our God!
    Constrain the earth to come;
Send thy victorious word abroad,
    And bring the strangers home.

6 We long to see thy churches full,
    That all the chosen race
May, with one voice, and heart, and soul,
    Sing thy redeeming grace.

376   *Self-consecration.*   *L. M.*

1 Now I resolve, with all my heart,
    With all my powers, to serve the Lord;
Nor from his ways will I depart,
    Whose service is a rich reward.

2 Oh! be his service all my joy!
    Around let my example shine,
Till others love the blest employ,
    And join in labors so divine.

3 Be this the purpose of my soul,
    My solemn, my determined choice,
To yield to his supreme control,
    And, in his kind commands, rejoice.

4 Oh! may I never faint nor tire,
    Nor wandering leave his sacred ways;
Great God! accept my soul's desire,
    And give me strength to live thy praise.

377   *Self-Dedication.*   *L. M*

1 Lord! I am thine, entirely thine,
    Purchased and saved by blood divine;
With full consent thine I would be,
    And own thy sovereign right in me.

2 Grant me, in mercy, now a place,
　Among the children of thy grace,
　A wretched sinner, lost to God,
　But ransomed by Immanuel's blood.

3 Thee, my new master, now I call,
　And consecrate to thee my all;
　Lord! let me live and die to thee,
　Be thine through all eternity.

———◆◇◆———

378　　　　*Covenant-sealing.*　　　*L. M.*

1 OH! happy day, that fixed my choice
　　On thee, my Saviour, and my God!
　Well may this glowing heart rejoice,
　　And tell its raptures all abroad.

Chorus.—Happy day, happy day,
　　　　When Jesus washed my sins away;
　　　　He taught me how to watch and
　　　　　pray,
　　　　And live rejoicing every day.

2 Oh! happy bond, that seals my vows
　　To him who merits all my love!
　Let cheerful anthems fill the house,
　　While to his altar now I move.

3 'Tis done—the great transaction's done;
　　I am my Lord's, and he is mine;
　He drew me, and I followed on,
　　Rejoiced to own the call divine.

4 Now rest, my long-divided heart!
    Fixed on this blissful centre, rest;
Here have I found a nobler part,
    Here heavenly pleasures fill my breast.

5 High heaven, that hears the solemn vow,
    That vow renewed shall daily hear;
Till, in life's latest hour, I bow,
    And bless in death a bond so dear.

---

379   *Christ's Presence Desired.*   *L. M.*

1 FAR from my thoughts, vain world! be gone,
    Let my religious hours alone:
Fain would mine eyes my Saviour see;
    I wait a visit, Lord! from thee.

2 My heart grows warm with holy fire,
    And kindles with a pure desire;
Come, my dear Jesus! from above,
    And feed my soul with heavenly love.

3 Blest Saviour! what delicious fare,
    How sweet thine entertainments are!
Never did angels taste above
    Redeeming grace, and dying love.

4 Hail, great Immanuel, all-divine!
    In thee thy Father's glories shine:
Thou brightest, sweetest, fairest one,
    That eyes have seen, or angels known!

380   *Institution of the Supper.*   **L. M.**

1 'TWAS on that dark and doleful night,
    When powers of earth and hell arose,
Against the Son of God's delight,
    And friends betrayed him to his foes:

2 Before the mournful scene began,
    He took the bread, and blessed, and brake:
What love through all his actions ran!
    What wondrous words of grace he spake!

3 "This is my body, broke for sin;
    Receive and eat the living food:"
Then took the cup, and blessed the wine;
    "'Tis the new covenant in my blood."

4 "Do this," he cried, "till time shall end,
In memory of your dying friend;
Meet, at my table, and record
The love of your departed Lord."

5 Jesus! thy feast we celebrate;
    We show thy death, we sing thy name
Till thou return, and we shall eat
    The marriage-supper of the Lamb.

----•◇•----

381   *Receiving New Members.*   **L. M.**

1 KINDRED in Christ! for his dear sake,
    A hearty welcome here receive;
May we together now partake
    The joys, which only he can give.

26

2 May he, by whose kind care, we meet,
　　Send his good Spirit from above,
Make our communications sweet,
　　And cause our hearts to burn with love.

3 Forgotten be each worldly theme,
　　When Christians see each other thus;
We only wish to speak of him,
　　Who lived, and died, and reigns, for us.

4 We'll talk of all he did and said,
　　And suffered for us, here below;
The path he marked for us to tread,
　　And what he's doing for us now.

5 Thus, as the moments pass away,
　　We'll love, and wonder, and adore;
And hasten on the glorious day,
　　When we shall meet to part no more.

—————

382　　*Remembering Christ.*　　*C. M.*

1 ACCORDING to thy gracious word,
　　In meek humility,
This will I do, my dying Lord!
　　I will remember thee,

2 Thy body, broken for my sake,
　　My bread from heaven shall be;
Thy testamental cup I take,
　　And thus remember thee.

3 Gethsemane can I forget?
    Or there thy conflict see,
  Thine agony and bloody sweat,
    And not remember thee?

4 When to the cross I turn mine eyes,
    And rest on Calvary,
  O Lamb of God, my sacrifice!
    I must remember thee:

5 Remember thee, and all thy pains,
    And all thy love to me!
  Yea, while a breath, a pulse remains,
    Will I remember thee.

6 And when these failing lips grow dumb,
    And mind and memory flee,
  When in thy kingdom, thou shalt come,
    Jesus! remember me.

--------⋄--------

383   *Christ's Love.*   C. M.

1 How condescending and how kind,
    Was God's eternal Son!
  Our misery reached his heavenly mind,
    And pity brought him down.

2 He sank beneath our heavy woes,
    To raise us to his throne;
  There's ne'er a gift his hand bestows,
    But cost his heart a groan.

3 This was compassion, like a God,
　　That, when the Saviour knew,
　The price of pardon was his blood,
　　His pity ne'er withdrew.

4 Now, though he reigns exalted high
　　His love is still as great;
　Well he remembers Calvary,
　　Nor lets his saints forget.

5 Here, let our hearts begin to melt,
　　While we his death record,
　And, with our joy for pardoned guilt,
　　Mourn that we pierced the Lord.

SABBATH.

384　　　*Sabbath Welcomed.*　　　**H. M.**

1 WELCOME! delightful morn,
　　Thou day of sacred rest!
　I hail thy kind return;
　　Lord! make these moments blest;
　From the low train of mortal toys,
　I soar to reach immortal joys,

2 Now may the King descend,
　　And fill his throne of grace;
　Thy sceptre, Lord! extend,
　　While saints address thy face:
　Let sinners feel thy quickening word,
　And learn to know and fear the Lord.

6 Descend, celestial Dove!
    With all thy quickening powers;
Disclose a Saviour's love,
    And bless the sacred hours;
Then shall my soul new life obtain,
Nor Sabbaths be bestowed in vain.

---

385   *Lord's Day-Morning.*   *C. M.*

1 LORD! in the morning thou shalt hear
    My voice ascending high;
To thee will I direct my prayer,
    To thee lift up mine eye:

2 Up to the hills, where Christ is gone
    To plead for all his saints,
Presenting, at his Father's throne,
    Our songs and our complaints.

3 Thou art a God, before whose sight
    The wicked shall not stand;
Sinners shall ne'er be thy delight,
    Nor dwell at thy right hand.

4 But to thy house will I resort,
    To taste thy mercies there;
I will frequent thy holy court,
    And worship in thy fear.

5 Oh! may thy Spirit guide my feet,
    In ways of righteousness;
Make every path of duty straight,
    And plain before my face.

26 *

386   *Sabbath in the Sanctuary.   7s. 6 lines.*

1 SAFELY, through another week,
    God has brought us on our way;
  Let us now a blessing seek,
    Waiting in his courts to-day;
  Day of all the week the best,
  Emblem of eternal rest.

2 While we seek supplies of grace,
    Through the dear Redeemer's name,
  Show thy reconciled face,
    Take away our sin and shame;
  From our worldly cares set free,
  May we rest, this day, in thee.

3 Here we come thy name to praise;
    Let us feel thy presence near:
  May thy glory meet our eyes,
    While we in thy house appear:
  Here afford us, Lord! a taste
  Of our everlasting feast.

4 May the gospel's joyful sound
    Conquer sinners, comfort saints;
  Make the fruits of grace abound,
    Bring relief from all complaints:
  Thus let all our Sabbaths prove,
  Till we join the church above.

387 *Day of Rest.* 7s.

1 WELCOME! sacred day of rest!
    Sweet repose from worldly care;
Day, above all days the best,
    When our souls for heaven prepare;
Day when our Redeemer rose,
    Victor o'er the hosts of hell;
Thus he vanquished all our foes;
    Let our lips his glory tell.

2 Gracious Lord! we love this day,
    When we hear thy holy word,
When we sing thy praise, and pray;
    Earth can no such joys afford:
But a better rest remains,
    Heavenly Sabbaths, happier days,
Rest from sin, and rest from pains,
    Endless joys, and endless praise.

---

388 *Sabbath Work.* L. M.

1 SWEET is the work, my God! my King!
To praise thy name, give thanks, and sing;
To show thy love by morning light,
And talk of all thy truth at night.

2 Sweet is the day of sacred rest,
No mortal care shall seize my breast;
Oh! may my heart in tune be found,
Like David's harp of solemn sound.

3 My heart shall triumph in my Lord,
  And bless his works, and bless his word;
  Thy works of grace,—how bright they shine!
  How deep thy counsels! how divine!

4 Lord! I shall share a glorious part,
  When grace hath well refined my heart,
  And fresh supplies of joy are shed,
  Like holy oil, to cheer my head.

5 Then shall I see, and hear, and know
  All I desired or wished below;
  And every power find sweet employ,
  In that eternal world of joy.

────◆────

389 *The Earthly and Heavenly Sabbath.* L. M.

1 THINE earthly Sabbaths, Lord! we love,
  But there's a nobler rest above;
  To that our longing souls aspire,
  With cheerful hope and strong desire.

2 No more fatigue, no more distress,
  Nor sin, nor death shall reach the place;
  No groans shall mingle with the songs,
  That warble from immortal tongues.

3 No rude alarms of raging foes,
  No cares to break the long repose,
  No midnight shade, no clouded sun,
  But sacred, high, eternal noon.

4 Soon shall that glorious day begin,
  Beyond this world of death and sin;
  Soon shall our voices join the song,
  Of the triumphant, holy throng.

390   *Sabbath, Pledge of Rest.*   **L. M.**

1 ANOTHER six days' work is done,
  Another Sabbath is begun;
  Return, my soul! enjoy thy rest,
  Improve the day thy God hath blessed.

2 Oh! that our thoughts and thanks may rise,
  As grateful incense to the skies;
  And draw, from heaven, that sweet repose,
  Which none but he that feels it knows.

3 This heavenly calm, within the breast,
  Is the dear pledge of glorious rest,
  Which for the church of God remains,
  The end of cares, the end of pains.

4 In holy duties, let the day,
  In holy pleasures, pass away;
  How sweet a Sabbath thus to spend,
  In hope of one that ne'er shall end!

391   *The Lord's Day.*   **C. M.**

1 THIS is the day the Lord hath made,
    He calls the hours his own:
  Let heaven rejoice, let earth be glad,
    And praise surround the throne.

2 To-day he rose and left the dead,
　　And Satan's empire fell;
　To-day the saints his triumph spread,
　　And all his wonders tell.

3 Hosanna to the anointed King,
　　To David's holy Son:
　Help us, O Lord! descend, and bring
　　Salvation from thy throne.

4 Blest be the Lord, who comes to men
　　With messages of grace;
　Who comes, in God his Father's name,
　　To save our sinful race.

5 Hosanna, in the highest strains,
　　The church on earth can raise;
　The highest heavens, in which he reigns,
　　Shall give him nobler praise.

————◦◇◦————

392　　*Sabbath, Foretaste of Heaven.*　　S. M.

　1 WELCOME! sweet day of rest,
　　　That saw the Lord arise!
　　Welcome to this reviving breast,
　　　And these rejoicing eyes!

　2 The King himself comes near,
　　　And feasts his saints to-day;
　　Here we may sit, and see him here,
　　　And love, and praise, and pray.

3 One day, amidst the place
  Where my dear God hath been,
Is sweeter than ten thousand days
  Of pleasurable sin.

4 My willing soul would stay,
  In such a frame as this,
And sit and sing herself away
  To everlasting bliss.

393   *Sabbath Worship.*   *8s, 7s & 4s.*

1 In thy name, O Lord! assembling,
  We, thy people, now draw near:
Teach us to rejoice with trembling;
  Speak, and let thy servants hear;
    Hear with meekness,
Hear thy word with godly fear.

2 While our days on earth are lengthened,
  May we give them, Lord, to thee;
Cheered by hope, and daily strengthened,
  May we run, nor weary be;
    Till thy glory
Without cloud in heaven we see.

3 There, in worship, purer, sweeter,
  All thy people shall adore;
Tasting of enjoyment greater
  Than they could conceive before;
    Full enjoyment,
Full, and pure, forevermore.

394   *Lord's Day Evening.*   *C. M.*

1 FREQUENT the day of God returns,
    To shed its quickening beams;
And yet how slow devotion burns!
    How languid are its flames.

2 Accept our faint attempts to love,
    Our frailties, Lord! forgive;
We would be like thy saints above,
    And praise thee while we live.

3 Increase, O Lord! our faith and hope,
    And fit us to ascend,
Where the assembly ne'er breaks up,
    The Sabbath ne'er shall end:

4 Where we shall breathe in heavenly air,
    With heavenly luster shine,
Before the throne of God appear,
    And feast on love divine:

5 Where we, in high seraphic strains,
    Shall all our powers employ;
Delighted range the ethereal plains,
    And share immortal joy.

395   *Close of Evening Service.*   *7s.*

1 FOR the mercies of the day,
    For this rest upon our way,
Thanks to thee alone be given,
    Lord of earth and King of heaven.

2 Cold our services have been,
  Mingled every prayer with sin;
  But thou canst and wilt forgive:
  By thy grace alone we live.

3 While this thorny path we tread,
  May thy love our footsteps lead;
  When our journey here is past,
  May we rest with thee at last.

4 Let these earthly Sabbaths prove
  Foretastes of our joys above;
  While their steps thy children bend
  To the rest which knows no end.

MINISTRY.

396　　*Ministers, Christ's Heralds.*

1 How beauteous are their feet,
    Who stand on Zion's hill!
  Who bring salvation on their tongues,
    And words of peace reveal!

2 How charming is their voice!
    How sweet the tidings are! ·
  "Zion! behold thy Saviour King,
    He reigns and triumphs here!"

3 How happy are our ears,
    That hear this joyful sound!
  Which kings and prophets waited for,
    And sought, but never found.

27

4 How blessed are our eyes,
    That see this heavenly light!
  Prophets and kings desired it long,
    But died without the sight.

5 The watchmen join their voice,
    And tuneful notes employ;
  Jerusalem breaks forth in songs,
    And deserts learn the joy.

6 The Lord makes bare his arm,
    Through all the earth abroad;
  Let every nation now behold
    Their Saviour and their God.

———❖———

397   *The Great Commission.*   *L. M.*

1 "Go, preach my gospel!" saith the Lord,
  "Bid the whole earth my grace receive;
  He shall be saved who trusts my word;
    He shall be damned who don't believe.

2 "I'll make your great commission known,
    And ye shall prove my gospel true,
  By all the works that I have done,
    By all the wonders ye shall do.

3 "Teach all the nations my commands,
    I'm with you till the world shall end;
  All power is trusted in my hands
    I can destroy, and I defend."

4 He spake—and light shone round his head
    On a bright cloud, to heaven he rode:
They, to the farthest nations, spread
    The grace of their ascended God.

---

398   *Ministers asking the Spirit.*   L. M.

1 POUR out thy Spirit from on high;
    Lord! thine assembled servants bless;
Graces and gifts to each supply,
    And clothe thy priests with righteousness.

2 Within thy temple where we stand,
    To teach the truth as taught by thee,
Saviour! like stars in thy right hand,
    The angels of the churches be!

3 Wisdom and zeal, and faith impart,
    Firmness with meekness from above,
To bear thy people on our hearts,
    And love the souls whom thou dost love:

4 To watch and pray, and never faint;
    By day and night strict guard to keep;
To warn the sinner, cheer the saint,
    Nourish thy lambs, and feed thy sheep.

5 Then, when our work is finished here,
    In humble hope, our charge resign;
When the chief Shepherd shall appear,
    O God! may they and we be thine.

399 *Prayer for Laborers.* **L. M.**

1 Lord of the harvest, bend thine ear,
For Zion's heritage appear;
Oh! send forth laborers filled with zeal,
Swift to obey their Master's will.

2 Our lifted eyes, O Lord, behold
The ripening harvest tinged with gold;
Wide fields are opening to our view;
The work is great, the laborers few.

3 Under the guidance of thy hand,
May Zion's sons to every land
Go forth, to bless the dying race,
As heralds of redeeming grace.

4 Bid all their hearts with ardor glow,
The Saviour's dying love to show,
And spread the gospel's joyful sound,
Far as the race of man is found.

400 *Death of a Pastor.* **S. M.**

1 Rest from thy labor, rest;
Soul of the just, set free!
Blest be thy memory, and blest
Thy bright example be!

2 Faith, perseverance, zeal,
Language of light and power,
Love, prompt to act, and quick to feel,
Marked thee till life's last hour.

3 Now, toil and conflict o'er,
   Go, take with saints thy place;
But go, as each hath gone before,
   A sinner saved by grace.

4 Lord Jesus! to thy hands
   Our pastor we resign;
And now we wait thine own commands;
   We were not his but thine.

5 Thou art thy church's head;
   And when the members die,
Thou raisest others in their stead:
   To thee we lift our eye.

---

401   *Death of an Aged Minister.*   *S. M.*

1 "Servant of God! well done!
   Rest from thy loved employ:
The battle fought, the victory won,
   Enter thy Master's joy."

2 The voice at midnight came,
   He started up to hear;
A mortal arrow pierced his frame,
   He fell—but felt no fear.

3 Tranquil amid alarms,
   It found him on the field,
A veteran slumbering on his arms,
   Beneath his red-cross shield.

27 *

4 The pains of death are past,
    Labor and sorrow cease ;
And, life's long warfare closed at last,
    His soul is found in peace.

5 Soldier of Christ ! well-done !
    Praise be thy new employ ;
And, while eternal ages run,
    Rest in thy Saviour's joy !

NATIONAL.

402   *God, the Nation's Trust.*   *C. M.*

1 IN thee, great God ! with songs of praise,
    Our favored realms rejoice ;
And, blest with thy salvation, raise
    To heaven their cheerful voice.

2 In deep distress, our injured land
    Implored thy power to save ;
For life we prayed ; thy bounteous hand
    The timely blessing gave.

3 On thee, in want, in woe, or pain,
    Our hearts alone rely ;
Our rights thy mercy will maintain,
    And all our wants supply.

4 Thus, Lord ! thy wondrous power declare,
    And still exalt thy fame ;
While we glad songs of praise prepare,
    For thine almighty name.

403   *Prayer for Country and Church.*   C. M.

1 SHINE on our land, Jehovah! shine,
   With beams of heavenly grace;
Reveal thy power through all our courts,
   And show thy smiling face.

2 When shall thy name, from shore to shore,
   Sound all the earth abroad,
And distant nations know and love
   Their Saviour and their God?

3 Sing to the Lord, ye distant lands!
   Sing loud with solemn voice;
Let every tongue exalt his praise,
   And every heart rejoice.

4 Earth shall obey her Maker's will,
   And yield a full increase;
Our God will crown his chosen land,
   With fruitfulness and peace.

5 God, the Redeemer, scatters round
   His choicest favors here,
While the creation's utmost bound
   Shall see, adore, and fear.

---

404   *God, in National Blessings.*   L. M.

1 GREAT God of nations! now to thee
   Our hymn of gratitude we raise;
With humble heart, and bended knee,
   We offer thee our song of praise.

2 Thy name we bless, Almighty God!
    For all the kindness thou hast shown
To this fair land the pilgrims trod,
    This land we fondly call our own.

3 Here Freedom spreads her banner wide,
    And casts her soft and hallowed ray;
Here thou our fathers' steps didst guide
    In safety, through their dangerous way.

4 Great God! preserve us in thy fear;
    In dangers still our guardian be;
Oh! spread thy truth's bright precepts here,
    Let all the people worship thee.

---

405   *Judgment Deprecated.*   **7s.**

1 WHY, O God! thy people spurn?
Why permit thy wrath to burn?
God of mercy! turn once more,
All our broken hearts restore.

2 Thou hast made our land to quake,
Heal the breaches thou dost make;
Bitter is the cup we drink,
Suffer not our souls to sink.

3 Be thy banner now unfurled,
Show thy truth to all the world;
Save us, Lord! we cry to thee,
Lift thine arm—thy chosen free.

406   *Thanksgiving.*   **7s.**

1 SWELL the anthem, raise the song,
  Praises to our God belong:
  Saints and angels! join to sing
  Praises to the heavenly King.

2 Blessings from his liberal hand
  Flow around this happy land:
  Guarded by his watchful eye,
  Peace and freedom we enjoy.

3 Here, beneath a virtuous sway,
  May we cheerfully obey,
  Never feel oppression's rod,
  Ever own and worship God.

4 Hark! the voice of nature sings
  Praises to the King of kings;
  Let us join the choral song,
  And the grateful notes prolong.

———◦◇◦———

407   *Praise from all Nations.   7s.   6 lines.*

1 GOD of mercy, God of grace!
  Show the brightness of thy face;
  Shine upon us, Saviour! shine;
  Fill thy church with light divine;
  And thy saving health extend
  Unto earth's remotest end.

2 Let the people praise thee, Lord!
  Be by all that live adored;

Let the nations shout and sing,
Glory to their Saviour King;
At thy feet their tribute pay,
And thy holy will obey.

——◄◆►——

408   *My Country, 'tis of Thee.*   *6s & 4s.*

1 My country, 'tis of thee,
  Sweet land of liberty,
    Of thee I sing:
  Land where my fathers died,
  Land of the pilgrims' pride,
  From every mountain-side
    Let freedom ring.

2 My native country, thee,
  Land of the noble free,
    Thy name I love;
  I love thy rocks and rills,
  Thy woods and templed hills:
  My heart with rapture thrills
    Like that above.

3 Let music swell the breeze,
  And ring from all the trees
    Sweet freedom's song;
  Let mortal tongues awake,
  Let all that breathe partake;
  Let rocks their silence break,
    The sound prolong.

4 Our fathers' God, to thee,
Author of liberty,
To thee we sing;
Long may our land be bright
With freedom's holy light;
Protect us by thy might,
Great God, our King!

- - - ◇ - - -

409   *"God Save the State!"*   6s & 4s.

1 God bless our native land!
Firm may she ever stand,
Through storm and night;
When the wild tempests rave,
Ruler of winds and wave,
Do thou our country save
By thy great might.

2 For her our prayer shall rise
To God, above the skies;
On him we wait:
Thou who art ever nigh,
Guarding with watchful eye,
To thee aloud we cry,
God save the State!

- - - ◇ - - -

MORNING.

410   *Morning.*   8s.

1 In this calm impressive hour,
Let my prayer ascend on high;

God of mercy! God of power!
　Hear me, when to thee I cry:
Hear me from thy lofty throne,
For the sake of Christ, thy Son.

2 With the morning's early ray,
　While the shades of night depart,
Let thy beams of light convey
　Joy and gladness to my heart:
Now o'er all my steps preside,
And for all my wants provide.

3 Oh! what joy that word affords,
　"Thou shalt reign o'er all the earth;"
King of kings, and Lord of lords!
　Send thy gospel heralds forth:
Now begin thy boundless sway,
Usher in the glorious day.

411　　*A Morning Invocation.*　　*L. M.*

1 AWAKE, my soul! and with the sun
Thy daily course of duty run;
Shake off dull sloth, and joyful rise
To pay thy morning sacrifice.

2 Wake, and lift up thyself, my heart!
And with the angels bear thy part,
Who, all night long, unwearied sing
High praises to the eternal King.

3 Glory to thee, who safe hast kept,
  And hast refreshed me, while I slept:
  Grant, Lord! when I from death shall wake,
  I may of endless life partake.

4 Lord! I my vows to thee renew;
  Scatter my sins as morning-dew;
  Guard my first springs of thought and will,
  And with thyself my spirit fill.

---

412 *Morning and Evening Mercies.* L. M.

1 My God! how endless is thy love!
    Thy gifts are every evening new;
  And morning mercies from above,
    Gently distill, like early dew.

2 Thou spread'st the curtains of the night,
    Great Guardian of my sleeping hours!
  Thy sovereign word restores the light,
    And quickens all my drowsy powers.

3 I yield my powers to thy command;
    To thee I consecrate my days;
  Perpetual blessings, from thy hand,
    Demand perpetual songs of praise.

---

413 *Morning Thanks.* 7s.

1 Thou that dost my life prolong!
    Kindly aid my morning song;
  Thankful, from my couch I rise,
  To the God that rules the skies.

28

2 Thou didst hear my evening cry;
 Thy preserving hand was nigh;
 Peaceful slumbers thou hast shed,
 Grateful to my weary head.

3 Thou hast kept me through the night,
 'Twas thy hand restored the light;
 Lord! thy mercies still are new,
 Plenteous, as the morning dew.

4 Still my feet are prone to stray,
 Oh! preserve me through the day;
 Dangers everywhere abound,
 Sins and snares beset me round.

5 Gently, with the dawning ray,
 On my soul, thy beams display;
 Sweeter than the smiling morn,
 Let thy cheering light return.

---

414   *Morning Gratitude.*   *C. M.*

1 ONCE more, my soul! the rising day
 Salutes thy waking eyes;
 Once more, my voice! thy tribute pay
 To him who rules the skies.

2 Night unto night his name repeats,
 The day renews the sound;
 Wide as the heaven, on which he sits
 To turn the seasons round.

3 'Tis he supports my mortal frame,
  My tongue shall speak his praise;
My sins would rouse his wrath to flame,
  And yet his wrath delays.

4 A thousand wretched souls are fled.
  Since the last setting sun;
And yet he lengthens out my thread,
  And yet my moments run.

5 Great God! let all my hours be thine,
  Whilst I enjoy the light;
Then shall my sun in smiles decline,
  And bring a peaceful night.

---

415   *A Morning Song.*   C. M.

1 LORD of my life! oh! may thy praise
  Employ my noblest powers,
Whose goodness lengthens out my days,
  And fills the circling hours.

2 Preserved by thine almighty arm,
  I passed the shades of night,
Secure and safe from every harm,
  And see returning light.

3 While many spent the night in sighs,
  And restless pains and woes,
In gentle sleep, I closed my eyes,
  In undisturbed repose.

4 When sleep, death's image, o'er me spread,
    And I unconscious lay
Thy watchful care was round my bed,
    To guard my feeble clay.

5 Oh! let the same almighty care
    My waking hours attend;
From every danger, every snare,
    My heedless steps defend.

6 Smile on my minutes as they roll,
    And guide my future days;
And let thy goodness fill my soul
    With gratitude and praise.

EVENING.

416   *Evening Hymn.*   *L. M.*

1 GLORY to thee, my God! this night,
For all the blessings of the light;
Keep me, oh! keep me, King of kings!
Beneath the shadow of thy wings.

2 Forgive me, Lord! for thy dear Son,
The ill that I this day have done;
That with the world, myself and thee,
My soul, this night, at peace may be.

3 Teach me to live, that I may dread
The grave as little as my bed;
Teach me to die, that so I may
Rise glorious at the judgment day.

4 Oh! may my faith on thee repose;
  May gentle sleep my eyelids close,
  That shall my frame more vigorous make,
  To serve my God when I awake.

5 Lord! let my soul forever share
  The bliss of thy parental care;
  'Tis heaven on earth, 'tis heaven above,
  To see thy face, and sing thy love.

----

417   *An Evening Song.*   C. M.

1 DREAD Sovereign, let my evening song,
    Like holy incense, rise;
  Assist the offerings of my tongue,
    To reach the lofty skies.

2 Through all the dangers of the day,
    Thy hand was still my guard;
  And still, to drive my wants away,
    Thy mercy stood prepared.

3 Perpetual blessings from above
    Encompass me around;
  But, oh! how few returns of love
    Hath my Creator found!

4 What have I done for him, who died
    To save my wretched soul?
  How are my follies multiplied,
    Fast as the minutes roll!

28 *

5 Lord ! with this guilty heart of mine,
      To thy dear cross I flee ;
  And to thy grace my soul resign,
      To be renewed by thee.

6 Sprinkled afresh with pardoning blood,
      I lay me down to rest,
  As in the embraces of my God,
      Or on my Saviour's breast.

418   *An Evening Meditation.*   L. M.

1 Thus far the Lord has led me on,
      Thus far his power prolongs my days ;
  And every evening shall make known
      Some fresh memorial of his grace.

2 Much of my time has run to waste,
      And I, perhaps, am near my home ;
  But he forgives my follies past,
      He gives me strength for days to come.

3 I lay my body down to sleep,
      Peace is the pillow for my head ;
  While well-appointed angels keep
      Their watchful stations round my bed.

4 Thus, when the night of death shall come,
      My flesh shall rest beneath the ground,
  And wait thy voice to rouse my tomb,
      With sweet salvation in the sound.

419 *An Evening Sacrifice.* L. M.

1 GREAT God! to thee my evening song
    With humble gratitude I raise;
Oh! let thy mercy tune my tongue,
    And fill my heart with lively praise.

2 My days, unclouded, as they pass,
    And every gently rolling hour,
Are monuments of wondrous grace,
    And witness to thy love and power.

3 Seal my forgiveness in the blood
    Of Jesus; his dear name alone
I plead for pardon, gracious God!
    And kind acceptance, at thy throne.

4 Let this blest hope mine eyelids close;
    With sleep refresh my feeble frame;
Safe in thy care may I repose,
    And wake with praises to thy name.

420 *An Evening Family-song.* 8s & 7s.

1 SAVIOUR! breathe an evening blessing,
    Ere repose our spirits seal;
Sin and want we come confessing;
    Thou canst save, and thou canst heal.

2 Though destruction walk around us,
    Though the arrows past us fly,
Angel-guards from thee surround us;
    We are safe, if thou art nigh.

3 Though the night be dark and dreary,
　　Darkness cannot hide from thee;
Thou art he who, never weary,
　　Watcheth where thy people be.

4 Should swift death this night o'ertake us,
　　And our couch become our tomb,
May the morn in heaven awake us,
　　Clad in bright and deathless bloom.

421　　　　*Repose and Devotion.*　*7s.*　*6 lines.*

1 Now, from labor and from care,
　　Evening shades have set me free;
In the work of praise and prayer,
　　Lord! I would converse with thee:
Oh! behold me from above,
Fill me with a Saviour's love.

2 Sin and sorrow, guilt and woe,
　　Wither all my earthly joys;
Naught can charm me here below,
　　But my Saviour's melting voice:
Lord! forg've, thy grace restore,
Make me thine for evermore.

3 For the blessings of this day,
　　For the mercies of this hour,
For the gospel's cheering ray,
　　For the Spirit's quickening power,
Grateful notes to thee I raise;
Oh! accept my song of praise.

422   *Day Ending.*   7s.

1 SOFTLY, now, the light of day
  Fades upon my sight away;
  Free from care, from labor free,
  Lord! I would commune with thee.

2 Thou whose all pervading eye,
  Naught escapes without, within,
  Pardon each infirmity,
  Open fault and secret sin.

3 Thou who, sinless, yet hast known
  All of man's infirmity;
  Now from thine eternal throne,
  Jesus look with pitying eye.

4 Soon, for me, the light of day
  Shall forever pass away;
  Then, from sin and sorrow free,
  Take me, Lord! to dwell with thee.

--- ❖ ---

423   *Twilight Prayer.*   C. M.

1 I LOVE to steal awhile away,
    From every cumbering care,
  And spend the hour of setting day,
    In humble, grateful prayer.

2 I love, in solitude, to shed
    The penitential tear;
  And all his promises to plead,
    When none but God is near.

3 I love to think on mercies past,
  And future good implore;
My cares and sorrows all to cast,
  On him whom I adore

4 I love, by faith, to take a view
  Of brighter scenes in heaven;
The prospect doth my strength renew,
  While here by tempests driven.

5 And, when life's toilsome day is o'er,
  May its departing ray
Be calm, as this impressive hour,
  And lead to endless day

424　　　*One Day nearer Home.*

1 A CROWN of glory bright,
  By faith's clear eyes I see
In yonder realms of light
  Prepared for me.

Chorus.—I'm nearer my home, nearer **my**
      home,
    Nearer my home to-day;
      Yes! nearer my home in heaven to-
      day,
    Than ever I've been before.

2 Oh! may I faithful prove,
  And keep the crown in view,
And through the storms of life
  My way pursue.

3 Jesus, be thou my guide,
  And all my steps attend,
Oh, keep me near thy side,
  Be thou my friend.

4 Be thou my shield and sun,
  My Saviour and my guard,
And when my work is done,
  My great reward.

---

425   *Coming Night.*   *8s & 7s.*

1 TARRY with me, O my Saviour,
  For the day is passing by;
See! the shades of evening gather,
  And the night is drawing nigh.

2 Many friends were gathered round me
  In the bright days of the past;
But the grave has closed above them,
  And I linger here at last.

3 Deeper, deeper grow the shadows;
  Paler now the glowing West;
Swift the night of death advances;
  Shall it be the night of rest?

4 Feeble, trembling, fainting, dying,
  Lord, I cast myself on thee;
Tarry with me through the darkness!
  While I sleep, still watch by me.

5 Tarry with me, O my Saviour!
    Lay my head upon thy breast
    Till the morning ; then awake me,
    Morning of eternal rest !

THE YEAR.

426   *New Year.*   *11s & 5s.*

1 COME, let us anew
    Our journey pursue,
    Roll round with the year,
And never stand still till the Master appear ;
    His adorable will,
    Let us gladly fulfill,
    And our talents improve,
By the patience of hope, and the labor of love.

2 Our life is a dream ;
    Our time, as a stream,
    Glides swiftly away,
And the fugitive moment refuses to stay :
    The arrow is flown,
    The moment is gone,
    The millenial year
Rushes on to our view, and eternity's here.

3 Oh ! that each, in the day
    Of his coming may say,
    "I have fought my way through,
I have finished the work which thou gav'st me
        to do !"

Oh! that each, from his Lord,
May receive the glad word,
"Well and faithfully done!
Enter into my joy, and sit down on my throne!"

------

427   *Our Times in God's Hand.*   S. M.

1 OUR times are in thy hand,
   O God, we wish them there;
Our life, our friends, our souls we leave
   Entirely to thy care.

2 Our times are in thy hand,
   Whatever they may be,
Pleasing or painful, dark or bright,
   As best may seem to thee.

3 Our times are in thy hand,
   Why should we doubt or fear?
A Father's hand will never cause
   His child a needless tear.

4 Our times are in thy hand,
   Jesus the crucified;
The hand our many sins have pierced,
   Is now our guard and guide.

5 Our times are in thy hand,
   We'll always trust in thee,
Till we have left this weary land,
   And all thy glory see.

29

428   *Year Opening.*   *L. M.*

1 GREAT God! we sing that mighty hand,
By which supported still we stand;
The opening year thy mercy shows,
Let mercy crown it till it close.

2 By day, by night—at home, abroad,
Still we are guarded by our God;
By his incessant bounty fed,
By his unerring counsel led.

3 With grateful hearts the past we own;
The future, all to us unknown,
We to thy guardian care commit,
And peaceful leave before thy feet.

4 In scenes exalted or depressed,
Be thou our joy, and thou our rest;
Thy goodness all our hopes shall raise,
Adored, through all our changing days.

5 When death shall close our earthly songs,
And seal, in silence, mortal tongues,
Our helper, God, in whom we trust,
Shall keep our souls, and guard our dust.

---

429   *Life Fleeting.*   *7s & 6s.*

1 TIME is winging us away,
To our eternal home;
Life is but a winter's day,
A journey to the tomb;

Youth and vigor soon will flee,
  Blooming beauty lose its charms;
All that's mortal soon will be
  Enclosed in death's cold arms.

2 Time is winging us away
  To our eternal home;
Life is but a winter's day,
  A journey to the tomb:
But the Christian shall enjoy
  Health and beauty soon above;
Far beyond the world's alloy,
  Secure in Jesus' love.

---

430   *Past and Future.*   *7s. Double.*

1 While with ceaseless course, the sun
  Hasted through the former year,
Many souls their race have run.
  Never more to meet us here:
Fixed in an eternal state,
  They have done with all below;
We a little longer wait,
  But how little, none can know.

2 As the winged arrow flies,
  Speedily the mark to find;
As the lightning from the skies
  Darts and leaves no trace behind,

Swiftly thus our fleeting days
    Bear us down life's rapid stream;
Upward, Lord! our spirits raise,
    All below is but a dream.

3 Thanks for mercies past, receive;
    Pardon of our sins renew:
From this moment, may we live
    With eternity in view:
Bless thy word to young and old;
    Shed abroad a Saviour's love:
And, when life's short tale is told,
    May we dwell with thee above.

---

431   *Time Short—Man Frail.*   *C. M.*

1 THEE we adore, eternal Name!
    And humbly own to thee,
How feeble is our mortal frame,
    What dying worms are we!

2 The year rolls round, and steals away
    The breath that first it gave.
Whate'er we do, where'er we be,
    We're traveling to the grave.

3 Great God! on what a slender thread
    Hang everlasting things!
The eternal state of all the dead,
    Upon life's feeble strings.

4 Infinite joy, or endless woe,
   Attends on every breath,
And yet, how unconcerned we go,
   Upon the brink of death!

5 Waken, O Lord, our drowsy sense,
   To walk this dangerous road;
And if our souls are hurried hence,
   May they be found with God.

DEATH.

432   *Asleep in Jesus.*   .   L. M.

1 ASLEEP in Jesus! blessed sleep,
From which none ever wakes to weep!
A calm and undisturbed repose,
Unbroken by the last of foes.

2 Asleep in Jesus! oh! how sweet,
To be for such a slumber meet!
With holy confidence to sing,
That death hast lost its venomed sting.

3 Asleep in Jesus! peaceful rest,
Whose waking is supremely blest!
No fear, no woe, shall dim that hour
Which manifests the Saviour's power.

4 Asleep in Jesus! oh! for me
May such a blissful refuge be!
Securely shall my ashes lie,
And wait the summons from on high.

29 *

433   *Burial of Saints.*   *L. M.*

1 UNVEIL thy bosom, faithful tomb!
   Take this new treasure to thy trust,
And give these sacred relics room,
   To seek a slumber in the dust.

2 Nor pain, nor grief, nor anxious fear,
   Invade thy bounds; no mortal woes
Can reach the peaceful sleeper here,
   While angels watch the soft repose.

3 So Jesus slept; God's dying Son
   Passed through the grave, and blessed the
      bed!
Rest here, blest saint! till, from his throne,
   The morning break, and pierce the shade.

4 Break from his throne, illustrious morn!
   Attend, O Earth! his sovereign word;
Restore thy trust; a glorious form
   Shall then arise to meet the Lord.

434   *Death, the Voice of Jesus.*   *C. M.*

1 WHY do we mourn departing friends,
   Or shake at death's alarms?
'Tis but the voice that Jesus sends,
   To call them to his arms.

2 Are we not tending upward too,
   As fast as time can move?
Nor should we wish the hours more slow,
   To keep us from our love.

3 Why should we tremble to convey
    Their bodies to the tomb?
  There the dear flesh of Jesus lay,
    And left a long perfume.

4 The graves of all the saints he blessed,
    And softened every bed:
  Where should the dying members rest,
    But with their dying Head?

5 Thence he arose, ascended high,
    And showed our feet the way;
  Up to the Lord his saints shall fly,
    At the great rising day.

6 Then let the last loud trumpet sound,
    And bid our kindred rise;
  Awake, ye nations under ground!
    Ye saints! ascend the skies.

---

435   *Dying in the Lord.*   *C. M.*

1 HEAR what the voice from heaven proclaims
    For all the pious dead;
  "Sweet is the savor of their names,
    And soft their sleeping bed.

2 "They die in Jesus, and are blessed,
    How kind their slumbers are!
  From sufferings and from sins released,
    And freed from every snare.

3 "Far from this world of toil and strife,
    They're present with the Lord;
  The labors of their mortal life
    End in a large reward."

436   *Death, the Gate of Life.*   L. M.

1 WHY should we start, and fear to die?
    What timorous worms we mortals are!
  Death is the gate of endless joy,
    And yet we dread to enter there.

2 The pains, the groans, the dying strife,
    Fright our approaching souls away;
  Still we shrink back again to life,
    Fond of our prison and our clay.

3 Oh! if my Lord would come and meet,
    My soul would stretch her wings in haste,
  Fly fearless through death's iron gate,
    Nor feel the terrors as she passed.

4 Jesus can make a dying bed
    Feel soft as downy pillows are,
  While on his breast I lean my head,
    And breathe my life out sweetly there.

437   *Death of the Righteous.*   L. M.

1 How blest the righteous when he dies,
    When sinks a weary soul to rest!
  How mildly beam the closing eyes!
    How gently heaves the expiring breast!

2 So fades a summer cloud away;
　　So sinks a gale when storms are o'er;
So gently shuts the eye of day;
　　So dies a wave along the shore.

3 A holy quiet reigns around,
　　A calm which life nor death destroys;
Nothing disturbs that peace profound,
　　Which his unfettered soul enjoys.

4 Farewell, conflicting hopes and fears!
　　Where lights and shades alternate dwell:
How bright the unchanging morn appears!
　　Farewell, inconstant world! farewell!

5 Life's duty done, as sinks the clay,
　　Light from its load the spirit flies;
While heaven and earth combine to say,
　　"How blest the righteous when he dies!"

438　　　*Mourners Comforted.*　　　8s & 7s.

1 CEASE, ye mourners! cease to languish,
　　O'er the grave of those you love;
Pain, and death, and night, and anguish,
　　Enter not the world above.

2 While our silent steps are straying,
　　Lonely, through night's deepening shade,
Glory's brightest beams are playing
　　Round the immortal spirit's head.

3 Light and peace at once deriving,
    From the hand of God most high,
In his glorious presence living,
    They shall never, never die.

4 Endless pleasure, pain excluding,
    Sickness there, no more can come;
There, no fear of woe, intruding,
    Sheds o'er heaven a moment's gloom.

5 Now, ye mourners! cease to languish,
    O'er the grave of those you love;
Far removed from pain and anguish,
    They are chanting hymns above.

————◆————

439   *A Funeral Hymn.*   *12s & 11s.*

1 THOU art gone to the grave, but we will not
        deplore thee,
    Though sorrows and darkness encompass
        the tomb;
The Saviour has passed through its portals
        before thee,
    And the lamp of his love is thy guide
        through the gloom.

2 Thou art gone to the grave, we no longer be-
        hold thee,
    Nor tread the rough paths of the world by
        thy side;

But the wide arms of mercy are spread to
    enfold thee,
And sinners may hope, since the Sinless
    hath died.

3 Thou art gone to the grave, and its mansion
    forsaking,
    Perchance thy weak spirit in doubt lingered
      long;
But the sunshine of heaven beamed bright
    on thy waking
And the sound thou didst hear was the
    seraphim's song.

4 Thou art gone to the grave, but we will not
    deplore thee,
    Since God was thy ransom, thy guardian,
      thy guide;
He gave thee, he took thee, and he will re-
    store thee;
And death hath no sting, since the Saviour
    hath died.

----

440   *Death awaiting All.*   *C. M.*

1 BENEATH our feet, and o'er our head,
    Is equal warning given;
Beneath us lie the countless dead,
    Above us, is the heaven.

2 Death rides on every passing breeze,
   And lurks in every flower;
Each season has its own disease,
   Its peril, every hour.

3 Our eyes have seen the rosy light
   Of youth's soft cheek decay,
And fate descend, in sudden night,
   On manhood's middle day.

4 Our eyes have seen the steps of age
   Halt feebly to the tomb;
And yet shall earth our hearts engage,
   And dreams of days to come?

5 Turn, mortal! turn; thy danger know;
   Where'er thy foot can tread,
The earth rings hollow from below,
   And warns thee of her dead.

6 Turn, Christian! turn; thy soul apply
   To truths divinely given;
The forms, which underneath thee lie,
   Shall live, for hell, or heaven.

----♦----

441   *Burial of an Infant.*   *8s & 7s.*

1 FARE thee well, thou lovely stranger;
   Guardian angels, take your charge;
Freed at once from pain and danger;
   Happy spirit set at large!

2 Life's most bitter cup just tasting,
   Short thy passage to the tomb;
O'er the barrier, swiftly hasting
   To thine everlasting home.

3 Rest thee here in gentle slumbers,
   Till the resurrection morn;
Then arise to join the numbers
   Who its triumphs shall adorn.

4 Soon, sweet babe, we hope to meet thee
   In the world of light above;
Oh, what rapture there to greet thee,
   And resound redeeming love!

5 Now, O Lord, to thee submitting
   We the tender pledge resign;
At the feet of Jesus sitting,
   We would have no will but thine.

JUDGMENT.

442 *Christ Coming to Judgment. 8s, 7s & 4s.*

1 Lo! he comes, in clouds descending,
   Once for favored sinners slain;
Thousand, thousand saints attending,
   Swell the triumph of his train:
         Hallelujah!
   Jesus shall forever reign.

30

2 Every eye shall now behold him,
　Robed in dreadful majesty;
Those that set at naught and sold him,
　Pierced and nailed him to the tree,
　　Deeply wailing,
　Shall the great Messiah see.

3 Every island, sea, and mountain,
　Heaven and earth shall flee away;
All who hate him, must, confounded,
　Hear the trump proclaim the day;
　　Come to judgment,
　Come to judgment, come away.

4 Now the Saviour, long-expected,
　See, in solemn pomp, appear!
All his saints, by man rejected,
　Now shall meet him in the air:
　　Hallelujah!
　See the day of God appear.

* * *

443　　*The Sinner Judged.*　　*8s, 7s & 4s.*

1 SEE the eternal Judge descending,
　View him seated on his throne!
Now, poor sinner! now lamenting,
　Stand and hear thine awful doom;
　　Trumpets call thee!
　Stand and hear thine awful doom.

2 Hear the cries he now is venting,
　Filled with dread of fiercer pain;

While in anguish thus lamenting,
That he ne'er was born again!
Greatly mourning,
That he ne'er was born again!

3 "Yonder sits my slighted Saviour,
With the marks of dying love;
Oh! that I had sought his favor,
When I felt his Spirit move!
Golden moments,
When I felt his Spirit move!"

4 Now, despisers! look, and wonder;
Hope and sinners here must part;
Louder than a peal of thunder,
Hear the dreadful sound,—"Depart!"
Lost forever,
Hear the dreadful sound,—"Depart!"

444 *A Vision of Judgment.* S. M.

1 I SAW, beyond the tomb,
The awful Judge appear,
Prepared to scan, with strict account,
The blessings wasted here.

2 His wrath, like flaming fire,
In hell forever burns;
And, from that hopeless world of woe,
No fugitive returns.

3 Ye sinners! fear the Lord,
　　While yet 'tis called to-day;
　Soon will the awful voice of death
　　Command your souls away.

4 Soon will the harvest close,
　　The summer soon be o'er:
　O sinners! then your injured God
　　Will heed your cries no more.

445　　　*The Judgment in Prospect.*　　S. M.

1 AND will the Judge descend?
　　And must the dead arise?
　And not a single soul escape
　　His all-discerning eyes?

2 How will my heart endure
　　The terrors of that day,
　When earth and heaven, before his face,
　　Astonished, shrink away?

3 But ere that trumpet shakes
　　The mansions of the dead,
　Hark! from the gospel's cheering sound,
　　What joyful tidings spread!

4 Ye sinners! seek his grace,
　　Whose wrath ye cannot bear;
　Fly to the shelter of his cross,
　　And find salvation there

5 So shall that curse remove,
    By which the Saviour bled;
And the last awful day shall pour
    His blessings on your head.

---

446 *Day of Judgment.* C. M

1 THAT awful day will surely come,
    The appointed hour makes haste,
When I must stand before my Judge,
    And pass the solemn test.

2 Thou lovely Chief of all my joys!
    Thou Sovereign of my heart!
How could I bear to hear thy voice
    Pronounce the sound—"Depart."

3 Oh! wretched state of deep despair,
    To see my God remove,
And fix my doleful station where
    I must not taste his love.

4 Jesus! I throw my arms around,
    And hang upon thy breast;
Without one gracious smile from thee,
    My spirit cannot rest.

5 Oh! tell me that my worthless name
    Is graven on thy hands;
Show me some promise in thy book,
    Where my salvation stands.

30 *

447 *Christ's Right Hand.* *C. P. M.*

1 WHEN thou, my righteous Judge! shalt come
To fetch thy ransomed people home,
  Shall I among them stand?
Shall such a worthless worm as I,
Who sometimes am afraid to die,
  Be found at thy right hand?

2 Blest Saviour! grant it by thy grace;
Be thou my only hiding-place,
  In this the accepted day;
Thy pardoning voice, oh! let me hear,
To still my unbelieving fear,
  Nor let me fall, I pray.

3 Among thy saints let me be found,
Whene'er the archangel's trump shall sound,
  To see thy smiling face;
Then, filled with rapture, shall I sing,
While heaven's resounding mansions ring
  With shouts of sovereign grace.

HEAVEN.

448 *I Would not Live Always.* *11s.*

1 I WOULD not live always: I ask not to stay,
Where storm after storm rises dark o'er the
    way;
The few lucid mornings that dawn on us here,
Are followed by gloom, and beclouded with
    fear.

2 I would not live always: no, welcome the
      tomb;
  Since Jesus hath lain there, I dread not its
      gloom;
  There, sweet be my rest, till he bid me arise,
  To hail him in triumph descending the skies.

3 Who, who would live always, away from his
      God;
  Away from yon heaven, that blissful abode,
  Where the rivers of pleasure flow o'er the
      bright plains,
  And the noontide of glory eternally reigns.

4 There saints of all ages in harmony meet,
  Their Saviour and brethren transported to
      greet;
  While anthems of rapture unceasingly roll,
  And the smile of the Lord is the feast of the
      soul.

---

449   *Rest for the Weary Soul.*   *S. M.*

1 OH! where shall rest be found,
      Rest for the weary soul!
  'Twere vain the ocean depths to sound,
      Or pierce to either pole.

2 The world can never give
      The bliss for which we sigh;
  'Tis not the whole of life to live,
      Nor all of death to die.

3 Beyond this vale of tears,
   There is a life above,
Unmeasured by the flight of years;
   And all that life is love.

4 There is a death, whose pang
   Outlasts the fleeting breath;
Oh! what eternal horrors hang
   Around the second death.

5 Lord God of truth and grace!
   Teach us that death to shun;
Lest we be banished from thy face,
   And evermore undone.

6 Here would we end our quest:
   Alone are found in thee,
The life of perfect love, the rest
   Of immortality!

———◦◦◦———

450   *Rest for the Weary.*

1 IN the Christian's home in glory,
   There remains a land of rest,
There my Saviour's gone before me,
   To fulfill my soul's request.

Chorus.—There is rest for the weary,
         There is rest for you,
         On the other side of Jordan,
         In the sweet fields of Eden,
         Where the tree of life is blooming,
         There is rest for you.

2 He is fitting up my mansion,
   Which eternally shall stand,
For my stay shall not be transient
   In that holy, happy land.

3 Pain or sickness ne'er shall enter,
   Grief nor woe my lot shall share;
But in that celestial center,
   I a crown of life shall wear.

4 Death itself shall then be vanquished,
   And his sting shall be withdrawn;
Shout for gladness, O ye ransomed,
   Hail with joy the rising morn.

5 Sing, O sing, ye heirs of glory;
   Shout your triumph as you go
Zion's gates will open for you,
   You shall find an entrance through.

---

451   *On Jordan's Banks.*   *C. M.*

1 On Jordan's stormy banks I stand,
   And cast a wishful eye
To Canaan's fair and happy land,
   Where my possessions lie.

2 Oh! the transporting, rapturous scene,
   That rises to my sight!
Sweet fields, arrayed in living green,
   And rivers of delight!

3 O'er all those wide-extended plains,
　　Shines one eternal day;
　There, God, the Son, forever reigns,
　　And scatters night away.

4 No chilling winds, no poisonous breath,
　　Can reach that healthful shore;
　Sickness and sorrow, pain and death,
　　Are felt and feared no more.

5 When shall I reach that happy place,
　　And be forever blest?
　When shall I see my Father's face,
　　And in his bosom rest?

6 Filled with delight, my raptured soul
　　Would here no longer stay;
　Though Jordan's waves should round me roll,
　　Fearless I'd launch away.

———•◦•———

452　　*Prospect of Heaven, Cheering.*　　*C. M.*

1 THERE is a land of pure delight,
　　Where saints immortal reign,
　Infinite day excludes the night,
　　And pleasures banish pain.

2 There, everlasting spring abides,
　　And never-withering flowers;
　Death, like a narrow sea, divides
　　This heavenly land from ours.

3 Sweet fields, beyond the swelling flood,
   Stand dressed in living green;
So to the Jews old Canaan stood,
   While Jordan rolled between.

4 But timorous mortals start and shrink,
   To cross this narrow sea;
And linger, shivering on the brink,
   And fear to launch away.

5 Oh! could we make our doubts remove,
   Those gloomy doubts that rise,
And see the Canaan that we love,
   With unbeclouded eyes.

6 Could we but climb where Moses stood,
   And view the landscape o'er,
Not Jordan's streams, nor death's cold flood,
   Should fright us from the shore.

━━━◆━━━

453   *That Beautiful Land.*

1 A BEAUTIFUL land, by faith I see,
   A land of rest, from sorrow free,
   The home of the ransomed, bright and fair,
   And beautiful angels, too, are there.

Chorus.—Will you go? will you go?
         Go to that beautiful land with me?
         Will you go? will you go?
         Go to that beautiful land?

2 That beautiful land, the city of light,
　　It ne'er has known the shades of night;
　　The glory of God, the light of day,
　　Hath driven the darkness far away.

3 In vision I see its streets of gold,
　　Its beautiful gates I too behold,
　　The river of life, the crystal sea,
　　The ambrosial fruit of life's fair tree.

4 The heavenly throng arrayed in white,
　　In rapture range the plains of light;
　　And in one harmonious choir they praise
　　Their glorious Saviour's matchless grace.

454　　　　*My Heavenly Home.*

1 My heavenly home is bright and fair,
　　Nor pain nor death can enter there;
　　Its glittering towers the sun outshine;
　　That heavenly mansion shall be mine.

Chorus.—Will you go? will you go?
　　　　Go to that heavenly home with me?
　　　　Will you go? will you go?
　　　　Go to that heavenly home?

2 My Father's house is built on high?
　　Far, far above the starry sky:
　　When from this earthly prison free,
　　That heavenly mansion mine shall be.

3 Let others seek a home below,
Which flames devour, or waves o'erflow;
Be mine the happier lot to own
A heavenly mansion near the throne.

4 Then fail this earth, let stars decline,
And sun and moon refuse to shine,
All nature sink and cease to be,
That heavenly mansion stands for me.

—◆—

455　　*Heaven Beyond the Tomb.*　　C. M.

1 THERE is an hour of peaceful rest,
　To mourning wanderers given:
There is a joy for souls distressed,
A balm for every wounded breast,
　'Tis found above—in heaven.

2 There is a home for weary souls,
　By sin and sorrow driven;
When tossed on life's tempestuous shoals,
Where storms arise and ocean rolls,
　And all is drear but heaven.

3 There faith lifts up her cheerful eye,
　To brighter prospects given;
And views the tempest passing by,
The evening shadows quickly fly,
　And all serene in heaven.

4 There fragrant flowers immortal bloom,
　And joys supreme are given;
There rays divine disperse the gloom;

Beyond the confines of the tomb,
Appears the dawn of heaven.

456   *Heaven alone Unfading.*   **L. M.**

1 How vain is all beneath the sky!
  How transient every earthly bliss!
How slender all the fondest ties
  That bind us to a world like this!

2 The evening cloud, the morning dew,
  The withering grass, the fading flower,
Of earthly hopes are emblems true,
  The glory of a passing hour.

3 But, though earth's fairest blossoms die,
  And all beneath the skies is vain,
There is a land, whose confines lie
  Beyond the reach of care and pain.

4 Then let the hope of joys to come
  Dispel our cares and chase our fears:
If God be ours, we're traveling home,
  Though passing through a vale of tears.

457   *The Worship of Earth and Heaven.*   **C. M.**

1 FATHER! I long, I faint, to see
  The place of thine abode;
I'd leave thine earthly courts, and flee
  Up to thy seat, my God!

2 Here I behold thy distant face,
   And 'tis a pleasing sight;
 But, to abide in thine embrace,
   Is infinite delight.

3 I'd part with all the joys of sense,
   To gaze upon thy throne;
 Pleasure springs fresh forever thence,
   Unspeakable, unknown.

4 There all the heavenly hosts are seen;
   In shining ranks they move;
 And drink immortal vigor in.
   With wonder and with love.

458   *Victory through the Lamb.*   C. M.

1 GIVE me the wings of faith, to rise
   Within the veil, and see
 The saints above, how great their joys,
   How bright their glories be.

2 I ask them whence their victory came;
   They, with united breath,
 Ascribe their conquest to the Lamb,
   Their triumph to his death.

3 They marked the footsteps he had trod;
   His zeal inspired their breast;
 And following their incarnate God,
   Possess the promised rest.

4 Our glorious Leader claims our praise,
  For his own pattern given,
While the long cloud of witnesses
  Show the same path to heaven.

————◆◇◆————

459 *Saints, one in Heaven and on Earth. C. M.*

1 COME, let us join our friends above,
  Who have obtained the prize,
And, on the eagle wings of love,
  To joy celestial rise.

2 Let saints below in concert sing
  With those to glory gone,
For all the servants of our King
  In heaven and earth are one.

3 One family, we dwell in him;
  One church, above, beneath;
Though now divided by the stream,
  The narrow stream of death.

4 One army of the living God,
  To his command we bow;
Part of the host have crossed the flood,
  And part are crossing now.

5 E'en now to their eternal home
  Some happy spirits fly;
And we are to the margin come,
  And soon expect to die!

6 Dear Saviour! be our constant guide;
    Then, when the word is given,
Bid Jordan's narrow stream divide,
    And land us safe in heaven,

------•>•------

460 *Heaven's Innumerable Throng.* 7s.

1 WHAT are these in bright array,
    This innumerable throng,
Round the altar night and day,
    Hymning one triumphant song?
"Worthy is the Lamb once slain,
    Blessing, honor, glory, power,
Wisdom, riches, to obtain,
    New dominion, every hour!"

2 These through fiery trials trod,
    These from great affliction came;
Now before the throne of God,
    Sealed with his almighty name,
Clad in raiment pure and white,
    Victor-palms in every hand,
Through their dear Redeemer's might,
    More than conquerors they stand.

3 Hunger, thirst, disease unknown,
    On immortal fruits they feed;
Them, the Lamb, amidst the throne,
    Shall to living fountains lead;

31 *

Joy and gladness banish sighs,
　　Perfect love dispel all fears,
And, forever from their eyes,
　　God shall wipe away the tears.

———◦◦———

461　　*The Bliss of Heaven.*　　7s.

1 HIGH in yonder realms of light,
　　Dwell the raptured saints above,
Far beyond our feeble sight,
　　Happy in Immanuel's love:
Pilgrims in this vale of tears,
　　Once they knew, like us below,
Gloomy doubts, distressing fears,
　　Torturing pain, and heavy woe.

2 'Mid the chorus of the skies,
　　'Mid the angelic lyres above,
Hark! their songs melodious rise,
　　Songs of praise to Jesus' love:
Happy spirits! ye are fled,
　　Where no grief can entrance find,
Lulled to rest the aching head,
　　Soothed the anguish of the mind.

3 All is tranquil and serene,
　　Calm and undisturbed repose;
There no cloud can intervene,
　　There no angry tempest blows:

Every tear is wiped away,
 Sighs no more shall heave the breast;
Night is lost in endless day,
 Sorrow in eternal rest.

------

462 *Heaven, a Dwelling with Christ.* L. M.

1 As when the weary traveler gains
 The height of some o'erlooking hill,
 His heart revives, if, 'cross the plains,
 He eyes his home, though distant still.

2 So when the Christian pilgrim views,
 By faith, his mansion in the skies,
 The sight his fainting strength renews,
 And wings his speed to reach the prize.

3 'Tis there he says I am to dwell,
 With Jesus in the realms of day:
 Then I shall bid my cares farewell,
 And he will wipe my tears away.

4 Jesus, on thee our hope depends,
 To lead us on to thy abode,
 Assured our home will make amends
 For all our toils while on the road,

------

463 *The Heavenly City.* L. M.

1 "WE'VE no abiding city here,"
 We seek a city out of sight:
Zion its name, the Lord is there,
 It shines with everlasting light.

2 "We've no abiding city here,"
　　This may distress the worldly mind,
　But should not cost the saint a tear,
　　Who hopes a better rest to find.

3 "We've no abiding city here,"
　　Then let us live as pilgrims do;
　Let not the world our rest appear;
　　But let us haste from all below.

4 O sweet abode of peace and love,
　　Where pilgrims, freed from toil, are blessed
　Had I the pinions of the dove,
　　I'd flee to thee, and be at rest.

5 But hush, my soul, nor dare repine,
　　The time my God appoints is best:
　While here, to do his will be *mine*,
　　And *his* to fix my time of rest.

—◆—

464　　　*The Shining Shore.*

1 My days are gliding swiftly by,
　　And I, a pilgrim stranger,
　Would not detain them as they fly,
　　Those hours of toil and danger.

Chorus.—For, oh! we stand on Jordan's strand,
　　　Our friends are passing over;
　　And just before the shining shore
　　　We may almost discover.

2 We'll gird our loins, my brethren dear,
   Our heavenly home discerning;
Our absent Lord has left us word,
   Let every lamp be burning.

3 Should coming days be cold and dark,
   We need not cease our singing;
That perfect rest naught can molest,
   Where golden harps are ringing.

4 Let sorrow's rudest tempest blow,
   Each chord on earth to sever;
Our king says come, and there's our home,
   Forever, oh! forever.

---

465   *The Saints in Light.*   7s.

1 PALMS of glory, raiment bright,
   Crowns that never fade away,
Gird and deck the saints in light,
   Priests, and kings, and conquerors they.

2 Yet the conquerors bring their palms
   To the Lamb amidst the throne:
And proclaim, in joyful psalms,
   Victory through his cross alone.

3 Kings for harps their crowns resign,
   Crying, as they strike the chords,
"Take the kingdom, it is thine,
   King of kings, and Lord of lords.'

4 Round the altar, priests confess,
    If their robes are white as snow,
'Twas their Saviour's righteousness,
    And his blood, that made them so.

5 Who were these? On earth they dwelt,
    Sinners once of Adam's race,
Guilt, and fear, and suffering felt,
    But were saved by sovereign grace.

6 They were mortal, too, like us:
    Ah! when we like them shall die,
May our souls, translated thus,
    Triumph, reign, and shine on high!

----

466   *In Heaven no Parting.*

1 AND may I still get there?
    Still reach the heavenly shore?
The land forever bright and fair,
    Where sorrow reigns no more.

Chorus.—Where there is no parting,
        And sorrow reigns no more.

2 Shall I, unworthy I,
    To fear and doubting given,
Mount up at last, and happy fly
    On angels' wings to heaven.

3 Hail, love divine and pure,
    Hail, mercy from the skies!
My hopes are bright, and now secure,
    Upborne by faith I rise.

4 I part with earth and sin,
  And shout the danger 's past;
My Saviour takes me fully in,
  And I am his at last.

467   *The Better Land.*   L. M.

1 THERE is a land mine eye hath seen,
  In visions of enraptured thought,
So bright that all which spreads between
  Is with its radiant glory fraught:

2 A land upon whose blissful shore
  There rests no shadow, falls no stain;
There those who meet shall part no more,
  And those long parted meet again.

3 Its skies are not like earthly skies,
  With varying hues of shade and light;
It hath no need of suns to rise,
  To dissipate the gloom of night.

4 There sweeps no desolating wind
  Across that calm, serene abode;
The wanderer there a home may find,
  Within the paradise of God.

468   *The Heavenly Jerusalem.*   C. M.

1 JERUSALEM! my happy home!
  Name ever dear to me,
When shall my labors have an end,
  In joy, and peace, and thee?

2 When shall these eyes thy heaven-built walls
　　And pearly gates behold?
　Thy bulwarks, with salvation strong,
　　And streets of shining gold?

3 Oh! when, thou city of my God!
　　Shall I thy courts ascend?
　Where congregations ne'er break up,
　　And Sabbaths never end.

4 Why should I shrink at pain or woe,
　　Or feel at death dismay?
　Jerusalem I soon shall view,
　　In realms of endless day.

5 Redeeméd saints and angels, there,
　　Around my Saviour stand;
　And soon my friends in Christ, below,
　　Will join the glorious band.

6 Jerusalem! my happy home!
　　My soul still pants for thee;
　Then shall my labors have an end,
　　When I thy joys shall see.

469　　　*Life in Heaven.*　　　*C. M.*

1 THERE is a place of sacred rest,
　　Far, far beyond the skies,
　Where beauty smiles eternally,
　　And pleasure never dies.

2 When tossed upon the waves of life,
  With fear on every side,
When fiercely howls the gathering storm,
  And foams the angry tide.

3 Beyond the storm, beyond the gloom,
  Breaks forth the light of morn,
Bright beaming from my Father's house,
  To cheer the soul forlorn.

4 The vision of that heavenly home,
  Shall cheer the parting soul,
And o'er it, mounting to the skies,
  A tide of rapture roll.

5 For there, adieus are sounds unknown,
  Death frowns not on that scene,
But life and glorious beauty shine,
  Untroubled and serene.

* * *

470   *Forever with the Lord.*

1 "FOREVER with the Lord!"
    Amen! so let it be:
  Life from the dead is in that word:
    'Tis immortality.

2 Here, in the body pent,
    Absent from him I roam;
  Yet nightly pitch my moving **tent**
    A day's march nearer home:
      Nearer home,
    A day's march nearer home.

32

3 My Father's house on high,
    Home of my soul! how near,
At times, to faith's far-seeing eye,
    Thy golden gates appear!

4 "Forever with the Lord!"
    Father, if 'tis thy will,
The promise of that faithful word,
    E'en here to me fulfill:
      Here fulfill:
E'en here to me fulfill.

5 So when my latest breath
    Shall rend the vail in twain,
By death I shall escape from death,
    And life eternal gain.

6 That resurrection word!
    That shout of victory,
Once more—"*Forever with the Lord!*"
    Amen! so let it be!
      Let it be!
Amen! so let it be!

------

471   *Heaven is my Home.*   **6s & 4s.**

1 I'M but a stranger here,
    Heaven is my home;
Earth is a desert drear,
    Heaven is my home;
Danger and sorrow stand
Round me on every hand,

Heaven is my fatherland,
   Heaven is my home.

2 What though the tempest rage,
   Heaven is my home;
Short is my pilgrimage,
   Heaven is my home;
And time's wild wintry blast
Soon will be over-past,
I shall reach home at last,
   Heaven is my home.

3 Therefore I murmur not,
   Heaven is my home;
Whate'er my earthly lot,
   Heaven is my home;
And I shall surely stand
There at my Lord's right hand:
Heaven is my fatherland,
   Heaven is my home.

---

472   *I'm a Pilgrim.*

1 I'M a pilgrim, and I'm a stranger;
I can tarry, I can tarry but a night;
Do not detain me, for I am going
To where the streamlets are ever flowing.

2 There the sunbeams are ever shining,
I am longing, I am longing for the sight;
I have been wandering forlorn and weary,
Within a country unknown and dreary.

3 Of that country to which I am going
  My Redeemer, my Redeemer is the light!
  There is no sorrow, nor any sighing,
  Nor any sin there, nor any dying.

473　　*Joyfully Onward.*　　*10s.*

1 JOYFULLY, joyfully onward I move,
  Bound to the land of bright spirits above;
  Angelic choristers sing as I come,
  "Joyfully, joyfully haste to thy home!"
  Soon, with my pilgrimage ended below,
  Home to the land of bright spirits I go;
  Pilgrim and stranger no more shall I roam,
  Joyfully, joyfully resting at home.

2 Friends, fondly cherished, have passed on
      before;
  Waiting, they watch me approaching the
      shore;
  Singing to cheer me through death's chilling
      gloom:
  "Joyfully, joyfully haste to thy home!"
  Sounds of sweet melody fall on my ear;
  Harps of the blessèd, your voices I hear!
  Rings with the harmony heaven's high dome,
  "Joyfully, joyfully haste to thy home!"

3 Death, with thy weapons of war lay me low,
  Strike, king of terrors! I fear not the blow;
  Jesus hath broken the bars of the tomb!
  Joyfully, joyfully will I go home.

Bright will the morn of eternity dawn,
Death shall be banished, his scepter be gone;
Joyfully then shall I witness his doom.
Joyfully, joyfully, safely at home.

474   *Death, the Victor, Vanquished.*   10s.

1 HAPPY the spirit released from its clay;
  Happy the soul that goes bounding away;
  Singing, as upward it hastes to the skies,
"Victory! victory! homeward I rise."
  Many the toils it has passed through below,
  Many the seasons of trial and woe;
  Many the doubtings it never should sing,
"Victory! victory!" thus on the wing.

2 Nor would we have it recalled from its home,
  Longer in sorrowing exile to roam;
  Safely it passed from its troubles beneath,
"Victory! victory!" shouting in death:
  And when its Lord shall descend from the
        skies,
  Calling its body from dust to arise,
  How it shall soar upon triumphing wing,
"Victory! victory!" ever to sing!

475   *Heaven Dawning.*

1 CHRISTIAN, the morn breaks sweetly o'er thee,
  And all the midnight shadows flee,
  Tinged are the distant skies with glory,
  A beacon light hung out for thee;
32 *

Arise! arise! the light breaks o'er thee,
    Thy name is graven on the throne,
Thy home is in the world of glory,
    Where thy Redeemer reigns alone.

2 Tossed on time's rude, relentless surges,
    Calmly, composed, and dauntless, stand,
For, lo! beyond those scenes emerges
    The height that bounds the promised land.
Behold! behold! the land is nearing,
    Where the wild sea-storm's rage is o'er;
Hark! how the heavenly hosts are cheering!
    See in what throngs they range the shore!

3 Cheer up! cheer up! the day breaks o'er thee,
    Bright as the summer's noon-tide ray;
The star-gemmed crowns and realms of glory
    Invite thy happy soul away;
Away! away! heaven is before thee,
    Thy name is graven on the throne;
Thy home is in that world of glory,
    Where thy Redeemer reigns alone.

DISMISSION.

476   *Dismission. 8s 7s & 4s, or 8s & 7s.*

1 LORD! dismiss us with thy blessing,
    Fill our hearts with joy and peace:
Let us all, thy love possessing,
    Triumph in redeeming grace:

Oh! refresh us,
Traveling through this wilderness.

2 Thanks we give, and adoration,
For thy gospel's joyful sound;
Let the fruits of thy salvation
In our hearts and lives abound;
May thy presence
With us evermore be found.

3 So, whene'er the signal's given,
Us from earth to call away,
Borne on angels' wings to heaven,
Glad to leave this cumbrous clay,
May we ever
Reign with Christ in endless day.

477　　　*Communion of Saints.*　　8s & 7s.

1 MAY the grace of Christ our Saviour,
And the Father's boundless love,
With the Holy Spirit's favor,
Rest upon us from above.

2 Let us thus abide in union
With each other and the Lord,
And possess, in sweet communion,
Joys which earth cannot afford.

478　　　*God's Benediction Sought.*　　L. M.

1 DISMISS us with thy blessing, Lord!
Help us to feed upon thy word;

All that has been amiss forgive,
And let thy truth within us live.

2 Though we are guilty, thou art good,
Wash all our works in Jesus' blood;
Give every burdened soul release,
And bid us all depart in peace.

————

DOXOLOGIES.

479 *L. M.*

PRAISE God, from whom all blessings flow;
Praise him, all creatures here below;
Praise him above, ye heavenly host;
Praise Father, Son, and Holy Ghost.

————

480 *C. M.*

LET God. the Father, and the Son,
    And Spirit be adored,
Where there are works to make him known,
    Or saints to love the Lord.

————

481 *S. M.*

YE angels round the throne!
    And saints that dwell below!
Worship the Father, praise the Son,
    And bless the Spirit too.

482 *8s & 7s.*

GLORY, honor, praise, and power
To the Lamb be ever paid;
Let new blessings, every hour,
Rest on his adoréd head.

---

483 *8s, 7s & 4s.*

GREAT Jehovah! we adore thee,
God, the Father, God, the Son,
God, the Spirit, joined in glory
On the same eternal throne;
Endless praises
To Jehovah, Three in One.

---

484 *7s.*

SING we to our God above,
Praise eternal as his love;
Praise him all ye heavenly host!
Father, Son, and Holy Ghost.

---

485 *H. M.*

To God, the Father's throne,
Your highest honors raise;
Glory to God, the Son;
To God, the Spirit praise:

With all our powers,
  Eternal King!
  Thy name we sing,
While faith adores.

----

486   *7s & 6s. (Iambic.)*

WE'LL praise thy name forever,
  Thou glorious King of kings!
Thy wondrous love and favor,
  Each ransomed spirit sings:
We'll celebrate thy glory,
  With all thy saints above,
And shout the joyful story
  Of thy redeeming love.

----

487   *7s & 6s. (Trochai*

FATHER, Son, and Holy Ghost,
  One God whom we adore,
Join we with the heavenly host
  To praise thee evermore:
Live, by heaven and earth adored,
  Three in One, and One in Three,
Holy, holy, holy Lord,
  All glory be to thee!

INDEX OF TOPICS.

3. Hope.

4. Love.

5. Depression.

6. Encouragement.

7. Walking with God.

8. Looking unto Jesus.

9. Longing for Home.

INDEX OF FIRST LINES.

Note.—The figures in parentheses refer to Psalms and Hymns in *Church Psalmist*; the other figures to the numbers of the Hymns in this book.